Catch Me, Kill Me
A Novel of Crime

Books by Bill Brooks

Dakota Lawman *series*
Last Stand at Sweet Sorrow
Killing Mr. Sunday

Quint McCannon Adventures
Leaving Cheyenne
Dust on the Wind
Return to No Man's Land

Novels
Catch Me, Kill Me
Moon's Blood
Bonnie and Clyde
Deadwood
The Last Law There Was
Stolen Horses
Bill Doolan: American Outlaw
The Stone Garden

Catch Me, Kill Me
A Novel of Crime

Bill Brooks

SPEAKING VOLUMES, LLC
NAPLES, FLORIDA
2019

Catch Me, Kill Me

ISBN 978-1-64540-069-1

For Diane, again.

Chapter One

*"I'll tell you what's wrong with society, no one drinks
from the skulls of their enemies"*
—Unknown

Nina waited in the car while Ray and Dime Bag went inside.

Not yet May and already it was hitting ninety. But at least today it was raining.

Ray and Dime Bag had left the car running—an old midnight blue Lincoln Continental with plush red velour upholstery that reminded her of the chair her daddy sat on in his living room to watch television. Ray joked he could put three dead bodies in the trunk, and did she want to see? Absolutely not, she'd said. He laughed like a hyena.

She was nervous and smoked a cigarette, lowering the window down a crack to let the smoke out. Ray had said they were going to Buzzard's place to score some dope, but she knew Ray didn't have enough money to buy a morning newspaper much less dope. And Dime Bag sure as hell had even less. So how were they going to score dope from Buzzard? She thought she knew and had tried to get out of going with them, but Ray had insisted, put on that old Ray charm—or thought he had—saying she brought him luck. And when she'd earlier questioned him about it, he'd said, "Not to fret, baby. Buzzard owes me from before on another deal and we'll work it out. He knows I'm always good for it once I get it unloaded. I triple whatever I buy off him, he gets more than fair market value and everybody is happy. Besides, I've already got a buyer lined up, a dude calls himself Geronimo, you know, like the Indian." Talking to her like she was stupid. "Got cash and plenty of it, too. Tell you what, soon's I do this deal I'll take you to Graceland. You always wanted to go there, right. Well, now we'll be able to baby. How's that sound?"

She'd always been a big Elvis fan, because her daddy listened to him and sometimes he and her mother would get up and dance in the kitchen listening to the King. Yeah, she'd always wanted to go to Graceland, and it was half the reason she went along with Ray even though she didn't believe him, tried to feign menstrual cramps at the last minute, thinking he'd take pity on her, said she wasn't feeling good. She had a dark feeling about going with him and his idiot friend.

"Take some Midol," he said.

She still resisted, she didn't want to get involved anymore with Ray and his drug dealings. Didn't want to even know about how he made his money, except he bragged a lot. She just knew that he never made a dime with honest work. One day he was loaded and the next he was flat broke.

She didn't know how he had such a hold over her, but lately she'd grown tired of living the up and down lifestyle. Ray might have been one of the best looking guys she'd ever met—even reminded her a little of Elvis, with the big sideburns—but his act was wearing thin on her. She was ready to move on, but she needed to find a way to get far enough that Ray wouldn't come after her. Ray spent lavishly on her when he was flush, but he didn't give her any money—nothing she could sock away. It was a dead-end relationship and she'd come to realize that—even if too late.

"Come on, now," he'd insisted. "Time's a wasting." He practically lifted her by her arm and guided her on out the door where Dime Bag sat behind the wheel of the Continental listening to that hard rock country shit he always listened to; bobbing his head so that his long greasy hair fell across his face. Playing air guitar, because, she long had thought, he's too stupid to do anything else.

It was a forty-five minute drive to Buzzard's and all the way over she kept telling herself to get them to pull over and let her out, but she knew it was useless and so sat between them in the front seat feeling trapped, nobody saying anything, but that music blaring loud enough to wake the dead. In the time it took to drive from Ray's to Buzzard's place, she had gone over her entire life until this moment—from an orphan child shuttled between foster homes until she became a drug dealer's girlfriend. What the fuck! she wanted to scream. The prescience of Ray had robbed her soul and only now was she really realizing the price she'd paid for being his "woman." Like that Bob Dylan song, "You Got to Serve Somebody." Well, that was her in spades.

They drove to that part of town guys like Buzzard live in—squalid, tenement apartments, junk cars lining the streets, those pimped out rides with wheels worth more than the damn car, barking dogs chained behind fences, every house a tragic story unto itself.

They pulled up and parked.

"Wait here," Ray told her. She was glad she didn't have to go in. Buzzard was the kind that raped you with his eyes.

They were inside Buzzard's about five minutes before they came out and she felt relieved to see it over with so quickly, but then Ray opened the passenger door while Dime Bag stood there in the rain like a dutiful dog, his hair wet and plastered to his head.

"Come on inside," Ray said.

"What for?" she asked.

"Just come on in. Buzzard wants to meet you?"

"What does he want to meet me for?"

Ray shrugged, shifted foot to foot as if he had to pee, but that was just who he was, always full of nervous energy. The only time she'd seen him be still was when he was zoned out on drugs or sleeping. But even in his sleep he tended to twitch. A fucking twitching Adonis, she thought.

Sometimes she'd watch him sleeping and twitching like that and get the urge to go into the kitchen and get the hammer he kept under the sink and bash him in the head with it just to get him to stop.

"He's just cautious is all," Ray said. "He needs to be assured things are copasetic, like to know everybody—thinks you could be a narc, I'm guessing is what it is with him."

"Narc! Did you tell him I was your girlfriend, Ray?"

Ray shrugged.

"Yeah, of course I did, Baby. I told him, but Buzzard's Buzzard, paranoid as shit all the time. Just come in and let him have a look so he'll chill out."

"I don't want to go in there, Ray."

"Will you please get the fuck out of the car and come inside so I can get this done! Shit, Nina . . ."

He reached in and grabbed her wrist and dragged her out of the car. She did her best to pull away, but she could see by the look on his face he wasn't fucking around. He'd hit her before.

"Goddamn it, Nina. This'll just take a minute, then we'll be on down the road. I'll take you out later and we'll get steak at Ponderosa, then head straight on up to Memphis. The guy is waiting for us, I got to get this done!"

"Us?"

"Me and Dime Bag," he said impatiently and led her into the shotgun shack set up on concrete blocks, with a loose wrought iron railing and a blistered door. Nina had noticed a grape colored new Dodge Charger parked at the side of the house. Looked like it was worth three times what the shack was worth. It would have been a cliché if it hadn't been real.

Ray swung open the door and pushed her in ahead of him. Dime Bag had stayed behind at the Continental, the radio turned up full blast. A couple of black kids halfway down the block were jiving on the sidewalk to their own music.

Buzzard was sitting on a green sofa, his bulk caving in the cushions. He was wearing a wife beater and blue boxer shorts and a pair of tan work boots with the laces untied. His elbows rested up on the back of the sofa, his muscled arms heavily tattooed. A beer bottle dangled from one hand while a joint smoldered in the other. He had a shaggy Osama beard to go along with his pitted face. His graying hair in braids reached nearly down to his beer gut. He looked like a demented Willie Nelson, she thought.

"See, I told you she'd come," Ray said pushing her forward.

"I guess you goddamn did," Buzzard said. Nina noticed then a blue teardrop tattooed near the corner of his left eye. It gave her chills the way he looked at her.

He sniffed and wiped his nose with the back of the hand holding the beer bottle then reached down and scratched himself unashamedly.

"Okay, then," he said and nodded to a package wrapped in gray duct tape and aluminum foil next to him on the couch. Next to that, she also noticed a large stainless steel revolver of some kind. Now she was really frightened.

Ray retrieved the package.

"I'll be back no later than midnight," he said and turned to go and Nina turned to go with him, but Ray stopped her and said, "Honey, I'm going to need you to wait here with Buzzard till I get back."

"No!" she said. "I'm going with you."

Suddenly Ray's eyes narrowed, and before she knew it, he'd clipped her with a backhand so hard she thought her jaw was broken. The blow caused her to stumble sideways where she fell on the sofa next to Buzzard who caught her and clamped an arm around the neck.

"We'll be waiting, Ray, Nina and me," Buzzard said. "Take your time, just don't show your skinny ass up without the money, else we got a problem."

Ray looked at her and then he was gone out the door and she was struggling to free herself from Buzzard's grip, when suddenly he came up with the revolver and pressed the muzzle to her temple.

"Now what the fuck you gonna do sweet girl? You think this shit is worth getting yourself shot over? You think I was just gonna let your boyfriend take off with my dope without any—what they call, collateral? Fuck, girl, you be tripping."

She couldn't hold back the tears of anger, fear, hatred, that suddenly spilled down her cheeks as Buzzard relaxed his grip on her but still kept the gun's muzzle pressed to her head.

"Now that is some motherfucker of a boyfriend you got there, Nina baby. I mean what sort of fucken guy would use his woman like he just done you? You want a drink or should we just get right down to it?"

"Please," she said. "I need to go."

"Go? Hell we both know that's not an option."

"I need . . . to use the bathroom . . ." she said, desperate to stop whatever he was planning. Then told him she was on her period, maybe that would put him off.

"Yeah, right," he said and shoved her face into his lap. "First off, you got to know I don't give a shit whether you're on the rag or not. Besides, there are lots of other ways of getting this shit done. Now whyn't you start getting it done . . ."

She was filled with disgust to go along with her raging anger. How could she have been so stupid? She should have left Ray a long time ago, but he always managed to draw her back in with promises and sweet talk, sometimes getting her to feel sorry for him, telling her he couldn't make it on the outside without her love and support, that she was the only good thing in his life. Telling her he'd kill himself if he had to be locked up again. Telling her, "You don't know the stuff that goes on in there, Nina. I can't go back in and, if you leave me, I'll end up fucking up and getting arrested again and that'll be it for me. I'll kill myself first."

Working on her pity, and each time she allowed him to get over on her. She had a dad she'd not seen in years because he too had been in prison and maybe that was part of her weakness for Ray's whining. Shad been shuttled from foster home to foster home until she was sixteen, then ran away and lived on the streets. Some of the kids prostituted themselves, but she never would. There was always some boy among them willing to help her out. Then she met Ray who came into her life like a storm and knew to say and do all the right things. He was older, owned a car, his own apartment. That was the start of it. With Ray she thought she'd found her true purpose—taking care of Ray. It was a sucker's game all the way. And now as Buzzard tried to force himself on her, she wished she'd never laid eyes on him.

Most of his acquaintances were freaks, like Dime Bag, with limited conversational skills. If they weren't talking about getting high, motorcycles or pussy, they didn't have anything to say. She did her best to reform Ray. And too late she learned the lesson of lots of women in her situation: you couldn't reform them. You either lived with it or you got away from it.

But what no one involved that day could have imagined was how Nina managed to get Buzzard's chrome-plated 44 Mag and shoot him to death even as she aroused him from the sleep of a sexually sated bastard. He'd barely time to see it coming

She'd pretended to fall asleep when he finished with her, pinned there on the sofa, her body wracked with pain, her head full of hot anger that matched the pain with every throbbing beat of her heart, every stifled breath.

7

She carefully extracted herself, fearing each second he'd stop his snoring and open his eyes. But he didn't, thanks to all the dope he'd consumed, pills and vodka. Then she eased the revolver from his hand and stood over him, cocked the hammer back, pressed the muzzle to his forehead and prodded him partially awake with it. His eyes fluttered open, crossed looking down the barrel before looking up at her. And when he realized the situation, he simply grinned and said, "Give me that gun, you stupid bitch!"

"Sure," she said and pulled the trigger. The bullet didn't have far to travel—an inch or two—then played pinball inside Buzzard's skull before exploding out the back splattering couch and wall behind couch with the poster of Marilyn smiling coyly and leaving the wall looking like a Jackson Pollock painting. She was too pissed to feel revulsion when some of the blood sprayed onto her as well, thought: One less prick to make the world a miserable place.

She went into the bathroom and washed the gore off her face and hands and forearms and stared for a moment into the mirror. The green eyes looking back at her where those of a stranger.

She went back out and found an afghan tossed in the seat of a recliner and dropped it over Buzzard's staring eyes and open mouth, then set a kitchen chair in front of the door and waited along with the big gun, partaking of one of Buzzard's cigarettes lying on the floor along with what was left in the vodka bottle.

As she smoked, she felt no sense of remorse or panic, or guilt. It was as if killing Buzzard had cleansed her of all fear, and there sure was something to be said for that. She held the big .357 in her lap like a pet.

Around two in the morning, headlights swept across the inside of the room as she heard a car pull up. She stood and glanced outside to make sure it was Ray and Dime Bag, then took a stance three feet in front of the door. She heard both car doors open and thud shut, heard the two of them talking loud and laughing outside, having a good time, they were. She cocked back the hammer of the Mag, holding it in both hands like she'd seen characters in movies like Clint do, and aimed it dead center of the door.

When Ray opened the door without even bothering to knock, she knew she'd never forget the look of surprise in his eyes.

"Hi, honey, you're home," she said and pulled the trigger.

The force of the bullet knocked him backwards into the trailing Dime Bag and they both went over the wobbly railing landing hard in what should have been a yard, but wasn't.

Dime Bag was screaming and cussing as she stepped out of the house and stood looking down at them. Ray was, for once, surprisingly quiet. Dime Bag was trying to get Ray off him, get to a gun he carried in his boot.

She took aim and fired again just as Dime Bag pulled free of his running buddy. Not exactly a clean shot, but it tore through Dime Bag's neck and he did his best to stop the spurting leak of his busted water hose of an artery.

He staggered about and then sank to his knees. He looked up. Nina stood over him aiming the Mag downward.

"You fucking bitch," he tried to say, but it came out, Ooo futtin' bish" and Nina said, "Yeah, you're right," and shot him through the top of his head.

The way she saw it, she'd done him a kindness. She didn't like to see things suffer.

She stood for a moment as if she was watching herself in some sort of crime movie, that she was one of the characters, but personally felt little for the dead, either in the house or without.

She heard her own breathing, the wetness of Florida rain falling on her and on them and on every goddamn thing in the world.

She looked around to see if anyone came out to see what the hell was going on. No one did, not in this neighborhood where gunfire was as common as it was on the Fourth of July.

She raised her face to the rain and stuck out her tongue, like when she was a kid and the rain still tasted the same—tinny. Her mother used to say that rain was God's tears, and, if you drank them, you had some of God inside you.

It was two days until Easter. She thought maybe she should go to confession; she hadn't gone in a long time—ever since meeting Ray. Another thing she disliked about him—the fucker wasn't religious.

She went back inside, stepped around Buzzard's outstretched feet, and searched the trailer. In the back bedroom she found four more packages like the one Ray had taken earlier. She found a roll of money wrapped with a thick rubber band. She didn't bother to count it, figured it to be several thousand dollars. She found another handgun and an assault rifle. She took the money and the drugs and carried them out into the kitchen, found a black plastic garbage bag and put the money and dope in it, then pulled the drawstrings tight and carried it outside and started to put it in Ray's Continental, then changed her mind and carried it over to the Dodge Charger and put it in the back seat. Then she climbed in behind the steering wheel and looked for keys, but there weren't any.

She sat a moment thinking, the rain doing a continuous tap dance on the car's roof and hood. She got back out and went inside the house—still nobody had come out of their places—glancing briefly at the two dead men in the yard, Ray especially, but with no regret. You get what you deserve in this life, she always believed.

Entering the open door, she searched through the pockets of Buzzard's crusted Levis tossed in a corner and found the keys to the Charger. She picked up the Magnum again and almost a full quart of Jack Daniels sitting on the kitchen counter, tipped it to her mouth and washed whatever that taste was out—blood, maybe—and spat it in the sink. Then she grabbed a grubby dishtowel and walked outside again carrying the bottle and dishtowel in one hand and the Mag in the other. She knelt next to Ray's body and found the money he'd got for the dope deal and put this in her jacket pocket, then walked to Ray's Lincoln—man he really loved that fucking car. She soaked the dishtowel in Jack Daniels, emptied the rest over the plush velour, lighted the cloth and set it on the seat, then walked over to the Charger, got in again and fired it up. It had a nice throaty sound, the engine did. She liked that, wondered how it was a car like that could make her feel better than a man could.

She sat there until the interior of the Continental caught fire, the flames jumping up off the seat and smoke curled inside as if looking for an escape route. The fire would destroy her fingerprints.

She put the Charger in gear and drove down the drive toward the highway thinking she'd just fucking drive and let the car take her to where it would. It was time she started trusting in something besides her own judgment for a time until she could figure out her next move.

She turned on the radio and dialed the knob and found "I'm So Excited" by the Pointer Sisters. The lyrics seemed apropos.

Wasn't quite how I imagined it going, Ray, she told herself. *But hey, listen, we can always still be friends, can't we?*

Chapter Two

"The Devil's name is dullness"
—Robert E. Lee

Bobby Lee sat bent at the waist on the trainer's table, his hands still taped when Max Gold came into the room wearing his sharkskin suit and slicked back hair that made it look like pencil marks on his scalp. Johnny Pearl came in with him. Johnny Pearl was Max's body man, his enforcer and flunky. Nobody knew for sure what all Johnny did for Max other than drive him around and hang at his elbow, but there were lots of stories floating around about him.

"You were supposed to go down in the eighth," Max said. "You didn't and I lost my ass betting on it. What the fuck is wrong with you—too many blows to the head? I'm not going to forget this you pug. No, you're going to pay me back one way or the other."

Bobby Lee had been waiting for Junior Cisco to come in and cut the tape off. He needed to soak his hands in ice water to take the swelling down. Slate Johnson was a big fucking dude with a head like granite and it was like beating his hands against a brick wall. But his ribs weren't so hard and from the second round on, Bobby had dug body shots to them. But then Slate said something only Bobby could hear and that was when he decided he wasn't going to throw the fight. Fuck whatever Max wanted him to do. He was tired of being Max's dog. That round he put Slate down with a shot that came up from his heels and snapped the guy's head like he'd run into a brick wall. When Bobby saw him fall face first to the canvas, he knew Slate wasn't going to get up again. Guys that go down like that, never do. Bobby also knew Max was sitting ringside watching the debacle. But Bobby was as finished as the other guy, only in a different way.

"Well, what the fuck you got to say for yourself, asshole?" Max said.

"Nice shoes," Bobby Lee said staring down at Max's black wingtips.

Max looked down then looked over at Johnny Pearl who stood by the door still, hands in the pockets of his leather coat.

"Now he's a fucken comedian, you believe this shit?" Then turning his attention back to Bobby, said, "You're cracking wise when I just lost a bundle of dough?" Max's face flushed red, and Bobby knew he wanted to take a swing at him, but he didn't have the cajones to do it.

Just then Junior Cisco came in, a short energetic little man in a satin jacket with short sleeves and stitching on the back, *Lou Sander's Gym*. He stopped short when he saw Max and Johnny Pearl.

"I can come back," he said and turned to leave, but Bobby Lee stopped him.

"I need this tape cut off, Junior. I need to soak my hands."

The trainer looked from Bobby Lee to Max, but Max didn't say anything, so Junior came forward stepping like he was walking across light bulbs.

"Sure, Bobby, hell of a fight, kid," he said unaware of the fix. Bobby held out his hands and Junior used the surgical scissors from his pocket and began cutting through the tape and gauze.

"So?" Max said growing more impatient by the second. His jowly face the same color of a man in the throes of a heart attack—darkening red.

"What do you want me to say," Bobby said. "I wasn't trying to knock the guy out, he just walked into it."

"Walked into it my ass. Like what am I, blind?"

"Think whatever you want, Max, but that's the way it happened."

"You know what I think, you jerkoff?"

Bobby said nothing, concentrating on Junior cutting the tape. One hand free, he flexed his fingers, they were so stiff and swollen he couldn't make a fist.

After a moment more, Bobby looked up, both hands free now, flexing and un-flexing them, not sure exactly what Max planned to do or when, but he was resolved to not give any more of himself to the fat prick.

***

"What do you think, Max, that you're going to kill me, have Johnny here break my legs, smash my hands with a hammer? Something like that?"

Max glared at him, then turned and in mock laughter said to Johnny Pearl "You believe this fucken mutt? Talking to me like that when I took him in and treated him like a son for chrissake?"

Johnny Pearl with a half smirk on his face.

"No Boss, I can't say as I do believe him."

"That's fucken right," Max said. "I can't either. Cisco, your services won't be required any longer—go and find yourself another fighter to train. Bobby here is retired. Johnny Pearl pulled a fold of cash from his coat pocket and peeled off two one hundred dollar bills and handed them to Junior who stuck them in the pocket of his black slacks, looked back at Bobby Lee.

"Good luck, Bobby, it was nice to have worked witcha."

"See you around, Junior."

Then they were alone, the three of them. Bobby slid down off the trainer's table and walked to the bucket of ice water and plunged his right hand in first because that was the one that hurt the most, the one he'd knocked out the guy with. Christ what a shot. Maybe the best one he'd ever thrown.

Max's accusation had been right, Bobby Lee *had* wanted to knock the guy out. He was one kind of man outside the ring, but inside it, he was a fighter with a fighter's mentality—it was like a switch flipped in him or something. But he was never going to admit to Max that he'd cold cocked the guy on purpose. Fuck Max and what he thought he knew.

Besides, it always felt good to put a guy out, especially one was supposed to be the next Tyson. But Bobby was still the champ, with a champion's heart and that was the thing guys like Max would never understand. So, yeah, fuck him.

"See you around," Max said and stormed out with Johnny Pearl pausing only long enough to make a gun with his forefinger and thumb and aim it at Bobby Lee.

***

"Too bad it's got to end like this, kid. You was a pretty good fighter, even though you was always an asshole and I'm going to enjoy ending you."

Bobby knew what was coming. They'd do it somewhere away from the arena. Probably fuck him up real bad so he'd feel the pain, and then kill him—either Max as a personal vendetta, or Johnny Pearl—stick a gun in his mouth and pull the trigger.

He finished soaking his hands and got dressed in a sports shirt and tan khaki trousers. He zipped his gym bag and went out and down the hall underneath the arena. Quiet now that the fight was over. Nothing but the cleanup people around. One of them, an old black ex-fighter with a horseshoe of cotton hair said, "Helluv a fight, Mista Lee. I had my money on you."

Bobby Lee nodded and muttered thanks, then went out the door that led to the parking lot. He looked around for any suspicious cars, didn't see any and headed for his pickup truck, got in, fired up the engine and drove away keeping a close eye on the rearview and side mirrors.

He needed to go see Augie, Max's bookie, and collect his money, then he needed to get the fuck gone. He wasn't sure where he'd go, but somewhere, far the fuck away and where Max would never think to look for him.

Seemed it had been that way his whole life. He did shit that put him directly in the way of danger. Like joining the Marines just when the country was going into the Gulf War. He nearly got his head shot off and blown up two or three times, saw good friends either dead or missing limbs and it scared the shit out of him at times. But what was worse was coming home and fighting the war within because the only enemy became yourself, the only demons, the ones you'd allowed to exist.

He'd read in a history book what his namesake Robert E. Lee had said war—*"It is a good thing that it is so terrible, otherwise we shall grow too fond of it."*

He cruised down Jackson Avenue keeping an eye out for Max's cream-colored Cadillac or Johnny Pearl's classic Chrysler Windsor Convertible. He passed Augie's place and circled once around the block and came back. Pulled ahead a couple of car lengths and got out and walked back to the store front—a pawn shop. There was a light on inside, but the front door was locked. Bobby went around and found the side door unlocked and quietly entered.

Augie was sitting at his gray metal desk in the office at the rear of the store, the room littered with various pawn items, his desk littered with paperwork. The bookmaker looked up.

"Jesus," he said. "You scared the shit out of me creeping up like that."

"Your side door was open," he said. "I came to collect my money."

On the desk was a half bottle of Seagram's and a paper cup.

"You want a drink, kid?"

"No, just my money."

Augie was a short slender man with a brushy gray moustache to match his brush cut hair. His eyes looked pinched in his lined face. Bobby knew that Augie's latest wife was a hell of a looker and couldn't figure what she saw in Augie—what any woman saw in him, really. She was maybe in her early twenties and here Augie was probably in his sixties. Had to be the dough.

Augie cleared his throat and spilled a little more booze into his cup, looked closely at what was left in the bottle then set it aside.

"There's a problem with your money, kid," he said.

"What kind of problem?"

"I can't pay you."

"What the hell you talking about?"

Augie drained what was in his cup and reached for his package of Luckies.

"I got a call ten minutes ago from Max."

"Max has got nothing to do with this. I laid a bet off with you, not Max. Now I want my money."

Fishing out a cigarette and putting it in this mouth, Augie snapped a green plastic lighter to flame, held it to his cigarette, drew in a lungful of smoke and exhaled blowing the smoke up toward the tiled ceiling.

Augie shook his head.

"You don't get it, do you, kid?"

"No, tell me."

"Max owns the operation, always has, from the jump. I work for him."

"I don't care if you suck his cock twice a day, I want my dough, Augie, or I'm going to bust you up."

"Easy now, kid," Augie said raising his palms. "It's Max you got the beef with, not me."

It was then that Bobby spotted the '60 customized Chrysler Windsor 300F, Johnny Pearl's. It had that ten-thousand dollar customized paint job all new white leather upholstery, matching drop top. The works. Johnny loved two things in the world—classic custom cars and boys. Johnny always bragging how much money he'd put into it, and there it sat, just waiting to be taken.

"That Johnny Pearl's car?" he said.

"Yeah, he dropped it off yesterday."

"What's wrong with it?"

"Nothing, he just wanted me to detail it." He lied about the blood cleanup. He's coming tomorrow to pick it up."

"Give me the keys."

"I can't do that."

"Then give me the money."

"I can't do that either, Bobby. Christ, don't you think I would if I could?"

He talked with the cigarette dangling from the corner of his mouth, the smoke curling up so that he had to squint in one eye, made him look like the cartoon character Popeye.

"You got about five seconds to give me my money or the keys to that car. I'm not fucking around with you, Augie. I've already knocked out one guy tonight, two would be a personal best for me."

***

Augie looked at Bobby Lee's swollen hands, the size of them.

"You wouldn't hit an old man would ya?"

Bobby closed the gap before Augie could take his cigarette out of his mouth and clipped him in the side of the jaw, not hard enough to break bone, but hard enough to send him sprawling out of his chair. Augie saw the constellations and his world dimmed before it brightened again.

"In . . . inna drawer," he pointed.

Bobby opened the desk drawer and found the keys to the car hanging on a silver fob, plus a wad of cash—also, a 1911 Colt .45, military style.

"What do you keep this for?" Bobby said holding it up.

"What the fuck you think? Protection."

"Yeah? Ain't doing you much good now is it?" He tucked the gun in his belt back behind his spine, and, well fuck it, why not, the cash too.

Augie, sitting there rubbing his jaw, the cigarette still in his mouth but crooked.

"You're in a shit load of trouble, kid. Rob me, you rob Max."

"Yeah, like I don't already know," Bobby said and walked over to the push buttons that operated the wide garage door where Augie took in cars and motorcycles on pawn, and the door cranked open. He got into the car and drove out onto Elm Avenue. He dropped it into first and stopped alongside his truck and got out his gym bag, unzipped it and dumped in the cash and the .45 then tossed it in the backseat of the Windsor and drove off.

All told it was a decent haul, but then why not, for his troubles as they were about to come. Hell, it might have even been his biggest payday as a fighter, what with Max's method of accounting.

***

Two hours up the highway just on the edge of Crossville, he was famished and weary. He pulled in to the Cascades Motel that had a restaurant across the parking lot. It looked like one of those rent by the hour sort of joint for trysts, the kind where some mid-level manager boss takes his secretary or aged married businessman his rent boy. It had a bed and a shower, and it was all he needed. He showered and went out again and deposited his gym bag in the trunk of the car, then walked across the parking lot to the restaurant to get something to eat. A nice juicy steak sounded good.

Nights with brightly lit restaurants are some of the loneliest places in the world, he thought as he went in and grabbed a booth.

The waitresses who served him wore a nametag that read, Jeanette: Middle age, not bad looking, some extra padding, nice smile, green eyes and reddish hair. Friendly, talkative like she was lonely maybe. In the end he paid his bill and went back to the motel across the way, pulled down the bedspread, turned up the a/c to full and climbed into bed.

What you going to do Bobby? You know that fucking Max is going to come for you. And Johnny Pearl, he'll kill you just for touching his car.

Shit if I know.

Better figure it out quick.

I know it.

He flexed his hands. They hurt. The world was a place full of hurt.

Chapter Three

"Let us consider that we are all insane."
—Mark Twain

One of the Ivory brothers drove up and saw police tape all around Buzzard's place, asked a neighbor woman in a Mumu standing there holding a fat little infant in diapers what happened. The lady said three guys were killed. She thought maybe it was a drug deal gone bad. "Least that's what I heard one of the cops say." The baby fussed.

"Me, personally," she said, "I won't miss that guy who lived there. Real troublemaker, you ask me. I was always worried they were cooking meth in there and would someday blow us all up. Good riddance, I say."

The dude quickly drove back to his brother's place, reported what happened, said, "Some neighbor said they killed three drug dealers, who the fuck *they* is."

The well-maintained guy skimming his swimming pool out back of his house said, "I know, I just saw it on the news. Showed pictures of them—in a state of life, of course. Buzzard, Dime Bag, and that little prick, Ray—called them 'known to the police.' "

"Then I bet the cops got the stash Buzzard was keeping in that dump of his, figuring nobody would ever rob him. I guess he was fucking wrong. You want a Dr. Pepper? I could go for one."

"No, but help yourself."

Then after a couple of minutes, the dude skimming his pool said, "What about that little chica Ray was running with? They didn't mention nothing about her on the news. Ray never went anywhere without her—like he was afraid she'd run off on him."

"Didn't see any broad around there," the other dude drinking the Dr. Pepper said.

"Yeah, but you'd think maybe she was with him when he ate a bullet? And if so, where is she now?"

"Good question."

"And, this is just a thought, but what if she didn't get killed, she went in there and got Buzzard's stash. Could that be a possibility?"

"Maybe. But she didn't look stupid enough she'd steal no fucken drugs off us, did she?"

"Listen to me, what I'm telling you. Given the right situation, everybody's a thief. You leave a "Hungry Man" frozen dinner laying around, even Mother Teresa, she's liable to grab it and scarf it down she's hungry enough. Don't kid yourself. Temptation is a mistress that will make you do shit you wouldn't ordinarily—and we all have our limits, how much we can resist. That little bitch, I seen her. I looked into her eyes once. I could tell that there was devils lurking in them."

"I don't know man. Ray had her pretty much dick whipped."

"Yeah, maybe when Ray was alive he did. But as so rightly pointed out, Ray is permanently incognito."

"Yeah, I can dig that."

"So we need to find out did she or didn't she. And even if she didn't, she probably knows who killed that cousin of mine, the stupid shit."

"I'm on it, dude."

"Make sure you drop the bottle in the recycle bin, huh?"

"Yeah, sure. Whatever."

"Oh, and don't come back to me in a couple of days and tell me you can't locate her. I don't want to hear that shit. Even if she is dead somewhere, I want you to take a picture and bring it to me. And if she ain't, I want to know where she is and what happened, and who took our goods out of that house. That's a lot of smack to just get legs and walk away. Somebody took it and I want you to start with her first."

"Hey boss,"

"What?"

"You missed a leaf over there."

"Get the fuck out of here."

"I'm already gone."

He needed to test the pool, see if it needed more chlorine, it was starting to look a little strange, the kids all pissing in it all the time, the little shits.

Chapter Four

"Freedom's Just Another Word For Nothing Left to Lose"
—Kris Kristofferson

Two years out of the pen and Jerry Summers was still trying to get used to freedom. The first couple of days was like a dream. He could go into any bar in town and get a drink. He didn't have to wake up anymore at a certain time or go to bed at a certain time. He could even be with a woman if that's what he wanted, but he still hadn't gotten over Mary Alice and his guilt.

He rented a small trailer in the Texas desert—a place where the wayward gathered in all manner of housing scattered over the desert's rough landscape—called Buscando Junction which was mostly a tire shop and one lonely ass little bar. Living out here nobody bothered you and yet if you needed help or something, somebody would always pitch in. The birds sang every morning like they were trying out for that TV talent show. And at night, it was so quiet you could hear yourself think. He had no TV, just a small transistor radio. He did have a telephone and a compost toilet and two metal lawn chairs he'd salvaged along the way. He had also acquired a lost black and white dog, a border collie that wasn't overly friendly, but seemed to like the place. Another refugee from society.

Twenty-two years he'd spent behind the wire. Was it worth it? This, a question he asked himself almost every day on the inside and every night on the outside. The answer always came back the same. Hell yes.

Was he bitter? No. Well, a little maybe. But truth was, he figured he'd already given too much of his life away on wasted second guessing and so he had to let the anger go.

Now he was content just getting up in the morning and sitting out under the awning with a cup of coffee and a cigarette, watching how the light changed as it passed over the landscape of yucca, honey mesquite, Mormon tea and all the rest, how it caused the pyrite to sparkle and swept dark shadows ahead of it out across the valley.

He tried not to think about her and that night all the violence broke loose. He tried not to think about it, but he did and each time it wounded him all over again. Robbie Winterfield, and the blood and screams, the crunching of bone and the splatter of blood as he beat Robbie to death with a hammer. And Christ, all the blood. Oh yeah, lots of that.

It was too late to save her, and after getting high on speed drove Robbie's body out into the desert and dropped him down an old mine shaft, then went back to the house and called the police. He was cradling her when they drove up and arrested his ass even though he told them what had happened. But when they asked him to show him where Robbie's body was, he couldn't remember. But of course the cops never believe a guy with a dead wife and the walls washed in blood.

They cuffed him, and riding in the back of the cruiser, thinking, well, so what, at least the son of a bitch who'd done it was dead. Mary Alice was gone as well, and to tell the truth, he hadn't much to live for now any fucken way. So take me to jail Mister *Po-leece* and lock me up and let me do the time 'cause it's all fucked.

So that was then and now it seemed like something that had happened to someone else, a story about a murder he'd read.

He hitched a ride to the bus station in Manzanita once in awhile and rode it to El Paso, to the cemetery and visited her grave and lay down next to it and talked to her. But less and less as the days went by, because he knew she wasn't really there, that her sweet soul had fled that violent night and she was living in glory far, far away from all the bullshit. It's where she deserved to be.

But the thing he thought about most was his only child, and a wild child she was too. He figured because he hadn't been there to finish raising her, and her care had been entrusted to the State of Texas, it must have been terrible for her. He'd lost contact after a couple of dozen different foster homes. The letters he sent were never returned nor answered but for one occasion that said she'd ran off soon as she turned sixteen.

Once he was released he had gone straight to the library in Buscando Junction—a spot in the road place had a gas station, feed store, combination bar and café and a little library about the size of his cell. But fortunately they had internet and one computer and he got the librarian to help him on the computer to try and find her, started searching the obituaries first, figured some guy would take advantage of her, or that she'd hit the streets like a lot of kids and maybe a pimp had gotten hold of her. His worst fears were imagined over and over again. But her name never came up—at least one that matched Nina Summers.

After that his life turned into the simplest existence. He checked out as many books as he could when the bookmobile came around, and between reading and his companion, the dog, Gus, he'd named him, all he could do was talk to the god up in the sky and ask for the girl's return or at the least somehow to contact him. He thought about her most of all. Oh, every once and awhile he hitched a ride into Manzanita right on the border—a real town because it had an IGA and a Dollar General, library and small hospital and such . . . And after a time he started visiting a woman whose name he'd been given in the beer joint by one of the men he'd gotten to know who mentioned about the woman, said her name was Nancy and that she was a good woman with a kind heart.

"She's not a prostitute as such," this Pete said. "Calls herself a comfort woman. I've known her for about four or five years now since she moved down here. A widow from Denver. Been going over there maybe once every couple of months. My wife don't know I go over there, and I'd never want her to because I love her and wouldn't want to lose her. You know how wives are . . ." then caught himself and apologized.

It was a slow night and still early yet when they got to talking over a game of shuffleboard.

"She don't have them lining up out the door, no sir, it ain't that at all. Far as I know, she has to take a liking to you to invite you in and let you stay in. How I met her was I went over there to fix some plumbing problems she was having in that old house and we got to talking and it just went on from there."

So the next time he went to Manzanita he went on over there and knocked on her screen door and she came to answer it with her hair tied up in a scarf like she'd been cleaning house or she was just hot, holding a glass of tea in her hand and peered down at him through the screen.

"Pete mentioned your name and I was wondering if maybe I could pay you a visit for a little while," he'd said that first time.

"What's your name?" she'd asked.

"Jerry Summers," he said.

"And what is it you want to visit with me for, Jerry Summers?"

"Tell the truth, I reckon it's just to be in the company of someone—a woman, I mean—that's nice and I could carry on a conversation with. Pete said you liked to carry on a good conversation. I do too. I had a wife, but she died some time back and I've been gone."

"Where you been gone to, Jerry Summers?"

"Up to state's prison, twenty-two long damn years. But I done my time and I'm a freeborn soul. That's to say I'm no problem to anyone. You could ask Pete about me, or anybody. I'm just lonely is what it is. Tired of my own company."

"You do know that there are plenty of girls goes to the roadhouse in Jonestown, don't you? All kinds of girls—young ones too."

"I reckon I did not know it, but I reckon I'd not be interested so much in such girls. And I understand if you turn me away. I really do. And if you want, I could just sit out here and we could talk through the screen. Even that I'd be grateful for."

She swung the screen door open, but had neither moved nor invited him in.

"What else did Pete tell you about me, Jerry Summers?"

"Told me you were a real decent and kind person. Told me he sometimes comes around to visit you. He spoke highly of you and I reckon that's what got my interest up—that he spoke so highly of you. Said you understood his situation, about him and his wife, I mean. That's all."

She stood appraising him as if he was something she was considering, like a Bible salesman trying to sell her a family edition of the Good Book.

"Well, come on in and I'll get you a glass of this tea and we can sit out back and talk. You caught me in the middle of spring cleaning, or is it summer? Hard to tell in south Texas." Her laughter was full throated, and she seemed to sway the way happy women sway and her happiness latched onto him and suddenly he felt happy too.

That's all they did, talk, mostly her asking him about why he'd gone to prison and he told her. She seemed to understand and accept what he told her. He'd gone back several times in the two years since his release and each time it felt to him like a happy marriage even if it was only for a few hours. And he was always happy the day when he got ready to go over there and he was happy when he left.

Nancy had three or four or five regular visitors, men like himself and Pete, by the way she spoke of them. Told him one or two she'd only see a couple of times a year—like the fellow out of Houston who came through selling farm equipment. She always made a nice lunch and, if the weather was good, they would sit out back at a small picnic table and eat and drink cold tea and talk about almost everything under the sun.

She was a great conversationalist and knew when to listen and when to ask questions or talk about things that interested her.

The lunch would be leisurely and then they would go inside and into her bedroom, which was in the back east side of the house where it was coolest that time of day, and she'd have the shades and curtains partially closed so that it was dim as well. Just a nice cool dim place. Then she would proceed to undress him as if undressing a child, slowly and all while humming some low soft tune, taking time only to kiss his mouth and touch his face, until she had his shirt off, his belt undone, trousers unzipped, then she would have him sit on the side of the bed and take off his shoes and socks and finish pulling off his trousers and then his underwear before having him lay back.

He would watch her undress because she had said the first time that she wanted him to watch her, that it felt good to have him watch her.

"I'd like it if you watch me undress. I'll do it slowly. My husband used to like that and it turned me on."

He'd never had a woman talk to him that way, act that way, treat him that way, not even his late wife and it touched something he hadn't know was there before.

Then she would lie down beside him and draw his hands over her nakedness and kiss him the whole while and like that for the next couple of hours. And when they'd finished, she would say, "Excuse me, Jerry," and rise from the bed while grabbing a nightgown she'd had hanging over the back of a chair and disappear into the bathroom, saying over her shoulder, "You can get dressed now. Just leave the money on the nightstand. Call me ahead when you want to visit again. Thank you, love, and goodbye for now."

The first time he wasn't sure how much to leave so he left pretty much what he had in his wallet, forty-two dollars.

Then the next time he'd visited he asked her about it there in the back yard as they were eating egg salad sandwiches and drinking iced tea this time.

"Well, one-hundred dollars is the minimum for my time . . . but I understand if you can't afford that much. But do let me know if you can't. I mean I don't want to sound mercenary, honey, but I'm trying to survive the best I can, and while I enjoy talking to you and everything . . . it's just not possible without. Well, you know."

He said that he absolutely understood and that the money wasn't a problem—even though it really was. But he wanted badly to see her time and again and so saved all he could between times and thought, that was how things were supposed to be, weren't they—that you didn't overindulge in a thing you liked to the point it lost its value to you?

And so for two years he'd found a form of salvation that fed his soul enough he began to feel human again in the way humans are supposed to—good and kind and whatever it cost him to see her, it was worth every cent.

Chapter Five

"Vices Are Their Own Punishment"
—Aesop

Johnny Pearl came rushing in yelling, "That fucker, that dirty prick, I'm going to kill him!"

Max was getting head from one of his girls there in the back room of his strip club, the new blonde he'd hired: twenty something and skinny, but big plastic boobs her biker husband had paid for with money you were better off not to ask its source. Max had a pudgy hand resting atop her bobbing head but took it off at the intrusion of his bodyguard.

She momentarily stopped, looked up too, but he said, "Keep going" and she resumed.

"Who the fuck you talking about?" Max asked Johnny.

"Bobby Lee, who else. I just got a call from Augie, the son of a bitch went over there trying to get his money, which you told him not to give to that mutt, so instead, he slapped Augie around, took the keys to my car and the cash Augie had on hand and got in the wind. I knew we should have taken care of this business sooner than later." Johnny being careful what he said in front of the dancer, because them broads were the worst gossips in the world.

"Don't worry," Max said. "I've taken care of it already."

"You've taken care of it? How the fuck'd you take care of it?"

"I put a call in to the Cowboy, he'll be here tomorrow. Then everything will be handled. So not to worry."

Max, shifting around in his leather swivel chair with the girl working on him, getting him close, starting to sweat, his eyes getting a bit dreamy.

"You didn't need to call him," Johnny said. "That's what you got me for."

"I got you to watch my back, be my body man, like the President's got, sort of a Secret Service butler, like that. I got the Cowboy for the heavy stuff that will keep the stink of the bad shit away from us. Now get the fuck out of here so Carol here can finish up and get back out there and earn her keep on the pole, will ya. She's got a new kid to feed."

"Looks like she's already earning her keep on the pole," Johnny said sarcastically.

Johnny went out shutting the door hard and walked down a short hall to the main room where the girls danced, sold customers drinks, lap dances, and whatever else they wanted. Just one rule, no sex on property; you had to take the men somewhere else you wanted to sell your ass. Cops were funny that way.

This being Saturday night, the place was full of all types from truckers to guys in suits. After all, pussy was pussy and men were men and, in this case, hardly ever the twain shall meet.

The music was loud, and the spotlight shone a miasma of swirling smoke as it highlighted the current dancer Chocolate Cherry, a black chick Max was grooming for himself. Couldn't say Max was discriminatory—he hired any girl who was under thirty and had a nice body, no matter their color. Oh yeah, and it helped if they could actually dance, or at least look like they were dancing while they were sharing their tits and beaver with a room full of drooling strangers. Max always said what he sold wasn't pussy, it was the dream of pussy. Over half the guys who walked through the door were married, but that didn't stop them from dreaming.

Johnny Pearl stopped at the bar and Levi served him his usual, gin, lemon and seven-up. Levi was a nice looking college type that Johnny, in his capacity of bar manager, had himself hired—one of the allowances

Max had given him, besides the other stuff he had him do because he knew Johnny's tastes ran, well, let's say, to the other side of the street. Max didn't care, as long as Johnny was loyal—and he was—and did whatever Max told him to, which he did. He was also Max's ex-wife's kid brother, Max being the generous sort, which he was when it came to said ex-wife, Irene, only because she was the one woman he had still had a real thing for, even if she had been the one who filed for divorce citing irreconcilable differences. Max would do anything for her.

So when he learned of Johnny's true nature, he simply said, "Look, everybody fucks somebody, and it don't matter to me who you do, okay." But when he'd given Johnny the job of club manager, he told him, "Don't let me catch you forcing the help to do your sexual bidding, you understand. I can't stand no fucken lawsuits." Johnny thinking, "don't do as I do, do as I say." That was Max.

"How's it going tonight," Mr. Pearl?" the new bartender shouted over the blare of the current number Cherry was dancing to—"I'm So Excited."

Johnny was still in a foul mood, but when he looked at that handsome boy's face, he mellowed.

"Good, you?"

The kid was jumping around trying to keep up with the drink orders the waitresses—who were the dancers not currently dancing—were bringing him.

The kid nodded as he poured.

"Yeah, busy!" he shouted back.

Finally the song stopped and Cherry exited the stage after picking up the dollar bills the cheap bastards had tossed her, and for a moment it was at least quiet enough to talk without shouting and a slight lull in the drink orders.

"Got my car stolen," Johnny said, maybe seeking some sympathy from the kid, you know, get him chatting so you can maybe work something out for later. Johnny glanced at his fake Rolex, it was about an hour to closing time.

"Gee, that's too bad," Levi said, pouring two shots, one for him and one for Johnny.

"What's this?"

"Tequila," Levi said. "Only way I know to forget your troubles. Salute."

Johnny raised his glass and touched it to Levi's. Jesus what a good-looking kid he was.

In a couple of minutes more, the blonde who'd been blowing Max in the office got up on stage, Carol, whatever the fuck her last name was—she went by the name Madonna and right away started dancing to "Like A Virgin" and Johnny thought, like hell. Anybody'd blow Maxie sure as fuck was no virgin, not even close. Max had a short fat prick no decent girl would let her mouth get within a mile of. Johnny couldn't figure what his sister ever saw in Max for the six months they were married, asked her once, said, "Sis what'd you ever see in Max for chrissake?" She said, "Money, dumbass. And don't talk so bad about your brother-in-law, I'm getting him to set you up. Don't bite the horse that feeds you." Johnny laughed, his sister was sweet, but dumber than a box of doorknobs, said, "Hand that feeds you." She just looked at him.

This was before her and Max got divorced. Johnny was surprised Max hadn't let him go after they split, but he hadn't and confessed Irene had this strange hold over him and that he loved her like a Catholic loves the Pope.

Anyway Johnny thought he'd hang around awhile, till closing, see couldn't he get somewhere with Levi after, even though Johnny was supposed to count the night's receipts after closing while Ginny the

34

Gimp, who was the other bartender on busy nights, had to clean up before they left. Maybe he'd send Ginny home so it could be just him and Levi there and they could talk, see how far and fast the young man wanted to get somewhere—assistant manager, maybe if he played along.

The only thing Johnny overlooked in his nefarious plan was how drunk he'd gotten by the time the night ended, drinking out of misery for his stolen car, for the fact Max didn't trust him to take care of that fucker Bobby Lee and instead called the Cowboy to take care of it. And besides the kid had shown no interest in Johnny's thinly veiled attempts since he'd started working at the club. It just made Johnny that much more determined to woo the kid over knowing that even straight guys were curious. Johnny had certainly had his share of those, too.

He was throwing them back one after another. And the next thing he knew, he awoke to someone shaking his shoulder, raised his head off the bar and saw a blurry figure wearing a large hat.

The Cowboy had arrived.

***

Max slept over at Chocolate Cherry's place after she got through dancing. She kept a fuck pad paid for by Max on the West end. What Johnny did not know, however was, that Max wasn't her only regular.

Besides Max, she had a hedge fund manager with a wife and three kids who lived in a nice waterside estate overlooking the Gulf. He had told her his wife's name, Amber, and the kids, Danny, Granger and Louisa, all privately schooled while mommy dearest spent most of her days at the spa, shopping and going to lunches with her equally privileged girlfriends. Like Cherry gave a shit, but she pretended to. Most likely, Cherry figured, the wife never had a hint her hubby of fifteen years kept a mistress the flavor of Chocolate Cherry, AKA Denise Waters. No baby, that shit don't fly.

Cherry let Ian, the hedge fund guy know when it was safe to come over, when neither Max would be there or that other equally well-off old dude, Foster, who was an accountant for the largest bank in the city, Peter Pringle, who had purchased her a nice used Caddy to get around with. She hadn't done too bad for herself only being in town less than a year. She danced the nights either of her mens, as she called them, would be coming around. The hedge fund guy was always middle of the day on his lunch hour, and the goofy little accountant who reminded her of Yodo, or whatever the fuck his name was in that Star Wars thing, was always the second Tuesday of each month. Thing with that old dude was all he wanted to do was to have her fondle him while she talked dirty to him. Oh, well, she thought, whatever works.

Max, was another matter. Max was her latest boss and she always worked them especially hard if they took a shine to her, because they were generally the easiest to get the cash from. A fuck pad was one thing, and a used Caddy another, but it was the green that really counted.

"Hey baby," she'd said when he came over that night, handing him a Makers Mark. "Come take care of mama, mama been needin' you, baby, real bad." It always got Max aroused the way she talked to him, like no other woman but his ex-wife.

So they were laying in the bed, morning light streaming through the window like ten police flashlights, when someone rapped on the door and rang the doorbell.

Max sat up. Cherry sat up, her large cocoa tits so beautiful Max thought they should be a National Landmark.

"Who be ringing my door this early?"

"Well, go see who the fuck it is," Max said.

He watched Cherry slip from the bed and throw on a terry cloth robe and go to the door in the other room. Then heard: "Max, Clint Eastwood's here to see you. Nice lookin' dude, too."

Max thinking: What the fuck, is she high?

Chapter Six

"Hell Is Empty.
All the Devils are Here."
—Shakespeare

She didn't know where she was at, nor did she much care. At least she'd cleared the spaghetti highways of Miami. She'd driven until she nearly fell asleep at the wheel and only the blaring of a sixteen-wheeler and bright glare of his headlights snapped her to in time to get back on her side of the road.

Fuck, she thought, I better find a place to pull in. The next place she saw emerging out of the darkness was a motel sign that said, VACANCY in bright yellow lights.

She eased the Charger into the slot next to the office and a fat woman in a robe and carrying a yappy little dog in her arms came out of the back and said, "How many?"

"Just me."

"Sign the register please."

She had a smoker's cough and between it and the little fucker barking at her, it didn't help Nina's headache one bit.

"Cash or credit?"

"Cash."

"Forty-two plus tax, comes to forty-seven fifty."

Nina took Ray's roll of cash out of her jacket pocket, snapped off the rubber band, and was glad to see there wasn't any blood on it and gave the woman three twenties.

"I don't got no cash till morning, if that's alright?"

"That's fine."

"You want up front or toward the back where it's quieter, don't get no noise from the highway."

"Back."

The woman handed her a key with a large green plastic fob imprinted with 120.

"Just one night?"

"Yeah."

"Okay then. No loud noises or men. You ain't the kind to have men in there are you? I don't run no cathouse. Some of them women like you try and use this place like that. It used to be before me and Eddy bought it. But I'm a Christian woman."

"Me too," Nina said and saw the woman's face change from stern to accepting.

"Good for you, honey. God bless and good night."

Nina eased the car down the parking lot until her headlight swept the right room number.

Goddamn she was starved. Saw a restaurant across the way. Later, she thought, I've got to shower first, make sure there's no blood in my hair or anywhere else.

She got out grabbed the garbage bag and gun then locked the Charger and entered the room. It was cold and lifeless and it took her several minutes to figure out the heating thing on the wall below the window. And when it came on it rattled. She waited until it got warm enough, then undressed and went into the bathroom, turned on the shower and got in, standing under the spray and getting it as hot as she could stand it.

She stood there for a long time crying, her palms pressed against the tiles, the water running off her back.

What'd I ever do so wrong as to have my life come to this—to kill three men? "Goddamn, Nina! Goddamn."

***

She finished washing with the small bars of soap and her hair with the tiny bottle of shampoo and sure enough, when she rinsed the first time, the water washed out pink from the splatter of blood there. Finally she got clean and got out using the small towels to dry herself off, got dressed again in her Metallica t-shirt and cut-off jeans, then slipped the athletic jacket on that Ray had given her once, never explaining where he got it, but it was new with the price tag still on it.

She was whipped but also very hungry, thought for a moment, killing fuckers sure gives you the munchies, laughed at her own sick joke.

She decided to walk over to the restaurant. Between the motel, there was a space of darkness, but after all, she had that big ass gun. Looked around, thought, nah, leave it and the garbage bag in the trunk of the car.

As she walked across the lot, the closer she got to the restaurant it reminded her of that Edward Hooper painting. She'd always had a thing for art. Hardly anybody in the place this time of night but a few lonely souls. She went in and the waitress said, "Sit anywhere you like, honey. You want coffee?"

"Sure, yeah."

She walked toward the back so she could keep an eye on anyone coming in. She wasn't exactly expecting anyone, but with what had transpired, she wasn't taking any chances.

Ray had told her a lot of bad stories about the shit drug dealers did when someone stole from them. It was scary, though half the shit Ray said was made up lies, so you really didn't know what was truth and what wasn't. Listening to him, you'd think he was a tough guy, but what he was was a worthless prick who'd used her as collateral for drugs.

She slid into a booth and the waitress brought her a glass of ice water and some coffee.

"Do you know what you want, hon?"

She was tempted to say, *A good man and a little house in the mountains, maybe a dog or two, some chickens. I always wanted me some chickens, oh, and yeah, kids. Cute little kids running around in the yard.*

Instead she said: "Whatever is good you'd recommend."

"Patty melt's pretty good, so is the meatloaf if there's still any."

"Either one sounds fine. You got onion rings?"

"Yeah, I'll get Sammy to whip you up some."

"Thanks."

She sat there sipping coffee, only slightly noticed the guy across the way, sitting against the opposite wall by himself, head down as if he was praying or something. Big guy. He looked slightly familiar but she didn't waste time trying to figure it out.

She kept thinking about the shooting. She still couldn't believe it had happened. It was more like she'd seen it in a movie, and the actress looked like her and the bad guys like Ray and Buzzard and Dime Bag. That she'd wake up tomorrow and everything would be as it had been.

She shuddered to think Ray would be there.

She glanced out at the poorly lit parking lot, the few cars, their headlights sweeping along the highway.

She took out a cigarette and smoked it then put it out when she saw the waitress bringing her food and set the plate down.

She leaned over.

"Hon, just so you know, there's no smoking in here."

She said it with a southern accent that reminded her of her late mother.

"Sorry," she said. "I forgot—all these new laws."

"It's okay. Bud is in the back counting receipts so he didn't see you and Sammy smokes out back every chance he gets. I used to smoke too."

She wore a lot of makeup and her lipstick was very bright red and she looked like she maybe once had a good figure but was a victim of middle-aged spread. Wondered briefly if the same would happen to her. Jesus, she didn't think so because she didn't think she was going to live that long—especially if those guys Ray and Buzzard were dealing drugs with caught up to her.

"Which way you heading, hon?"

"North," she lied.

"I've always wanted to live in Arizona where the sun shines all the time. Maybe someday if I could ever get Jimmy off his ass. Jimmy's my husband in case you haven't guessed. Been married going on thirty years, but don't ask me why. We don't have a living thing in common anymore. Sometimes it feels like I'm living with my brother. Can I tell you something?"

Nina nodded, thinking: You've already told me more than I care to hear.

"If you ever get married to a man, live with him for about six, seven years so you know everything there is about him and whether you like what you know. That way there'll be no surprises later on—like he's a damn big couch potato that never wants to go nowhere or do nothing. Well, I got to get back up front. You need anything just wave."

Christ, Nina thought. What is it about me that attracts them? She was starved and wolfed down the sandwich and every one of the greasy onion rings and washed it down with coffee and ice water.

She got up and walked to the front and the waitress made out her check then rang it up and Nina paid with cash, the waitress saying as she went out the door, "Have a safe trip, hon. And if you cross Arizona, say hey for me."

Then at the last second, Nina asked if there was a payphone.

"Sure, hon, right around the corner there, just before you get to the restrooms.

Nina laid a twenty on the counter and asked for some of it in change, quarters and dimes and nickels. Then scooped it up and disappeared around the corner to the payphones, lifted the receiver and gave the operator the number she wanted to dial and was told how much money to deposit. Each coin was like the tolling of the bells.

She listened to the muted ringing at the other end, nearly hung up, but no, she'd come too far. Then a man's gruff sleepy voice.

"Yeah?"

"Daddy."

Chapter Seven

"Lead Me Not Into Temptation
I Can Find the way Myself."
—Rita Mae Brown

For some reason he was attracted enough to watch her rise from her booth and go to the front and stop at the cash register, saw the waitress ring her up and chat for a bit then watched the girl turn around the corner figuring she was hitting the john.

He didn't know what it was about her, but she reminded him of an old flame, Julie McKowski. Jesus how that woman broke his heart. He was so damn in love with her he just couldn't believe it when she told him the truth two weeks before they were to get married.

"How can you love another woman when you've been with me for six months and agreed to marry me?"

She told him she didn't know. Told him she was conflicted.

"Conflicted? Goddamn, I guess."

She told him it was just something she'd always felt but until she met Jill, her boss at work, she didn't realize how much she was who she truly was.

They drank two bottles of wine that night sitting on her living room floor and the firelight flickering across her face just made her so fucking beautiful he cried, and she did too.

"Just be my friend, Bobby," she'd pleaded. "I don't want to lose you as a friend. Please?"

She really was too good a person to reject entirely and they had remained friends for a few years until she and Jill and their adopted child were killed in a car wreck. He couldn't fuck believe that either. It had hurt him a hundred times worse as the news she told him about herself. He wept at her funeral and was one of the pallbearers and said almost like a prayer: "I'm carrying you home, baby. I'm carrying you home."

After that he enlisted into the Marines for four years and that's when he got into boxing. Long time ago, seemed like another century now.

But it was Julie McKowski who caused him to take notice of the girl. They looked enough alike to have been sisters, except Jill had only one brother.

He waited until she appeared again, the waitress telling her goodnight, then he rose and went and paid his bill, leaving a ten on the counter and hearing, "Gee, darlin' that's real sweet of you" as he exited the door a few dozen steps behind the girl who walked fast.

He didn't try and catch her. Didn't need to.

A group of young guys hanging out by the office, whose light was now out, saw her coming too and intercepted her.

"Hey baby. You working tonight?" one of them said.

"Get the fuck away from me," she said.

They gave a mock "Ooooh" and held up their hands. But they were blocking her from getting into her room.

"I mean it assholes," she warned.

Again, they mocked her.

That's when Bobby caught up to her, said, "There a problem here, Miss?"

"No problem, these jerkoffs were just being jerkoffs."

Now it was on and Bobby could see that it was, because A, he was a man and he understood men, especially mouthy punks, and B, he was tired and needed rest, and C, he just didn't like the motherfuckers.

They braced him.

"Whatcha going to do muthafucka?" the biggest of the lads said in that tough guy way he must have seen tough guys on television or the movies say it.

"Just this," Bobby said and took out the forty-five and aimed it at him.

They both fled like spooked rabbits. He put the gun away, said, "You alright?"

"Yes. You're from the restaurant?"

"Yeah, I guess we're the only two out having a good time tonight." Caused her to smile a little.

"Thanks. Why aren't these dildoes at home eating fruit loops instead of harassing people?"

"Hell if I know," he said. "Name's Bobby. I'm staying in room nine. You want, I'll wait till you get inside and lock your door. I'm going to have a smoke out here anyway."

"In this?"

It had begun to rain lightly the way Florida rain is at night.

"I'll stand under the eaves. I like being outside."

"You got a spare one?"

"Last I knew they came twenty in a pack, I got half a pack, so that leaves ten, five for you, five for me."

"Just one, thank you."

He shook one out of the pack and she took it, then one for him and he flicked the Zippo to flame, the same lighter he had in the Corps, in the Gulf War, had a bronze eagle and globe on it.

They stood under the eaves and the yellow bug lights and smoked and watched the rain drip.

"I noticed your hands," she said.

"Yeah. I fought a guy earlier tonight—in the ring, I mean. I'm not sure I hadn't had this piece on me I could have whipped those guys it came to it. I can't hardly open and close them."

"You know I think maybe that's where I seen you—on TV, boxing. My . . ." she started to say her boyfriend, but quickly changed it instead to: "My ex-boyfriend was always watching boxing matches, even the Pay-for-view, betting on them, like everything else, him and his homies, as he called them. He'd make me watch them with him. Oddly enough I found it pretty exciting watching men beat the shit out of each other. But I can't remember your name or anything. Are you famous?"

"Hardly," he said. "I mean I fought some pretty top notch guys, and was in the top ten in my class, so maybe you did see me once in awhile."

"Bobby?" she said. "So what's you're last name?"

"Lee," he said. "My old man had this thing he thought we were related somehow to the Civil War general—Robert E. Lee. I always thought he was nuts. He named me for him, so I mean what the hell, huh? Say I didn't catch your name, fair is fair."

She thought about it a second.

"Kelly" she said. "Kelly Smith, from Hollywood—the one in Florida." Where she came up with that, she didn't know, but it sounded good.

"Nice to meet you, Kelly Smith from Hollywood, the one in Florida."

"You, too, Bobby."

She flicked the cigarette butt away, said, "Well, I better get to bed, get an early start. Going to visit my daddy. Haven't seen him in awhile."

"I bet he'll be glad to see you, then," he said. "Goodnight, Kelly."

He watched her head to her room, waited till she got a large garbage bag out of her car and carried it in and closed the door. He smoked another cigarette. She seemed like a real nice girl. But this time of night, out alone, sharp looking car like that Charger, she had a story to tell, that was a fact. He'd known girls like that before, the live hard die young type. Wondered what her story was, then told himself, he didn't want to know.

***

He found the key to get into his room and cranked up the air because it was stuffy, then stripped out of his clothes and threw himself on the bed, so exhausted he could barely move, exhausted and the pain from the blows he'd taken in the ring starting to chew on him. He lay listening to the air conditioner rattle and blow, it sounded almost like the engine of a Model A he thought.

He fell asleep. How long he'd been out, he didn't know, but was awakened at someone knocking on his door. Sat up, reached for the piece under his pillow, the .45, hoped it wasn't the cops, or worse, someone sent by Max. Went from bed to door in his shorts, that gun in his hand behind his back. He slipped the chain on the latch and opened it a crack ready to shoot whoever it was in the face in case some fucking how Johnny Pearl had caught up with him.

It wasn't Johnny Pearl. It was the waitress from the restaurant.

"Hi," she said. "Could I come in?"

He didn't know what to say, but let her in.

"Wondered if you wanted company," she said. She pulled a bottle of Jim Beam from a paper sack.

"This place have a glass?"

He went into the bathroom and got her a glass and when he came out she'd kicked off her shoes and was sitting on the side of the bed. He handed her the glass and watched as she poured it half full, then took a drink and offered him one. He took it. She patted the bed beside her, said, "Why don't you sit down, I won't bite."

So he did because he didn't know what else to do.

48

"I just want to talk," she said. "I get so damn lonely to talk to another human, a man, I mean. There in the restaurant, I got the vibe you might be interested, thought, what the hell, give it a shot. I mean, I know I'm older than you, but some guys like that. Do you like that?"

He watched as she took another drink of the whiskey and held the glass out to him, but he didn't take it from her.

"Would you like to kiss me," she said, taking his hand and putting it on her breast. And before he could do anything, she kissed him hard on the mouth.

"No," he said softly when she broke off the kiss. "I mean if I didn't already have someone waiting for me, I'd be interested for sure. But I'm a one-woman man."

Her face seemed to crumple and she let loose of her hand, said, "That's okay, I didn't figure I stood a chance. But I mean ,what the hell, it was worth a try, huh?"

He didn't say anything.

"Well," she said standing up, the sacked bottle in her hand. "I guess, I'll get going. Thanks for being true to your sweetheart. Not many men are. Whoever she is, she's lucky. See you around, sugar."

He stood thinking, Man that could have gone sideways in a hurry. Then felt badly for her, a woman that lonely, anybody that lonely. Went and laid down on the bed hoping he could get back to sleep. Truth be told, it was in a way tempting, and flattering in a way that such things are in the middle of the night in a strange place with strangers.

Chapter Eight

"Never Lie Down With a Woman
Who's Got More Troubles Than You"
—Nelson Algren

He didn't know how long he'd slept, but was awakened at someone knocking on his door again, prayed it wasn't the waitress again.

Once more he reached for the .45, the weight of it in his hand comforting, a little anyway. Stood and walked to the door thinking it could be Johnny Pearl. But how the hell had he found him? Well, duh, the Windsor. A car like that was so rare it was probably the only one in the state. He should have ditched it, but then he'd be out what it was worth, what he could sell it for whenever he got to where he was going, which, by the way, was yet to be determined.

If it was Johnny with some of Max's guys, he was going to empty the whole damn clip on them if he had to. He could barely get his swollen forefinger in the trigger guard.

But then again, it was more likely just a Jehovah's Witness. He lowered the piece and held it down behind his leg as he slipped the chain on the door and opened it slowly.

It was Kelly from Hollywood in Florida from last night. She looked upset. "You believe this shit!" she yelled. "Some bastard stole my car. Jesus fucking Christ! I bet it was those pricks from last night."

She stood there pointing back in the direction of her room and he stepped out just in his boxer shorts and that .45 in his hand still, forgetting it was there.

He didn't see the Dodge.

"Come on in, let me get dressed and we'll call the police." Then he thought, shit, do I really want the police asking me questions? But fuck it, for her sake, yeah.

She came in, her room key in her hand and closed the door behind her.

"No police," she said.

***

He stopped and stood there and her eyes did not avert away from his near nakedness, but for those boxers and the handgun.

"Looks like one of us had a good night anyway," she said.

"What do you mean?"

"You got lipstick on your mouth. Was it that waitress? It looks like her shade of lipstick."

He rushed into the small bathroom, grabbed a washcloth. From the other room he heard her said: "I didn't take you for the MILF type."

He finished washing off the lipstick and came out and said, "What?"

She was laughing. He threw the gun on the bed, pulled on his trousers and then a shirt, was buttoning it, said, "What's a MILF?'

"Jesus, you retarded?"

"No, just brain damaged, a little," he grinned. "So what do you want to do about your car?"

"Nothing. It wasn't mine to begin with. "

"Is there some reason you don't want the cops involved?" he said.

"You mean besides the fact I stole it from my boyfriend? Well, not exactly my boyfriend, but a friend of his—the kind of guy you don't want to steal a car from. I mean if he were alive, which he is not. But he's got friends who he does business with who might like to get it back. Jesus, listen to me yak on, like I'm in confession and you're Mother Teresa or something. Where are you headed?"

"Fuck if I know, but out of Florida, that's for damn sure."

"Me too. Let's go together, least until we get out of this fucken place."

"Fine with me," he said.

"Good, then it's settled."

"I thought you were going to see your father?"

"I am. He lives in Texas way out in the desert. I don't think the guys who'd be after me would find me there. Least I hope not."

"How bad do these guy want to find you?" he said buttoning his shirt. "Bad or real bad?"

"Real bad."

"Go get your things and I'll drive over and pick you up."

He waited while she hauled out the big garbage bag and put it in the back seat then climbed in.

"You ready slick?"

"Name's Bobby Lee, case you forgot."

"I didn't."

"You're a wiseass."

"Yeah, tell me something I don't already know."

He dropped the car in gear and eased out of the parking lot looking both ways at the street entrance, not so much for the traffic as for Max's gold Caddy El Dorado, had all that chrome trim he had put on extra. Bobby didn't see it.

"Which way?"

"Left, I think."

"You don't know?"

"Do I look like I know anything from anything? I've been with this asshole boyfriend of mine so long. He did all the direction thing."

He turned left, the tailpipes giving a throaty rumble.

"Jesus Christ, this is like from the Ice Age or something," she said looking around the interior of the car, "but pretty fucken cool too."

"We'll find a gas station and get an Atlas," he said.

"You sure you don't want to swing by the restaurant for breakfast, see your girlfriend?"

He glanced at her.

"You really are a piece of work," he said.

"You know something, Chipper, you're not the only one's got a gun."

"I told you my name is Bobby Lee. And what the fuck do you mean?"

She showed him the chrome .357 revolver she'd taken from her jacket pocket.

"Jesus Christ, put that away." She did. "Where'd the fuck'd you get that?"

"Same place I got the car. I told you, Ray's friends—that's my boy-friend, or used to be—were some real badass people."

He pulled into a big Sunoco out the edge of town, the kind sold everything plus gas. She went in with him.

"In case you need backup," she said when he shot her a look.

"I'm not planning on robbing the place, just buy an Atlas," he said.

"You just never know Skippy."

He shook his head, found an Atlas, took it to the counter, asked for two packages of Chesterfields, pack of gum, was about to pay when here she came carrying a bottle of flavored ice tea, package of potato chips and one of beef jerky and dropped them next to his stuff.

"I'll treat next time," she said. "I left my money in the car."

He arched a scarred eyebrow, then paid for the works.

He studied the Atlas sitting in the car, said "Need to get up to I-10 then head west."

"Aye-aye, El Capitan."

Once they got onto Westbound I-10 he said, "What's in the bag?"

"My life's work," she said.

"Oh, you're an artist or something?"

"Yeah," thinking you damn right I am. Took down those goons hadn't I? She was tired of being used by men. Time to turn it around. Like now, with boxer boy driving her hopefully to see her old man, a veritable stranger who'd killed her mother. He proclaimed he was inno-cent, that it was some other dude who he'd then killed. And as a child, at first she believed him. But later when she researched it, there was one article in the newspapers that said it was a lover's triangle and that her mother had been caught sleeping with the guy her father had killed. Fuck, who knew what the truth really was. She thought maybe now was the time to find out if killing was in the family blood.

She wondered about this dude driving. Maybe ten years older than her. He'd sure had his face knocked around in the ring but oddly he still looked pretty handsome in a rugged way. At least he wasn't some punk like Ray turned out to be.

"Were you any good as a boxer?" she said.

"Why do you want to know?"

"Well, I'm no expert or anything, but sitting here looking at you, you don't look like you won too many fights. What was your record."

"I won more than I lost."

"Does your face hurt?"

He touched it with the tips of the fingers on his right hand, his other on the wheel.

"Nah."

"Well, it's killing me!" she yelped in laughter.

"What're you, like nine?"

"Honey, I bet when I was nine I was more woman than you were man when you were nine."

"That, I don't doubt."

They drove the next hundred miles without talking but she did turn on the radio playing rock and roll music, something he didn't much care for and after about half an hour he turned it off, said, "You're making my eyes bleed."

"*Sooory*," she mewed. "I forgot you're an old hide."

He wished now he'd had gotten something to drink too, watching her chug that iced tea with beads of sweat forming on the outside. But he kept driving until near noon when he saw a truck stop that looked like an eighteen-wheel convention and a big ass restaurant and pulled in.

"I could use something cold to drink and maybe a burger," he said turning off the ignition.

"I thought you'd never ask. I've got to pee so bad my back teeth are floating. Last one in's a monkey's uncle."

"Jesus, should I get you a plush toy in there?"

She tossed him the finger and went in ahead of him. He called out, "Get a window seat. I'd like to keep an eye out for certain people."

She acted like she hadn't heard him, but by the time he got inside, she was already in a window booth and looking at the menu. He sat down opposite, noted a lot of the big lugs sitting at the counter had turned halfway around to stare at her in those cut-off jeans.

The waitress came over with her order pad and asked what she could get them to drink, he said just ice water, two glasses, and Nina said she'd have a Pepsi, then quickly changed her mind and said to make it a root beer float instead.

"Y'all decided what you want to eat?"

"Steak and baked potato," Bobby Lee said without waiting for Nina to answer first figuring she'd talk all damn day, but she didn't, spoke up and said, "Is the taco salad good here?"

"I think so," the waitress said.

"Then that's what I'll have, thank you."

The waitress nodded and went away.

"Taco salad and root beer float?" Bobby said.

"Yeah, sure, why not, it's a free country."

While they waited, Nina chewed a stick of gum she took from her purse and tapped her fingernails on the tabletop.

"So what's your story, anyway, Jack. I mean above what you've thus far shared." Bobby thought she called him everything but his name just to agitate.

"Why do you care?"

"I like to know who I'm keeping company with."

"Considering your carrying a gun, I can see why."

She offered him a facetious grin, said, "Like you're not" then she leaned over the table and conspiratorially asked: "You kill somebody?"

"Not yet."

She offered a knowing grin.

"I suppose you have?" he said.

She leaned in even closer, said, "You really want to know the truth?"

He wasn't so sure he did, said, "Yeah."

"I shot three of them and I am pretty fucken sure they have all met their maker by now, and if I'm any judge of such matters, their maker is not too happy to see any of them. Like the way I look at it (pause) I did the world a favor."

Jesus, what he needed was more trouble. No doubt Max had loosed the hounds on his ass by now and they were right this minute sniffing out his trail. Max had contacts all over the county and could track almost anybody. Thought, Need to keep moving. But . . . What about her?

Their food came and each watched the other eat.

"Let's take a walk," he said after, reaching into his wallet to pay the bill with some of the money he took from Augie, his money the way he saw it, and they went outside.

"Look," he said. "I'm in some deep shit and the last thing I need is more trouble than what I already got. Why did you murder three guys?"

"I wouldn't exactly call it murder," she said.

"What is it called when you shoot guys dead?"

She paused to light a cigarette. "One of them raped me. So he sure fucken deserved it. The other two were my ex and his pal, a real goon, because they left me with the guy who raped me so they could do a drug deal—in other words, I was used as collateral to assure my sweetheart returned with the drug money. Some boyfriend, huh?"

Cars and trucks went zipping by up and down the highway, blowing heat and dust. Eighteen wheelers with their diesels knocking like a bucket of bolts, families getting out of their cars, little old people getting in their Cadillac's, the truck stop restaurant a beehive of activity so that it felt like the entire world was swirling around the two of them.

"Look," she said. "It wasn't like I had any choice. I knew Ray, after what he pulled, they would have probably sold me to some biker gang next. You want to know something, else?"

He sucked in air, expelled it, said, "Why not?"

"I used to be a good student, got straight A's, never gave my folks any trouble, the whole ball of wax. Then my father was accused of killing my mom, tried and found guilty and sent off to prison on a manslaughter charge when I was just eight. Bounced from place to place until I took off at sixteen. It was Ray who basically saved me from being on the streets. We were together for almost three years before he found he liked dope better than me. And if you've ever known a junkie, it only gets worse. That's my story, Jack."

He shook his head.

"I keep telling you, my name is Bobby, goddamn it!" He was angry, and he wasn't sure why. It was all just building up in him. Thirty-nine years old, and no future. What do washed up fighters do with their lives with no viable skills. Shooting people, like he had as a Marine Corps sniper was not a job skill Lowe's was interested in when you filled out an application. Shit!

"Okay, Bobby Lee," she said. "I've told you my story, now tell me yours."

So he told her about how he was supposed to throw the fight so his manager could win and thus promote the next big thing, but that he had knocked the guy out instead of the other way around. And how he was pretty sure Max would have him off'd because of it.

"Wait, you're telling me some guy is going to have you killed because you won a fight? That makes absolutely no damn sense," she said.

"Tell me what does in this world anymore," he said.

"Well, shit, maybe you should have killed him first," she said with a slight smile.

"Let's go," he said.

"They got in the car.

"How about I drive you someplace where you can rent a car and you can go on down to your father's place in Texas and I can go on to wherever I'm going," he said as he pulled out of the place and back onto the expressway.

"You're afraid if they catch me, they'll catch you with me and kill us both, is that it?"

"Kinda what I was thinking."

"Yeah, they probably will."

"Give me a smoke, huh?"

She took one out and lighted it for him and then handed it over. He didn't look at her as he drove, kept it at the legal speed limit.

"So," she said. "Is that true or not, the way you see it. They catch up to you, I'm just collateral damage?"

"Yeah, so it's even more reason we should split company."

"Fine, drive on, Jeeves."

He nodded and drove on.

Chapter Nine

*"The Only Thing Worse Than Wanting Something
Is Getting It"*
—Oscar Wilde

Max came out of the bedroom wearing one of Cherry's robes, a pink one with fuzzy cuffs and a pink boa collar—the nearest thing he could grab because he knew the Cowboy didn't like waiting, and in fact, started ringing up his fees the minute he boarded the plane in NYC—and he always travelled first class.

Johnny Pearl had even questioned the sanity of spending that kind of dough for a hit man when he, Johnny, said he'd kill Bobby for free for stealing his car.

"What's so important about that damn car you want to murder him over it for?" Max had inquired.

"Nothing!" Johnny swore petulantly.

"What'd you get your first piece of man ass in it or somethin'?"

Johnny's entire neck and face turned scarlet when Max said that. Sputtered and stammered.

"Oh, what, you didn't think I knew you smoked the sausage?" Max went on now that he had Johnny flustered. "Fuck I knew before I even hired you. I don't usually make it a habit of hiring fags, but Irene was my wife and you're her boy and we didn't hold back much from each other while we was married. Relax, goddamn it, don't be such a drama queen."

Cherry was in the kitchen fixing herself some toast or some shit and Max asked her to put on the coffee.

"Slavery went out like a hundred years ago. I look like some damn Bob Evans, or shit?" she called from in there.

***

Cowboy was sitting in the elegant wingback in her living room, his Stetson resting atop his knees, for as he abided by the Western Heritage, a gentleman takes his hat off indoors.

His suit was purely Western as well, a gray gabardine with "smiley" pockets on the jacket and dark ribbing across the yoke. His cowboy boots were brown and pointed in the toes and had roses stitched into the shafts. Max thinking whenever he saw him, which thankfully wasn't more than once a year—that he reminded him of that Jon Voight character in Midnight Cowboy, what was it, oh yeah, Joe Buck. And when Max thought about it all, well that was about a queer too.

"Nice gown," Cowboy said, "though it might be a size too small for you, or large, depending on how you look at it, Max."

"Jesus, Christ, I didn't want to have to make you wait around or I could have gotten dressed."

"No, that's okay. I sort of like you in pink."

He knew Cowboy was fucking with him—at least he thought he was. These days you never knew.

"Cherry, you fixing coffee?" Max called.

"Yeah, yeah," she called back. "I'm just a slave, always gonna be a slave and nothin' but a slave."

"Stop your pissing and moaning," Max said. "You make two, three hundred a night, plus I'm paying for everything else. I'd hardly say *you're* the slave. More like me and these other dumbasses who shove money in your cooch are the slaves."

He heard her give a short hard laugh and mumble something, like, "You got that right you honky motherfuckah."

"So what's the job, Max?" Cowboy said.

"Just a minute," Max said and got up and walked back into the bedroom, noticed just then what the air smelled like—expensive perfume, sweat and lust spent never to be revitalized at least for a few days—and reached inside his suit jacket, took out the envelope and walked it back into the living room, handed it to Cowboy, who opened it, saw the piece of paper with the name Bobby Lee written on it along with Bobby Lee's last known address, an apartment on Mill Street above a bakery, plus the usual five-grand retainer.

"He's probably not there anymore," Max said sitting down on the couch again. They never are when they run. But I trust you will locate him and do what is called for—usual fee of course."

"What'd he do to deserve me?" Cowboy said.

Cherry brought in a silver tray with matching pot, two hand painted china cups, sugar bowl and creamer and set it down on the coffee table, said, "There you go massa Max. I's got to go now and pick a field of cotton." Then she disappeared back in the bedroom closing the door behind her.

Max looked at Cowboy who sat staring after her, said, "I know, right? It's not like the old days, is it?"

Cowboy shrugged, said, "Nothing ever is, Max," and stood to his full six-feet four inches, broad-shouldered and truly looking like he could have been starring in Westerns—except they weren't making them anymore, but if they were . . .

"Soon as it's done, let me know and I'll wire the rest of the money to your account."

Cowboy settled that El Presidente 100X Sliverbelly just so on his head, the brim slightly tipped forward, so he looked real badass. And make no mistake about it, Max thought, he *is* real badass.

Max sat and sipped the shitty coffee Cherry had brewed and wondered how anybody could fuck up Starbuck's Dark Roast.

Yeah, he thought, this Bobby Lee thing was costing him a bundle on top of what he lost on the fight, but what was a guy supposed to do, just let it go? No, people had to respect you in his, or any other kind of business. They saw you were weak or a pushover and could get away with shit, they'd eat you alive, and before you knew it, you'd be working in some sub shop making sandwiches for losers wearing those little cheap-ass plastic gloves and saying, "What kind of bread?" and "Six inch or foot long?" and "You want that toasted?" Because that's where a guy who didn't get respect ended up. No, fuck that.

He set the half-drunk shitty coffee down again, thought, look at this, I buy her a silver set and she can't make decent coffee.

Stood, went into the bedroom and found her in the shower, ready to read her the riot act for showing him no respect in front of Cowboy, ready to raise ten kinds of hell on her, but then he saw the outline of her through the icy shower glass, those upright tits and that ass you could rest a beer glass on, well. And the woman could screw the lid off a pickle jar.

He stood there, his resolve softening while the rest of him hardened. She paused and turned to look at him through that glass and the steam, he dropped her pink robe on the bathroom floor and got in there with her reaching for the bar of soap.

Through the showerhead's hiss of water, she said, "Oh, massa, you's want sompin' from yo lil' ol' slave, does you?"

"Yeah, I sure the fuck do. Now turn around and lean your hands against the wall."

"Yes, massa."

He allowed her to play her games, as long as he got what he wanted from her.

Then, when he was working against her from behind and about to finish, she said, "You shoulda ask Mr. Eastwood to join us, honey."

"Yeah, whatever," Max grunted.

And when he had finished and climbed out and found a towel to dry off, she stepped out, said, "See, I know you was like that, Max."

"Like what?" he said.

"Like what I said in there and you said, 'Yeah, whatever'—about getting Clint to join us next time?"

She was fucking with him again. Always pushing the boundaries with him.

"You want to keep working for me?" he growled.

She fell silent.

"Then shut the hell up with that kind of talk. You sure as hell ought to know by now, I'm not gay."

"I know you ain't, baby. I was just fucken with you."

But later when he was asleep on the bed from exhaustion, she leaned over him and said in his ear: "Then why you like it so much that way, huh, Maxie? 'Cause I sure as hell don't like it like that."

When he woke again around one in the afternoon, Cherry was gone, probably out shopping or getting her hair and nails done. He wondered if she talked about him to her girlfriends, and what she said about him.

He sat up and looked down at his protruding white belly and fat legs and small pale feet. And for some reason, in spite of having the world by the ass, he felt lousy.

Why was that? he asked himself.

Why the fuck was that?

Chapter Ten

It's a hell of a thing, killing a man. You take away all he'd got
And all he's ever gonna have.
—The character William Munny

The detective Frank Dodge, old school, riding the desk that night because he had just twelve hours left until he retired, turned in his gun and badge for a fly reel and a cabin on a lake somewhere peaceful, where the fishing was good and the living was easy.

On the other end of the line, a nasally voice reported a couple of dead guys sprawled in front of one of those shacks on Old Cove Street.

"I heard shots too," the caller said, and hung up right away so as not to get involved. Frank couldn't tell if he meant, too, or two.

And seeing as how it was only Frank and the new detective on duty because everybody else was out west of the city working a derailed train on fire, Frank saw no choice but to take the call and said he and the new detective should ride out to check the veracity of the caller's claim.

"Let's take a ride," he told the other dick, whose name of all things was, Ivanhoe, Joe Ivanhoe. Well, to be precise, Joseph Ivanhoe the Third.

They rode out there in the dark rain, neither saying much except for when Joe Ivanhoe Three said, "Lousy deal you catching this a day before you retire, Sarge."

"They're all lousy days being a homicide cop," is what Frank Dodge replied. "But keep in mind, the murdered always have a worse day. And let's face it, murder is our raison d'etre, Detective Ivanhoe. Without crimes of the capital punishment sort, you and I would be collecting our unemployment checks and food stamps. Thank Jesus for killers."

"True that," Ivanhoe said.

"True that, indeed."

***

It took twenty minutes to arrive at the given address—a dump of a place—one of those concrete jobs built the shape of a trailer, among several of its brethren both sides of the street. Lining the curb were cars no younger than the previous decade, lonely and wet under the rain that beaded their steel skins like sweat. And sure enough, there in the front of the place on a mostly bare lawn, a couple of unmoving people looking as if they'd just fallen from the sky.

"I count two," Ivanhoe said.

"Education is a wonderful thing, detective. But let's not be overly hasty in our assessment here, there could be more in the house or, and I hope and pray there is not, the shooter waiting to drop a couple of homicide dicks. It's become almost de rigueur to off a cop these days."

They exited the car, raised the collars on their all-weather coats then drew their Glocks—just in case all the shooting and mayhem had not yet been completed—and stepped cautiously onto the wet patches of grass as if it was full of landmines and they didn't want to get their nuts blown off.

They shined their lights on the latest of the city's dead, one face down and the other face up, mouth sprung open like a busted trap, eyes staring into the wet abyss and nary a flinch from the rain tapping his corneas. Frank Dodge looked from the dead to the open door of the house, said, "This right here is why our mothers warned us about hanging with the wrong people."

"True that."

"Maybe better if you go around back while I take what is known as the ingress of that door, just in case anyone in there wants to make the egress."

"You sure enough talk funny for a cop," Ivanhoe said.

"I sure enough talk funny for anybody my wife Wendy always said, or did until she became my ex-wife."

Ivanhoe moved off toward the back keeping his gun two-handed along with the flashlight trained on the house while Frank Dodge held his position, but glancing down at the guys on the ground. Something off, familiar maybe about the dead man face down. It was that silky dark blue jacket with *Jerry's Lounge* stitched across the back. He'd seen it before but couldn't right away place where. He bent down while still keeping an eye and gun trained on the front door in case some fucker came out screaming Geronimo or some stupid shit, guns blazing.

He grabbed the shoulder of the dead guy and turned him over, shined his light down in his cold dead face, dropped his grip and stepped back.

What the fuck? He knew the guy. In fact he knew him pretty damn well, said, "You dumb shit, Ray. What the fucked you get involved with that got you done this way? Goddamn it!"

He heard Joe Ivanhoe calling from the back, "Door's secured, locked."

He went steadily and with due deliberation to the open front door calling, "Police. Come out with your hands in the air!"

No answer.

He shined his light in. Nothing.

"Ray, you motherfucker, I hope this isn't the night we both end up dead."

Did the usual cop approach to entering a building, gun right, then left, flashlight braced in line with the muzzle. Called a warning once more, listened. Nothing. Called for Detective Ivanhoe to come around front and waited to be joined by his new best black friend.

"Anything?"

"Graveyard still," Frank Dodge said. Ivanhoe looked at him strangely.

"I'll go in first," Frank said. He did, with Ivanhoe behind him and found their raison d'etre flopped on the couch, all two-hundred and fifty pounds of him. He could have been a poster boy for any number of biker gangs.

They stepped up closer, saw the blood, the cracked gourd of a skull to go along with the tats along his arms and around his neck.

"You ever notice," Frank Dodge said, his heart still pounding from the recognition of the guy out front, Ray, "how these guys all look the same and yet they strive to be 'individuals?' "

"Yeah, I have," Ivanhoe said. "Christ it stinks in here."

He examined Buzzard's tattoos, noted that half of them were the kind you got in prison and the other half you got at bike rallies, and maybe one or two you had your old lady do if she liked you and you got her drunk enough.

"I guess our work here is done," Frank said walking back outside to catch a smoke while Ivanhoe called it in, saying they need the meat wagon and being told Good luck with that detective, everything's tied up at the site of the train wreck.

Ivanhoe found his own cigs and lighted one and drew deeply and exhaled, said, "You recognize any of these guys, Sarge?"

Frank thought a moment, said, "No. My guess is they were running drugs and they pissed off somebody. Find who's behind the powder and pills and you'll find out who they pissed off and vis-à-vis shooter or shooters."

Dawn was just breaking in the eastern sky, slate gray with the hint of promise now that it had stopped raining. By the time they finished their notes and the coroner's van finally pulled up along with a crime scene team. Frank watched them load the dead, Ray being the first to get zipped into a body bag, his young screwed up life nothing more now than a slab of beef, thought , You just had to go and break your sweet sister's heart didn't you, Ray. Now I've got to be the one to deliver the news—and just when we were able to start talking to each other again without screaming our brains out.

"Thanks a lot, fucker."

Ivanhoe standing there conversing with a uniform cop, turned and said, "What'd you say, Frank?"

"Nothing. Just talking to myself. You know how old guys get."

"Not yet," Ivanhoe replied grinning. "You want to stop on the way back to the station and get some breakfast? Grand Slam sounds damn good to me."

Frank shook his head. He had other business to conduct, like going and telling Wendy her punk brother was officially no longer walking the earth.

"Take a rain check."

"Rain check? Frank you haven't forgotten in another few hours you'll be a civilian again?"

Then it fully dawned on him. Ivanhoe was right.

"Well, hell, that doesn't mean we can't get a grand slam together sometime," he said with all seriousness, which cracked Ivanhoe up, said, "You some crazy mutha, Frank."

And thus it began, a whole new set of troubles and travails for one Frank Dodge, soon to be civilian Frank Dodge and not Detective Frank Dodge and his soul felt the color of the lead sky and the coming of new morning after a miserable night of a rain and murder, shattered skulls and shattered dreams.

Like what Eastwood said in that movie, *Unforgiven,* *"It's a hell of a thing, killing a man—you take away all he's got, and all he's ever going to have."*

True that.

Chapter Eleven

"You're either at the table or on the menu"
—Alphonse Capone

They rode on mile after mile, now and then changing drivers, stopping for gasoline and some food, burgers and potato wedges, Root Beer, cigarettes, candy for her, Frank flexing his hands still stiff from the fight even though it had been over twenty-four hours ago. A sign he was getting older, the time it took for his aches and pains and stiffness to go away.

She played the car radio as they drove, finding a station that she liked then running out of reception and starting the search over again—rock, rap, politics—but he had a feeling she was waiting to hear news of the guys she'd shot. He knew he would be.

But not a word.

"Maybe we're too far from there," he said.

"Or, maybe they were just faking it, or maybe I didn't kill them and they're in the hospital recovering. Or, maybe I just dreamt it all."

"You really believe any of that?"

She looked glum and not so pretty that way. He'd thought a hundred times about dropping her off somewhere and letting her make her way, but each time he brought it up she came up with a reason of not yet.

"Let's wait a little while. I don't want the cops nabbing me. I don't think I could stand jail. My father was in jail. Did I mention that?"

"Yeah."

"Oh.

"He didn't do it," she said.

"Isn't that what they all say?"

"I suppose it is."

"How long was he in?"

She shook her head.

"I am not exactly sure, something like twenty some years. I'd get letters from him now and then, but I never answered any of them."

"I'm guessing it was hard on you?"

"Yeah. I'm thinking my problems with men all stem from my lack of having a father around. I don't know. I read that somewhere, about girls like me."

"So you're going home to see him?"

"Yes," she said fiddling the knob on the radio then giving up after all she could find coming in clear was religious stations. "I found his address and telephone number on the internet. Did you know you can find just about anybody on the internet?

"So I've heard."

"What, you got something against preachers wearing Rolex's?" he said when she turned off the incessant preaching.

"No. It's just all gibberish to me—ghosts and the blood of the Savior and all that. I ask you, where was God when that big ape was raping me?"

"Better question might be, where was He when you shot the big ape and took his life?"

"Yeah, exactly. If God existed, then why did he let it happen and why did He let me kill the son of a bitch?"

"You're asking the wrong man," he said. "I never much got into religion. I asked some of those same questions when I was over in Iraq with a sniper rifle and watching my buddies die."

"What about you?" she said.

"What about me, what?"

"How'd you grow up, where?"

"Nebraska, on a farm till my old man lost everything to the bank."

"You ever get married?"

"Once."

"Where's your wife?"

"Hell if I know."

"She leave you, you leave her, what?"

"Don't quite remember."

Darkness fell slowly at first and then suddenly they were surrounded by it. He looked over and she was curled up asleep with her head against the window. His headache had started up again and he'd told himself he should have bought aspirins at the last gas station. In the last year or so he'd been getting really bad headaches, figured all the blows he took in the ring had finally caught up with him.

So when he saw the lights of a town floating ahead in the long distance he felt a sense of relief.

He found a motel on the main drag of liquor stores and not much else. Pulled into the motel's lot, said, "Go in and get us a couple of rooms, huh. I've got to get something for this headache."

"Sure," she said sleepily and unwound herself from the ball she'd curled into.

He stood out of the car, the air felt fresh on his nearly fevered skin, didn't know if he was coming down with something, but walked the block or so up to a liquor store, asked if they sold aspirins. The clerk pointed toward a dispenser of tins and Bobby grabbed one.

"Jim Beam?"

The clerk pointed, said, "Third isle on your left, second shelf."

With his purchases in hand, he started walking back toward the motel. It was a seedy looking area. He stopped in a doorway, unscrewed the bottle and snapped open the aspirins, swallowed three with the Beam, the liquor burned his throat, but in a good way. He used to drink pretty good back in the day when he was in the Corps. He even got drunk once on some of that homemade hooch. He smiled at the memory, stepped out of the doorway and suddenly there were two guys coming up the street toward him.

Did his best to think they were just guys, like himself, out for a stroll. But see that was the thing, they weren't, and something deep down told him this and he thought to himself, Goddamn as he slid the pint into his back pocket and the tin of aspirins into his front and prepared himself for what was coming.

They stopped right in front of him blocking his way, and he'd be damned if he was going to try and walk around them. Thing was, he'd left the gun in the car, under the front seat and hadn't thought about taking it when he got out.

"Hey man," one of them said.

He said nothing back.

"Hey man. You got the time?"

"Night," he said.

They grunted, they giggled, they shifted nervously, with anticipation, he supposed, of robbing him, of maybe beating him up a little.

"No," the gangly dude said. "I mean the time of the hour" pointing at his bare wrist.

"That makes no sense what you just said—time of the hour," he said, buying another second or two to set himself.

"Well just give me your watch and I'll look at it myself," his partner said. That was when Bobby Lee stepped in and caught him with a straight right cross that snapped his head and damn near knocked him off his feet. But just as he did, the gangly one swiped at him and he felt the hot burn of being cut just as he saw the streetlight's glint off the blade. The warmth of freshly released blood traveled down his left forearm. But he had been cut before, many times in the ring and so it was nothing new or

74

shocking, the feel of his own blood, and he brought a left uppercut so hard he heard bone break—or, possibly teeth and the guy dropped straight down like a hundred and twenty-pound sack of shit.

The other one was trying to gain his bearings and balled his fists and Bobby Lee said, "Really?" going into his boxer's stance. "That first one wasn't enough for you dumbass?"

The guy dropped his hands, turned and sprinted off.

Bobby looked down at the guy on the sidewalk not moving but breathing through a bloody mouth. He stepped over him and went on back to the motel where he stopped in the office and asked which room his friend rented, the lady looked at him and the blood dripping from his fingers.

"Are you hurt?"

Bobby looked down, said, "Got any paper towels, I seemed to have cut myself."

She went into the back and came out with a roll, he ripped off several and packed them to the cut under his sliced open jacket sleeve.

"She's down in twenty-eight," the woman said. "You sure you don't want me to call for an ambulance."

"I'm sure, but thank you."

He went out and down the way, found the Chrysler parked in front of twenty-eight and knocked on the door. She opened it a crack until she saw it was him, then opened it wide, he walked in, straight into the bathroom and got out of his jacket and shirt.

"What the hell happened to you?" she said standing in the doorway looking on.

"A couple of guys braced me," he said.

"Braced you?" She'd never heard the term. It was an old cowboy word because Bobby's favorite reading was Western paperbacks. It meant confronted.

It was a pretty good cut, a bleeder, but nothing serious.

"Rip one of the pillowcases into a bandage for me, will you?"

She did as he took the pint bottle of Jim Beam out of his jacket pocket, unscrewed it and spilled some over the cut. Then she bandaged the cut and washed off the rest of the blood.

"You're in pretty good shape for an old dude?" she said as they went out and sat at the small table in the room, Bobby sitting with his shirt off.

"Old?" he said. "I'm like thirty-eight."

"Daddy Jack, to me that's fucken old," she laughed and poured them each some whiskey in plastic cups taken from the bathroom, sipped hers made a face, said, "Needs some Pepsi."

"That's just plain sacrilege what you just said."

"Old school, new school," she countered.

"Which other room did you get," he said. "I think I'll go and take a shower and get some rest."

She shrugged.

"This was the only room they had left. Woman at the front desk said everything is sold out on account of a rodeo in town."

He got up, went to his coat pocket and got his cigarettes and lighter, came back and sat down again. Lighted one up and offered her one and she lighted one up, too.

"So'd you fuck those guys up, or what?" she said smiling mischievously.

"I don't think they'll be pulling anymore strong arms tonight."

She smiled more, said, "Goddamn."

"I detect a certain amount of cruelty in your voice," he said with a half smile.

"Not cruelty," she said. "I just enjoy when bastards get what's coming to them."

"So who gets the bed tonight?" he said noting the single queen-sized.

"Flip you for it," she said.

"Okay."

She got into her purse and found a Susan B. Anthony dollar, said, "I hate these damn things. You can't tell them from a quarter. I can't tell you how many times I realized that too late."

He spilled some more in their cups, said, "Hell, I forgot, I bought some aspirins at that liquor store, took a couple before those dudes came along. I could use a few more."

"I'll fetch them for you, Tiger, you just stay there. You're kinda old and fucked up for moving around."

He shook his head at her cheekiness, waited until she came back and snapped the lid open. He took two more and washed them down with the Beam.

She watched him curiously as he offered to refresh her drink, but she shook her head.

"Flip the coin," he said. "Because I'm plumb burned out from driving all day and nearly getting my arm sliced off."

"Oh, men are such big babies," she mocked and flipped the coin, caught it and slapped it on the back of her hand. "Call it?"

"Heads," he said.

She lifted her covering hand just enough so she could see the coin, said, "Sorry Pops. You get the chair, looks like, or floor if you'd rather."

"Let me see," he said.

But she dropped it back in her purse before he could look.

"Alright," he said wearily. Arose and went to the bed and grabbed a pillow and started to take it to the chair when she laughed, said, "I was just fucking with you. Get in the bed."

"No, it's okay, I don't mind. I've slept in plenty of chairs in my life."

"Well, just lay down until I shower, then," she said.

He was going to shower himself, but to tell the truth, he was just plain out of gas. Stood, then sat on the side of the bed, kicked off his shoes and lay down as she went into the bathroom and mercifully hit the lights to the living room.

He remembered hearing the shower running, her singing softly, closed his eyes and that was it.

Until he felt the bed move, then she slid up behind him and put her arm around him. No words, just that, and he closed his eyes and went off to La-La land.

Chapter Twelve

"Everybody's a gangster until a gangster walks in the room."
—John Gotti

Cowboy rang the number of a friend of his on the local PD, a guy named Ivanhoe. They'd served in Iraq and Afghanistan for a PMF— Private Military Force after regular tours in the Army. And yeah, they'd shot some hajjis who were coming at them in a beat-up white Toyota truck and wouldn't stop. Cowboy got off the first and most rounds and killed all three of the guys in the cab thus saving Ivanhoe's ass when his rifle jammed.

So there was that between them. But after that shithole experience, they went their separate ways: Cowboy into the murky underworld still doing what he liked best—being a mercenary—and Ivanhoe got on with the Miami PD and had since worked his way up to Detective.

"You still arresting crack heads?" Cowboy laughed on the other end of the phone.

"I'm a murder cop now, don't have nothing to do with crack heads until after they have been neutralized," Ivanhoe said, smiling on the other end. He could just see Cowboy and that fucking Stetson he wore even though it wasn't standard issue, but then what was in the PMF. Guns, right? Yeah, fucking guns. Guns and grit and the willingness to maybe one minute be guarding some high up hajji and the next minute cutting loose on a truck load of the fuckers. It was an insane fucking war no matter how you looked at it. Ivanhoe figured he'd seen enough decapitated heads to last him this lifetime and the next, if there was one. Thought the crazy cocksuckers were still living like five millennia ago.

"Listen," Cowboy said. "I could use a favor."

Ivanhoe was silent a moment before answering. He was a straight up guy now, doing God's and the PD's work.

"What is it?" he asked softly.

"Nothing major," Cowboy said. "I don't want you to smoke nobody. I just wonder if you can put out an APB for a stolen car."

"Yeah, I suppose so. What's the license plate number and description?

So Cowboy told him and Ivanhoe scribbled the info in his little notebook in the next blank page after his most recent notes on the three fuckers shot to death and wondered silently if this stolen car had anything to do with the shooting. Wondered if that was why Cowboy was suddenly popping up from wherever the fuck he had been since the last time he'd heard from him, what was that, two, three years ago when Ivanhoe was still a street cop and they ran into each other by sheer accident, ended up having a few beers and trying to relive those days in the hot-ass desert where water was as rare as pussy.

"May I ask why it is you're interested in this, was it your car that was stolen?"

"No, looking into it for a friend, you know."

"Yes, I think I do. But I have to ask. Me and my partner caught a triple homicide the other night. Would it have anything to do with that?"

"What were the vics names?"

Ivanhoe hesitated, but then told Cowboy the names of the dead.

"Nah, never heard of them before. And besides, where that car was, wasn't even close to where you say your shooting was. No, this guy I'm looking into it for is a straight shooter, no wants, not warrants."

"How do I locate you in case I get a hit on the car?"

Cowboy gave him a cell number—a burner he'd dispose of once he got what he wanted.

"Okay, I'll let you know," Ivanhoe said.

"Hey, my man. Let's grab a beer sometime, shoot the shit. Half of me wishes I was still over in hajji world."

"And the other half?" Ivanhoe said.

"Well, fuck the other half," Cowboy laughed. "Thanks for the favor. I owe you, Joseph."

***

Then the phone went dead and Ivanhoe hung up the receiver of his desk phone, but continued to look at the tag number and description: 1976 Windsor, aqua marine in color. Thought, now why is a damn stolen car so important, you want in on it, Cowboy? This ain't your kind of shit. Your kind of shit is taking care of folks who need taken care of, folks other folks pay damn good dough to see the work done. And last I know, you is a top shelf item among all the other mercenaries running around out there.

But hell, a promise is a promise and I ain't about to go back on my word to a brother no matter how he makes his living. Fuck it, and dialed the phone.

Meantime, back at the suburban ranchero of his ex-wife, Frank trudged up the sidewalk and rang the bell. There was something very fucking odd about ringing the doorbell to be allowed into a home you once owned and lived in. Your wife now like a county clerk giving you shit every time you came to conduct business.

Wendy came to the door in a bathrobe, opened it, but not all the way, said, "Frank, what are you doing here?"

He had not failed to notice the strange car in the driveway, a nice new Buick sedan. He knew of nobody personally driving one.

She held the robe clutched just there at her breastbone, her hairstyle just out of bed and most likely post coital as well. He remembered just what a fucking lunatic for sex she was once you got her into the sack. Wear out a football team. Told him once, "I can't help it when I get started." It was in part what had broken them up in the first place—the *urges* that overcame her when he left her alone too very long. Had caught her once with the tennis pro, said at the time, "I hope that son of a bitch is paying you and not the other way around." It was quite a row—maybe their worst.

"Can I come in, Wendy?"

She looked over her shoulder, then over his.

"Well, this isn't really a good time," she said.

"Just take a minute, I have some bad news."

Her face crumbled into full-on fear and worry, said, "Is it Ray? Does it have something to do with Ray?" her voice rising. She knew her brother had been in trouble practically his whole life.

"Yeah, he's dead, honey"

"Oh, Jesus God!" she screamed and fell toward him and he took hold of her as she sobbed and cried out the now defunct brother's name, first time he'd held her close in nearly a year, and even under the conditions, feeling her up next to him got him aroused.

"Hush, hush, honey," he said stroking her head as she bawled against his shirtfront. He didn't know what more to say than that.

A man appeared from back where the master bedroom was. A man wearing fucking boxer shorts—in his house, already! Son of a bitch, he thought. This wasn't turning out to be a very good fucking day, was it.

"Wendy?" the man said. "Something wrong?" the guy looking at him holding her. Young guy, too. Young and athletic and Frank wondered if he was another tennis instructor. Woman loved her tennis. But Frank felt himself coming to a boil at the sight of this asshole, whoever he was.

"Go back inside," Frank said harshly, and he watched as the guy stood there hesitating, before Frank added: "I'm her husband (not precisely true) and her brother's been murdered. Go back inside goddamn it!"

The guy disappeared back into the bedroom. Surprisingly Kay hadn't tried to correct him on that husband label, but then she was too awash in tears to berate him and let him know that they weren't together anymore. It was really a fucked up time, Frank admitted to himself.

She sobbed a bit more then suddenly stopped and leaned back, said, "Murdered?"

Frank nodded.

"Yes honey, he was shot sometime last night—him and two other men. We think drugs might have been involved and somebody shot them over that."

She stood staring in disbelief. He got her inside because neighbors were coming outside to get their papers, and watching everything going on like a hawk, a neighborhood just the opposite of the one where baby Ray—as Frank had been wanting to think of him—had eaten his last lunch. Over there nobody gave a shit as long as it wasn't them ducking bullets.

He got her to sit on the sofa while he took a seat waiting for the next questions to pour forth, but none came. She sat frozen and he couldn't help but wonder why she didn't see it as a relief; everyone who knew Ray knew two things about him: he was never going to live long, and his death was bound to be real bad. And thus, it had come true. His was an inelegant and not quite a Greek tragedy.

Finally she looked at him with that frozen stare, said, "Will you take me to see him, Frank?"

He nodded.

"Sure. Whenever you're ready. But are you sure you want to see him that way, Wendy? It won't be pretty."

Again she nodded.

"Yes," she said. "I watched all his life how he lived, there is no reason to not see how he died."

Frank couldn't help but wish they were still together. Wendy was a tough woman and every man feels lucky to have a tough woman.

She went to the bedroom and he heard their murmured voices and felt slightly embarrassed to listen but couldn't help it, got up and got himself a glass of water from the kitchen, noticed she'd had new countertops installed—quartz and was running his fingers over them when he heard a door close, footsteps and then the front door open and close.

"Frank," she called from the bedroom and he went back there, the door open now and she was standing there with her arms reaching around her back trying to zip up a black dress, like the one they'd gone dancing in a couple of years back, the one that made her look like the sexist woman alive with her short blonde hair and that black dress contrasting. He was always struck how much she reminded him of the actress Meg Ryan—not just in looks but in other ways too.

He walked into the room.

"Can you help me with this?" she said, her cheeks stained wet from the tears.

He stepped behind her and zipped up what she couldn't quite reach and he was tempted to lean and brush aside her hair and kiss her neck and see if she responded at all, but then as quickly thought: hell, she just slept with that guy and I've just told her that her only living relative is dead. Doubt she'd be in the mood for romance, you dumb fuck.

She grabbed a shawl and wrapped it over her shoulders and he walked her out to his car, held the door open for her, then got in behind the wheel, started the ignition and put it in gear.

And as he drove to the city morgue, it dawned on him he was no longer a cop, and he was no longer married to the only woman he loved and had just witnessed her post *in flagrante delicto*.

The world had become, in Frank Dodge's opinion, truly fucked up.

Chapter Thirteen

"If you can't find something to live for
You best find something to die for."
—Tupac Shakur

Max looked up. This time was he being given no blowjobs by one of the dancers. In fact, it was just after one o'clock in the afternoon and he had a corned beef and pastrami sandwich on marbled rye with a nice fat dill spread out on butcher's paper from the deli uptown he fucking loved—Gold's. They made the best pastrami anything and had in Max's words, "Jews and Jew lovers lined up for blocks" trying to get their daily allotment of sandwiches and soups, the Matzo and chicken noodle soups. You walked in the place and the smells alone would make you cream your jeans, Max thought happily as he dug in.

It was Johnny Pearl brought him the sandwich, as more or less a surprise, Max saying, "Jeez, thanks Johnny, I was getting ready to go out and up the street to that hot dog vendor guy. Nice of you to think of me with this."

"No problem," Johnny said and sat there and watched Max eat like he did everything else, full on, no holding back, like a damn—well, he was thinking *hog,* but since they were both Jewish, hog seemed a little unholy—like a, oh fuck it, like a pig, Johnny finally determined. Johnny himself didn't eat kosher all that much, preferred Italian and, believe it or not, Hungarian. His last boyfriend was Hungarian, Eddie Barna. Eddie could cook like a mother and he wasn't a bad kisser either.

"What the hell you smiling about?" Max said looking over at the wistful henchman.

"Nothing," he said.

"You look like the cat that just finished eating the bird, that, what's it."

"Canary," Johnny said.

"Yah, that fucking thing. So why the shit-eating grin, you know something I'm supposed to know?"

Johnny shook his head. The reason, as yet unspoken for his visit, sandwich in hand wasn't for sure out of kindly thoughts toward Max. Hardly. No, he had something he figured he better tell Max about that car got stolen, something Max might not be too happy to hear, but if he got wind of it after the fact, well, Max might be a lot less happy. So after a rather hasty night at the Ball Room, a gay club over on the eastside, he decided to break it to Max, what was in that car.

"Max, I got to tell you something."

Max more or less grunted as he continued to devour his lunch, his cheeks bulging and a little black rye seed clinging to the corner of his mouth; Max waving his half eaten pickle around like a limp green dick, which, from what Johnny had observed of it when some dancer was giving him a Mr. Happy, was about the same size as Max's.

"Yuh, mmmmfff."

"My car—the Windsor that was stolen by that prick lousy fighter of yours . . ."

Max stopped chewing and swallowed what he had and gulped a slug of beer, then thankfully wiped whatever else that was on his mouth away with a paper napkin, said, "What the fuck about it, John Boy. What are you going to fucken tell me—there was a dead broad in the trunk or somethin'?"

Johnny thought maybe he might wet himself when Max said that— like he had a second sense about these things, said, "No, nothing like that, Max. It's just that there might be some incriminating evidence against me I wouldn't want to get out, is all."

"What kind of evidence we talking here?"

Max could be very intimidating when he wanted to, for the same reason he could order a guy shot and his body dropped in the bay, after
whoever shot him chopped him into little pieces first and dropped one at
a time from the bridge into that cold fucking water. Johnny was scared
shitless of drowning and he knew that getting shot and chopped to pieces
you wasn't going to notice how cold the water was, but just the thought
of it—drowning like that, piece by fucken piece, getting eaten by the fish.
It gave him shivers.

"Ah, it's nothing," Johnny said. "I shouldn't even have brought it up,
Max. I mean it's my problem not yours."

Max sat there staring at him intently, Johnny trying desperately to
come up with a cover story for the dead girl in the Windsor's trunk.

"No seriously, Max, it's just you know . . ."

"You thought it important enough to mention it, so I assume there
was a good fucken reason you did. Now spill it."

Max had become extremely red in the face, a sign of how agitated he
was. *Think, Johnny, you stupid prick. Think.*

"There was some stuff in there about me, is all it was. You know—
that thing."

"You better spit it the fuck out or I'm going to cram the rest of this
sandwich down your fucken throat and then shoot you in the face."

Johnny wanted to say, What the fuck, Max, chill out you fat bovine,
but said instead: "About the fact I'm into guys." Johnny acting all bashful
and shit to put on a good act for Max. "I had a lot of gay men's maga-
zines in there and some other stuff, leather masks and gag balls."

Max's face relaxed then and he picked up the half eaten sandwich in
those fatty little hands and held it halfway to his mouth.

"That all? Shit, I bet half the guys in this town know you smoke the
pony, John. That ain't no big fucken deal. Not with me it ain't—unless,

of course, you get funny ideas and try something." Max filling the room with laughter. The guy was really a manic depressive. Johnny had described Max's behavior once to an Emergency Room doctor he'd met at one of the gay clubs and saw a few times that looked like it might go somewhere but never did. So that's how he knew.

"Okay, well, don't worry about it," Max said before gnawing on his sandwich again like a beaver working on a birch tree. "I got Cowboy out there looking for Bobby and if he finds him he finds your ride."

"Okay," Johnny said. "I just thought I ought to tell you."

"Okay," Max said, with all that chewed food in his yap so that Johnny could see that mess inside. "Go get laid and forget about it."

***

Johnny nodded and walked out and didn't even stop at the bar to speak to Levi, but went outside and got in his rental car, a six-year-old Chevy something or other and headed back to his place trying to think what the fuck to do about the body in the trunk of his car if the cops found it. They'd think Bobby Lee might have killed her, but he could probably prove that he didn't. It'd be a long shot, especially since the car was registered to Johnny to begin with. No, he couldn't take that chance.

Why did that fucken hooker have to be a real woman instead of a transvestite like he thought she was when he picked her up the night of the fight, just before he got to the arena—feeling horny as fuck, desperate to get laid and saw her hanging in the area where they were known to be working the streets.

There she was looking hot but very mannish in that red number, pumps, the whole nine yards, blond wig—only it wasn't a wig after all. And what sealed it for him, what got him to invite her into the car for a ride was that husky voice. Said, "Shit, bitch, you got to do better than that fake ass voice you want guys to think you're a chick."

They'd parked in an alley over in the industrial section of town about five blocks from the arena, a seedy side of town if ever there was one.

She'd laughed then, said, "Honey, what you be talking about? There ain't nothin' wrong with Sonya, baby."

He was in too big a hurry for conversation and had to be down at the arena before the fight was over. He quick reached for her package up under that skirt and found out, guess what—she wasn't a tranny after all, but a real woman.

He'd jerked his hand back like what she had down there had burned it.

"Goddamn, what the hell?" he'd shouted.

"What the hell yo'self" she replied. "What was you wantin'? 'Cause mama can be whatever you all is into."

She tried kissing him on the mouth, but he slugged her instead. She slugged him back harder and he punched her again, this time in one of her ample breasts and she screamed and pulled a knife on him, said she was going to cut him wide and deep.

That's when he pulled the derringer out of his boot top and shot her in the eye, and she slumped like a ragdoll.

"Fuck!" he yelled as his mind went into overtime. Looked around in the near darkness of that alley, heard voices coming, got out and dragged her from the car, popped the trunk and got her crammed into it, then quickly drove to Augie's body and repair shop, also a chop shop, and gave Augie the keys and told him to clean the blood off the front bucket seat and anywhere else and he'd be back for it later. And to make doubly sure Augie didn't go snooping around in the trunk, took that key with him, said, "Don't go snooping around in that fucken' trunk, neither, and I'll see you get paid five bills for taking care of it."

"Yeah, I'm hip," Augie said, the old fucken hippy still talking that shit from the what was it, the 60s? Before Johnny was even a gleam in his old man's eye. Augie, *Hip* with his gray pony tail and almost bald on top—his biggest claim to fame was he had gone to Woodstock. Johnny never even heard of the place. Augie telling him of all the young pussy he got there, told him about the rain and mud and a guy named Jimi Hendrix. Johnny Pearl doing his best not to act bored.

So that's how it stood when Johnny Pearl found out his car had been stolen and ever since he'd been trying to figure out how to get it back before the cops did.

I got to take care of this shit myself, he thought. I got to try and find out where that asshole went. Remembered this broad Bobby was banging part-time, spoke highly of her. What was her name, anyway. Think, you idiot.

Roxanne something, that was it. She sometimes came into the gym and watched Bobby work out, and afterwards, petting on him like he was a dog or something.

But how the hell to find her. Junior Cisco. Anybody'd know it would be him on account of him working with Bobby in the gym, wrapping his hands and so forth.

Johnny drove over to the gym, found Junior unwrapping a fighter's hands, a new kid looked like he was carved out of ebony. Jesus, the muscles on that kid. Johnny told himself he could use some of that. Went over to Cisco, said, "I need to ask you something."

Junior Cisco, pug ugly, had been around boxing all his life and was now hovering on seventy years old and looking like he'd got beat with an ugly stick, Johnny would say. "You look like you been beat with an ugly stick, there Cisco." Cisco never laughed, but instead looked at Johnny with eyes from under scarred brows that were feral—like some bush animal that wanted to kill and eat him.

"Sure, sure," Junior said, because he didn't want to aggravate the boss's right-hand guy. "What is it you need to know?"

"That girl who used to come around and drape herself all over Bobby Lee, the redhead. You remember her?"

Junior had to think. He liked to say his brain didn't work too good these days. Whether or not that was true or he was just faking it, nobody knew but Junior.

"Yah, I think so, what about her?"

"What was her name?"

Junior twisted his mouth and squinted one eye trying to summon the girl's name, said, "She was a real nice girl, that one was. Sure had a thing for Bobby Lee. Usta come to his fights."

"Yeah, yeah, but what was her name?" Johnny urged.

"Let's see." Long pause, Johnny getting impatient as hell. "Was it something like Beverly something?"

Cisco's brain was as slow as a check from the government.

"I believe it was," Cisco said.

"Do you recall her last name, where she lived?"

Junior did some more thinking, the black fighter sitting there waiting for the trainer to get the tape off his hands, his body slick with sweat.

"Nah," Cisco said. "But I heard her say she does hair over at that place, what was it? Yeah, I remember, it's called Hair Today or somepin' like that. I think she used to cut Bobby's hair and that's how they got to know each other."

Junior was still gazing at his feet, still thinking, and when he looked up Johnny Pearl was gone.

"Hey man, you gonna cut this tape off, or what?" the black fighter said.

"Sure, sure," Junior said reaching for the scissors in his jacket pocket.

***

Bev Schwartz didn't pay any attention to the guy out front of her apartment. She was upset that Jonathon said he was going to shut the place down and go to Hawaii with his husband.

"Randy just loves it over there and it's a make or break deal for us— we're right at that seven-year mark and you know what they say about the itch," Jonathon said to the girls after they closed the doors. "You ladies have been wonderful, but I can't let this lead to a divorce."

It had been emotional because it meant they'd all have to find other jobs. Three of them stopped at the Cribbage Lounge for cocktails and commiserated with each other for a couple of hours until Anne said she had to get home to her hubby and kids and Mandy said the same.

Bev was thinking about all this when she unlocked the door to her apartment and reached back to shut it, but instead was shoved into the room by somebody holding a gun.

"Don't worry," Johnny said. "I'm not going to hurt you. I just need to ask you some questions."

"Please don't rape me," she pleaded.

"Honey, the last thing in the world I would do is rape you."

She waited for the questions.

"Bobby Lee, the boxer you used to mess around with," Johnny said. "Tell me where he might head if he was on the run?"

She swallowed.

"How would I know?"

"You two talked didn't you, it wasn't all just screwing?"

"We never did. I wanted to, but he was still grieving for an old girl-friend got herself killed in a car wreck.

"You better come up with something better," he warned, "or I'm going to do bad things to you."

"You promised not to hurt me."

This one was a real ditz.

"I'm going to do things to you that you don't even read about in those medieval books," he threatened.

"Those what?"

"Give me a destination where he might go!"

She was, of course, on the verge of full blown hysteria.

"Let me get my address book, I write everything down in it. Maybe he told me something once . . ."

He waved to her with the gun and she got to her feet, went to a drawer in a stand by the couch and opened it, thought: I should shoot her for being so stupid. Beauty but no brains. God half blessed her and half cursed her, like most broads. Dumb women. He was thankful he was gay and didn't have to live with one.

She found a notation next to Bobby's name and apartment phone number—Dunham Lee, *Coral Reef FL*. What she remembered was that was his father, but she thought she recalled the guy had died. Still, anything to get this goon away from her. Showed it to Johnny who ripped out the page, stood there looking at her, said, "Get naked."

"What?"

"Are you deaf as well as stupid? Get undressed—all the way."

He stood looking on as she slipped off her dress, then unsnapped her bra and finally stepped out of her panties and stood before him.

"You're going to rape me," she cried, her voice cracking, her chin quivering, and all the rest that fear instills. "You're going to rape me and then kill me. Please don't. Please. I'll do anything you want. I won't fight you, I won't even report this to the police. Just don't hurt me."

He drew in a sharp breath, said, "I'm leaving now, but if you call the police, I'll come back and do all those things to you and more. Am I clear?"

She nodded.

"Go in the bathroom and shut the door and don't come out for one hour."

She rushed in the bathroom and shut the door and he left with what he'd come for. The striptease was just for humiliation and to instill fear, he no more wanted her than the bubonic plague.

Now if she'd been the black boxer—well that was another story.

Chapter Fourteen

"There's no such thing as good money
Or bad money, there's just money."
—Lucky Luciano

He awoke to raging thunderstorm replete with requisite booms and crashes that felt like the Devil himself was coming for him. It took a second to realize where he was, then realized she was there in the bed with him, her back now to him, knees drawn up and when he turned to look at her, he saw the still healing scars on her back, wondered who'd done such a thing to a woman, any woman.

He swung his legs over the side of the bed, sat for a moment more getting his bearings. The room was still in semi-darkness but for the flashes of lightening. It smelled also, of other people, cleaning solutions, stale cigarettes.

He'd stayed in a hundred rooms just like it, traveling for his fights because Max was too cheap for better.

"Soon as you win the title, kid, this will all change, this is just the grind every fighter goes through on his way up. Problem was, it never did change even when he was winning some real money fights. Seemed like Max always had reasons why there wasn't more: "Gotta pay the team, your trainer, a cut man, gloves, shorts, shoes, your robe. Then too, there is the expense of renting a gym everywhere we go, eats, gasoline, and it just never fucken ends. You think I'm making anything out of this, kid? I'm not, believe me, I'm not making a dime. I only wish I was.

"But it's like that fable about the turtle and the rabbit, you ever read that, Bobby, about them two racing? Everybody bet on that rabbit but it was the turtle won because that thing stopped to take a crap and then laid down for a nap and that turtle came along and won. That's me, you and me Bobby. We're the turtle, just going slowly along till we win the belt, then you'll see how it will all be different. Patience, kid. Trust me." So saith Max in the beginning, but a year ago Bobby realized he wasn't in Max's best financial interest.

Yeah, trust you Max to screw me over for the last two years while you robbed me blind and I paid for it with my blood and sweat, while you sat your fat ass in the third row with some bimbo, chewing on that cigar and watched me take a beating or give a beating. It wasn't you had your nose broke in the second round against Rodriguez, or your jaw broken in the tenth against Delano, was it? And now you want to kill me because I stood up and knocked that fucker out you thought was the next coming of Ali? Fuck you Max. Fuck you.

He walked to the window and parted the drapes enough to look out at the gloom and deluge, the rain hammering so hard it was dancing in the parking lot like a million tiny glass fairies, the sky a gloom of lead mixed with the blackest clouds.

Maybe it was a good thing, he thought amusedly, because he knew that a mere rainstorm was not going to stop whoever Max was sending for him. He flexed his hands, and though they were still stiff and sore, they were better.

He could do with a cup of coffee and a smoke, and soon as it quit raining go find a place to eat breakfast. He was a man used to eating big meals when he wasn't training. For some reason he'd dreamed of Beverly Schwartz last night—in fact he sat straight up in bed, but he didn't know why. They were not close, not at all like him and Julie McKowski were, and he hadn't even thought about her for a year. And now standing looking out at a medieval looking Louisiana sky, he wondered why he would have had a dream about her that startled him awake.

She would come to see him in the gym sometime and once in a while he'd spot her in the audience in one of his local fights. Pretty woman, for sure, and they'd dated on and off for a time not too long after. She was good in bed, but couldn't boil an egg. She wasn't dumb, exactly—had more resolve to get what she wanted and a lot of charm to go with it. She'd pursued him pretty hard after he'd gone in and gotten a haircut from her on the recommendation of a friend, said she did a great job and very personable. So then the next time he needed a trim, that is where he went and she seemed to just latch on to him. She was just one of those girls you run into once in a while—not someone you'd want to marry, not someone you'd even want as a friend, but not someone who did anything wrong either. But she was not memorable like Julie was. Boy what a shame how that turned out, he thought.

It got him thinking about his almost ex-wife again—not the sad stuff of her getting killed in a car crash—but the good stuff, before she broke the news she was into women, an "epiphany" she called it. She was otherwise great in every way, kind, gentle, smart, sassy, adventurous.

He found himself smiling thinking of her, thinking, where did you go darling Julie—up there in the storm?

"Hey," Nina from the bed calling to him in a sleep husky voice.

He turned.

"Hey what?"

"What're you doing?"

"Looking out the window."

She laughed, said, "I can see that, dodo. I mean why?"

"The storm woke me, that's all. It's like the third world war with all the sound and fury."

"You want to come back to bed?"

He turned, looked at her lying there, propped up on one elbow, the sheet pulled up under her arm, but he could see she didn't have anything on.

"You want me to come back to bed?" he said.

A crack of thunder startled them both.

"Yeah, I think so," she said. "I'm sorta scared." With a sheepish grin.

He went back to bed, she held the sheet open for him to get in and he did. She moved against him, kissed him tenderly on the mouth. He tried not to respond, but he did anyway. Passions were like beautiful tigers that ate you up.

He kissed her back, and then their hands and mouths sought the unknown territory of first time lovers. They kissed and touched a long time before she turned on her back and invited him in. And when he did everything turned sweet and surreal. She cried out in a sharp gasp that inflamed him all the more.

Time became irrelevant, passed unnoticed, but somehow when they finished, it seemed to have passed too quickly, and their lovemaking had not transported them to another time and place, had not washed away their sins and made them new again. They were still Bobby Lee and Nina Summers.

He reached for his cigarettes, offered her one and lighted them with the brushed chrome lighter and sat propped up on the bed smoking, wordlessly for a time.

Nina wondering what she'd ever done that for, maybe because in a way he was her protector, or maybe because she just needed to be needed and there was no better way in her mind than to have a man make love to her. She was surprised at how tender he had been for all his muscle and size and brutal features. She didn't know, really, and wasn't sure if she regretted it, told herself maybe she just needed to prove that being raped by Buzzard wasn't going to destroy her—yeah, maybe that is what it really was. But then as quickly told herself, Hell no, she just wanted to be close to this guy.

Bobby Lee was surprised at how much he enjoyed it with this rather strange girl, the fact she had shot and killed three guys just a couple of nights before. Told himself maybe she was nuts, a psycho, but then he didn't really believe that she was. She had stuck up for herself, fought back, and that was something he could both admire and appreciate. She might look like ninety pounds soaking wet, but she had lots of grit.

"You remind me of some of those Mexican fighters," he said.

"What, because you think I look like a Chihuahua?"

He laughed, said, "No, because you're tough."

"Oh. Gee, I guess that's supposed to be a compliment," she said. "You could have just said you found me attractive."

"Well, some of those guys are too," he teased.

"Shut the fuck up," she said. "Let's get dressed, I'm starved."

"Yeah, me too."

He dressed while she used the bathroom, then she came out in just her panties to get dressed and there was something almost stunning about seeing her like that, said, "You're right, I should have just said, I think you're attractive."

"You mean like this," she said. "Prance around in a pair of panties and men turn into dancing bears." She turned her back on him and started getting dressed while he used the bathroom.

They started out. It was still pouring rain like crazy. She had the bag with the stolen dope in her hand.

"You want I can carry that while you run and get in the car. She tossed him a suspicious look.

"No thanks, Jimbo, I'm a big girl, I can carry my own bag."

He shrugged, said, "Suit yourself, just trying to be helpful."

He ran out to unlock the doors and got in reaching across to unlatch her side, thinking, I wouldn't want to offend you by being a male chauvinist. He drove up to the office and got out and went in to pay their room and drop off the key. The man behind the desk asked him if he wanted a receipt. No. Then Bobby asked him for a place to eat heading West and the fellow told him there was a Waffle Shack about half a mile just before he got back on the interstate.

He finished paying the bill and ran out and got in the car and started it up, said, "I hope you're into waffles"

"Whatever," she said. "You made me hungry,"

"I bet you say that to all the guys," he said as he pulled out of the parking lot and made a left on the street.

"Listen, bub, I'm not some whore. So don't ruin it, okay?"

It caught him by surprise, her sudden flash of anger.

"Sorry," he said, "I just meant it as a joke."

"Just don't joke about that, okay. Ray used to call me all sorts of things, being a whore was his big one. Always thought I cheated on him. I never did."

"Sounds like a real asshole that boyfriend of yours," he said.

She turned to stare out the rain-streaked window thinking about him. Even though she shot him didn't mean she didn't still keep a little feeling for him, made all the more so by the fact that she *had* shot him. Something about killing a person ties you to them forever, she thought. But she hoped that wasn't the case.

He reached over and sympathetically touched her bare knee.

"I really am sorry, I was . . . well, I apologize," he said.

The rain was almost biblical in its intensity and the wipers of that beast of a car worked like hell trying to keep up. He flipped on the radio and got just static so shut it off again and looked for the waffle place, thinking, You had to go and screw it up Bobby by making a bad joke.

Chapter Fifteen

"I'm here to kick ass and drink whiskey
and Pilgrim, I'm all out of whiskey."
—John Wayne

The phone on Max's desk rang. He was in a funk and he didn't know why, telling himself, I got everything a man could want, except for a big cock, some more height and maybe fifty pounds less. I got plenty of dough, all the pussy I can handle and I'm in love with a black chick. My old mother would turn over in her grave. All she ever talked about when she was still alive, she would have referred to Chocolate Cherry as a *shikse* and wouldn't have liked it, would have still been hounding him to find a nice Jewish girl. Max was in a way glad Miriam had passed on, God rest her soul.

But this whole thing with Cherry showing her ass to other men was starting to get to Max. But he'd be damned if he would give her the upper-hand by telling her as much.

"Hello" he growled into the phone. On top of everything else he was having gastric problems—probably that Greek food he'd had the other night, the shank of lamb, the way they cooked it, *Ovey*.

"Max, just want you to know I've got some good leads on your missing fighter and I'm hoping in twenty-four hours to get eyeballs on him."

"What's with the eyeballs," Max complained. "I don't want you to put nothing on him or in him except a couple of them things you carrying in that six-shooter, Cowboy. Where you at now?"

"Panama City."

"What a shithole that is. Last time I went through there, I couldn't get out of there fast enough—nothing but horny drunken sailors all over the fucken place."

"Max, I think you're thinking of Pensacola."

"Whatever. I don't even consider that part of the state to be Florida, tell you the truth. What the fuck you doing there anyway, getting some of that college cooze from Spring Break?"

"Max, I don't think its Spring Break yet."

"Jesus Christ, will you listen to this guy."

"I've been hitting the gas stations, asking anybody seen that car of Johnny's and nobody has till I find this old fuck in greasy coveralls and drinking a can of Rolling Rock out front sitting on a pop crate, got Mick stitched on his hat.

"So I ask this Mick if he's ever seen a 1970s Chrysler aqua marine convertible with white leather top, and he looks at me like I just asked if Elvis had stopped in for a Milky Way, grins and shows me the teeth he's got left, spits and says, 'Yup.'

Max thinking as he listened to Cowboy tell it; the fucker usually doesn't say shit if he's got a mouthful is now telling this long winded story about some guy in greasy clothes named Mick.

"So I ask him," Cowboy continued, "did the driver look like a guy who just had a fight a few days ago, you know, did he have bruised eyes or a band aide over his eyebrow or something. Guy goes, 'Yup. Filled 'er up and I checked the earl and water.' Said earl instead of oil like country people say it. So I say, you see which way he went, and he just sits there looking at me like a dumb ox . . . ."

Max is about ready to blow a gasket if Cowboy doesn't hurry it along. He's getting fidgety sitting there listening to the guy; worse than listening to a book on tape. Max is starting to wish one of the girls would come in and ask him something, or better still, want something so he could do a little tit-for-tat, or more like a little tit-for-Max. But it's not even noon yet and nobody's in the place but him and the janitor out there mopping up the spilled beer and who knew what all in the back room and toilets.

"So I figure," Cowboy continued, "that he's wanting to get paid for any further information and I peel him off a pair of twenties, which, by the way, will be part of my bill, and he looks at them, both sides like it's counterfeit or something, and then he finally tucks 'em into the pocket of his coveralls and points toward the west. Like that was all he had to fucken say, but he didn't. I should have taken him out back and shot him like some old worthless dog. But at least I got a hit on our boy and I know he's going West, but to where I'm not exactly sure yet. However, I've got a call into a cop I know who's running an all points on the car."

"Aw jeez, that's fucken great, Cowboy. West. Well that ought to narrow it down. Couple of more years and you should catch up with him swimming in the Pacific with the fucken walruses and shit."

Max hung up the phone, said, "Fuck!"

A knock on the door gave Max hope maybe one of the girls came in early.

"It's open!" he yelled.

But it was just Ruiz, the old Cuban that had escaped two jumps ahead of Castro taking over way back when. Come in there to mop up and empty the wastebaskets.

"How ju, today, Mister Max?"

"The Jew's okay," Max said making fun of the Hispanic's manner of speaking. "How you doing?" Ruiz stopped and gave a quizzical look, but Max waved him off and picked up the phone and dialed Cherry. It rang about ten times before she answered, sounding all out of breath.

"Who you got over there?" Max said.

"Ain't got nobody, sugar."

"Like hell. How come you're out of breath then?"

"I was, oh, I was helping my neighbor move her couch, that's why it took me so long to answer the phone, you know Mimi from across the hall . . ."

"No, I sure as hell do not. I want to come over."

"Well, now honey, now might not be such a good time. I's just ready to go out and buy some groceries and shit. Maybe get my hair done, too. They got a new stylist over to the Razor Kut."

"There's something serious I want to talk to you about."

Cherry could always tell by a man's voice what his mood was and Max sounded mighty desperate, his voice rising to that of a ten-year-old girl demanding her some money.

"Can't you just tell me over the phone what it is, baby?"

"No, goddamn it. I'm having a helluva time and I want to talk to you. So make other plans and I'll be over there in twenty minutes." Then he slammed the phone down just as Ruiz finished emptying the wastebasket by his desk, the big one. The two men locked eyes. Max suddenly felt sorry for the poor bastard, but he didn't know why he did. Something just came over him, a rare wave of compassion, said, "How are you doing, Ruiz?"

The old man looked at him, said, "Ju already ask me, Mr. Max."

"Oh, that's right." Max thought briefly about giving him some money, thought about it, changed his mind as the old fellow shuffled to the door, then called to him and when he turned around, Max stood and walked over and handed him a one-hundred dollar bill."

"This is for you, Ruiz, for the good job you do, for your family. Your wife loves you?"

The old man nodded, said, "Si, most of the time."

"Yeah, women," Max said. "You can't shoot them and you can't live without them."

Ruiz smiled as if he was in agreement, Max going out smiling to himself at his own sudden and rare generosity.

He liked to think of himself as a good guy, and now maybe that old mop swinger would think of him as a good guy too.

Chapter Sixteen

"In the end, we only regret the chances we didn't take."
—Lewis Carroll

The body under the sheet was just a body like any other body until Frank said to his ex-wife, "You ready, honey?"

Through the glass not so darkly, but rather in a radiant white light, the surprisingly normal looking guy in the smock stood ready to remove the sheet from the naked body of one Ray, AKA Ray DeSanto, the now dead guy. The only thing Frank felt bad about was his ex-wife had to witness this.

She nodded slowly and squeezed Frank's hand and Frank nodded then to the coroner's assistant and he pulled the sheet back to Ray's bare shoulders, but not so far that the crude stitch job they used to sew the Y of the autopsy incision back up so that if you did not know any better, said loved one simply looked asleep.

She gasped, but surprisingly that was her total reaction. The assistant watched her through the glass until Frank gave him the okay to cover the corpse again and close the curtain.

They walked out of the basement world of the deceased, with hollow footsteps following them, passing closed doors, and under steam pipes and toward a distant light they hoped was of sunshine and life again.

And once outside she looked almost as pale as her deceased brother, pale and stark and fragile as he'd ever seen her and could not help but think that just an hour ago she'd been in the throes of—well, who knew, maybe she wasn't in the throes of anything; maybe her and that asshole had just been sleeping together.

"You want to get a coffee?" he said.

Silently she accepted and they drove to one of those silver diners looked like an Airstream, went in and sat in a back booth, Frank ordered them each coffee and didn't even bother watching the young waitress's backside as she left, because that is usually what divorced guys like himself did. Instead, his full attention was on his ex-wife sitting across from him, her mind a million miles away, or at least a couple of miles to where the morgue was.

When they'd gotten their coffee, he watched as she poured in cream, no sugar and stirred slowly, almost methodically, but certainly wordlessly. He waited.

Then she lifted her gaze from the mirror inside her cup, said, "Tell me who did this to him, Frank?"

"Don't know yet, honey." Frank felt completely impotent. "I know you don't know this, but this morning was my last day on the job. I'm retired. I just happen to be on duty last night when the call came in. Me and another detective were the first ones on the scene."

Her eyes searched his as if to pull answers from him that weren't there. But none were forthcoming—easier for a camel to pass through the eye of a needle, Frank thought.

Frank took a swallow of coffee. It was, he noted privately, lousy coffee, but worth it not to be sitting in one of those places where the hipsters went with their laptops and sat around like young potentates enjoying life while the rest of the world was out working for a living. His father would have shot him stone cold dead if he'd paid three bucks for a cup of coffee. Good old pops, himself now deceased, thank God. He would have gone ape shit at what was going on in the world these days, because he went ape shit when he was alive and the streets weren't nearly as bad.

"We hadda guy gave us trouble, we just took him in the alley and gave him an attitude adjustment. Believe me, we straightened out a lot of guys that way. Now days you even look at a prick cross-eyed they file a complaint. Shit, I'm glad I'm not a cop no more." Yeah, that was pops. Frank didn't want to be like him, but he still loved him.

"At least one of the guys was a known drug dealer and there was some evidence found, a crack pipe, syringes, the usual paraphernalia to suspect it could have been a robbery—maybe Ray was just at the wrong place at the wrong time." He was lying through his teeth and suspected Wendy knew it too. He just wanted to save her from the cruel truth, and truth is almost always cruel.

"No," she said. "He was probably mixed in it somehow." Shook her head. "Ray was a good kid—I mean he had a good heart, Frank. You know that." He didn't. Had never liked the little prick, but he nodded, said, "Yeah, Wendy, I know that."

"He got mixed up with the wrong people," Wendy continued. "He was an easy mark and others saw that in him and took advantage. I did my best to keep him straight, but he just ran off the rails." She said it with such finality.

"Well," Frank said. "I'm sure the police will catch the guy who did this."

She'd started to pick up her cup but set it back down.

"Do you love me, Frank. I mean do you really down deep still love me in spite of everything?"

He didn't even have to think about it, said, "Yes. You know that I do." He had never wanted the divorce to begin with. It was Wendy who'd grown restless, fearful he'd get killed on the job, and started acting out by getting with other men. How many he didn't know, but he did know one of them. She was never meant to be a cop's wife. Took a special kind of woman and Wendy wasn't that kind.

She reached across the table and took his hands.

"I love you too, Frank. I've always loved you and I know now getting a divorce was a mistake. That man you saw in my place, our place, he was just a friend, someone who I can talk too when I need to. But he's no replacement for you."

Frank was tempted to say, Is that what you call what you were doing at the house with the guy in the boxers, talking? But he held his tongue.

Her eyes welled up as she professed her feelings for him. He wanted to believe her, he really did.

"I don't understand why you wanted the divorce if you felt that way," he said feeling emotional for the first time in a couple of years.

"You know why," she said. He did know why.

"If you love me, Frank, and if you think there is a second chance for us, I want you to take care of this. I need to know whoever did this gets what's coming to him."

"Like I said, honey, I'm retired as of this morning."

She lowered her voice to just a whisper, said, "Fuck the police. I don't want the party responsible to be arrested, get a free attorney, have it plead down to second degree or manslaughter. They killed my only living family, Frank. They took that from me."

In a way he was surprised she was asking him to commit murder. She never even used to like having his service weapon in the house, was kind to everyone, loved animals, got involved in about every humane cause.

"If you do this for me, Frank, it is all I'll ever ask you as long as we both shall live." Funny way of putting it, he thought.

"You're saying you want to get back together?"

"Yes. I've missed you so much and have lain awake nights crying over you. I want you to come home, Frank. We'll go and live down in the Mexican Rivera if you want, or that place, that Sea of Cortez you talked about. Get a condo overlooking the ocean. We got plenty of good years in us, Frank—let's not waste them."

Before he knew it, they were back at the house, undressed, in bed, making love—perhaps the best he'd ever experienced, and she gave it her all until they both fell exhausted.

They lay there for a long silent time until she rolled herself into him, said, "Frank. Will you do what I asked? Will you come back to me?"

Kill a guy, or maybe a bunch of guys to have your wife back again? It wasn't who he was, but, he sure as hell wanted to be with her, especially now that he was retired. And a condo, say, in paradise was real tempting to be sure.

"Yes, baby, I'll take care of it, then we'll pack our bags and cross the border like those old time outlaws."

She reached up and kissed him full and long on the mouth, said, "You think you're up for another round?"

He didn't know that he was, said, "What took you so long to ask."

The second time wasn't as good, didn't last as long, the thought of just killing guys for the purpose of vengeance, especially for that dick, Ray, intruded itself into the physical pleasure, diminished it, or, maybe it was true, he just wasn't as young as he used to be and even her firm middle-aged body couldn't wring from him that same pleasure or stamina.

And then it was time to go—again her standing at the door in her robe and it gave him a sinking feeling that just a few hours earlier she'd been with another man. It was true, he thought, she had an insatiable sexual appetite, had always had it, and still had it. And what if he couldn't keep up, would she cheat on him again?

Or, he wondered, was this all because she wanted to have him go forth and take lives to assuage her pain of her no good brother's death. A death he likely deserved, for Ray was the bearer of pain and heartbreak on others many times, had not a single good bone in his body.

Now he had a choice to make, turned back to look at her standing in that robe knowing what was underneath and knowing how bad he wanted that.

Goddamn, Wendy, why'd you have to go and do that? Show me what I'm missing most in life?

Chapter Seventeen

"Never love anyone who treats you like you're ordinary."
—Oscar Wilde

They drove out of the rain and crossed into the piney woods of Texas. The sun seemed to turn the land to fire, each of them in thought, no conversation or radio, Bobby Lee driving, trying to decide just what he thought of the woman with him.

"Like intimate strangers, you and me," he said.

"What?"

"Just that we don't really know each other, and yet we know each other more than a lot of people do."

She turned from facing out the passenger window to looking at him.

"You talking about what happened, the sex thing?" she said.

"Yeah, that *sex* thing as you call it."

"It was okay," she said.

"Just okay?"

"What do you want me to say? I mean I didn't expect that much, you know, the difference in our ages and all that—but you held your own. Stop off at the next truck stop and I'll buy you a trophy for your dash."

"I was just trying to put a name to it."

"To what?"

"You and me."

"You think there is a you and me, Griswold?"

"Why do you call me everything but my name?" he said.

"I don't know. It just seems to work out that way."

"Who the hell is this Griswold, an old boyfriend or somebody?"

She laughed.

"You're such a lamebrain," she laughed again. "Clark Griswold from the movie Family Vacation. Like that."

He was lost as to what she was talking about.

"What, you never seen it?"

"No. I don't see a lot of movies. 'Sides, why would I watch a movie about people going on vacation?"

She laughed, said, "Man what do you do with all your spare time?"

"I'm always in training, and when I'm not, I'm too tired to go sit in a theater for a couple of hours just to have people cough on me."

"Getting punched in the face can't be much fun either."

"I like to read."

"You?"

"You find that hard to believe?"

"No, I guess not. You just don't look much like a guy who likes to read."

"What's a guy who likes to read look like?"

"You're screwing with me," she said. "What kind of books?"

"Any kind, mostly Westerns, but Shakespeare too."

"Yeah? Quote me something."

"What, you don't believe me?"

"Sure, but quote me something."

He cast a quick glance at her, could see she was just waiting for him to make a fool of himself, that she didn't trust a guy whose nose had been broken several times and had scar tissue around his eyes would know how to add two plus three.

"Okay," he said. "Here's something: '*To say the truth, love and reason keep little company nowadays.*'"

"What the fuck's that mean anyway?"

"Now it is you who are fucking with me," he said.

She sat there staring at him and he felt pretty smug about it, said. "I'm not just a pretty guy who gets hit in the face." Said it with a smile.

"Goddamn, Delbert, you sure as hell are not. I'm impressed."

"Try again, this time you pick a subject."

It took her a few seconds but then she said, "How about betrayal?" thinking of Ray and what he'd done to her; thinking about that was the only way she kept from grieving over what she'd done.

He thought for a moment, said, "Okay then. 'Though those that are betrayed, do feel the treason sharply, the traitor stands in worse case woe.' "

"Well that sure as shit sounds like Ray."

"You sorry now you did it? Kill him?"

"Only if the police catch me. I hear the bull dykes in prison are worse than men and I sure as shit ain't into that woman thing."

He looked over at her, could see she was tense. Scared, maybe of being caught, but also scared for what she'd done. She might put on a tough veneer, and he'd no doubt she was tough, but she was also very much a person, and he assumed that even the Devil wept now and then.

"You're pretty interesting," she said.

"Yeah? I'd say you are too."

"Let's be lovers."

He laughed, said, "I thought what we did made us thus."

She sat back, put her bare feet up on the dash. He smiled thinking Johnny Pearl would have a shit fit to see some woman's feet on the dash of his expensive ride. She had small pretty feet, the first time he'd noticed them.

"So what's the plan, Stan?" she said.

"You know what it is. We find you a ride and split company."

"What about you?"

"Fuck if I know. I might have to keep moving for a time. Thought about Hawaii, but maybe I need to go on down to South America, live in the jungle, turn native and all that."

"Yeah? I can just picture you living in some grass hut with some hot little chick feeding you grapes while you swing on a hammock," she said.

"Might not be too bad," he said, but without cheer because he didn't believe it, no fucking way.

They drove till noon and stopped at a root beer stand, pulled in and ordered through a speaker.

"I haven't been to one of these places since I was a kid," she said.

"Yeah, like that was a long time ago," he said.

A girl in a uniform on roller skates took their order, then brought their tray and he cranked the window half way up for her to rest it on, gave her a ten-dollar bill, then they ate while he kept an eye out for anybody who might be suspicious, but there were just people with kids, an old gray-haired couple, a couple of teenagers. It gave him a sense of nostalgia.

When they finished, he pulled out just as the teenage boy in the other car said, "Hey, that's a hell of a ride old man."

"See, I told you," Nina said.

"Told me what?"

"That you're an old man." Laughing. She had a nice laugh and it was good to see her enjoying herself, even if it was at his expense.

It got him to thinking that maybe they should get rid of the flamboyant ride, he said to her as they pulled onto the highway, "We got to get rid of this ride."

"Why, it's a beautiful ride, Pops."

He shook his head at still another name she called him by. Kids, he thought. Even though he figured she wasn't that much younger than him, ten, fifteen years maybe, he felt old and she looked and acted young sometimes—if, he overlooked the fact she'd killed three guys.

"It draws too much attention," he said.

"Will you let me pick the next one out?"

"No." She feigned a pout as she sucked at the straw of her to-go cup of root beer. Yeah, it really felt like he was hauling his daughter on down that lonesome old highway, but then he thought about this morning, told himself, she sure as hell wasn't a kid and certainly not his daughter. But then why did he feel these waves of guilt?

An hour later they came into a small town—Arrowhead—the sign said, POP 2600.

Just there on the outskirts about a mile past the town proper—such as it was—he saw some red, white and blue plastic banners flapping in the hot dry wind and about two dozen cars on a red dirt lot.

"Let's try this place," he said. She roused from her sleepy state and sat up, said, "I've got to pee."

He barely got the ignition turned off when a man came out of the trailer office extending his hand before a beaming smile on a face that looked made out of lard. His faded blue gabardine suit seemed a size too small across the shoulders and his belly slung over his belt like he was about eight months pregnant.

"How do, folks. That is some fine looking automobile, yes sir."

"You have a restroom?" Nina asked.

The sales guy appraised her like she was a pimp's Cadillac he'd like to take a drive in.

"Yes sir, little Miss. Right inside there."

When he'd finished watching her climb the set of steps and disappear inside, he turned back to Bobby Lee.

"So, you fixin' to trade that classic in? I can sure make you a good deal on that one alright."

From the eagerness in his voice and the look in his eyes, Bobby knew the guy would try and screw him on whatever he traded for, but shit, it didn't really matter.

"Yeah, I was thinking about maybe a truck. I see you got a couple of them over there."

"Sure do. Let's go over and take a look."

They looked at both the trucks, one was a GMC and the other a Ford.

"Which one runs best?" Bobby asked.

"Well, they both go good, that Ford's got a few less miles. Belonged to a woman whose husband passed. Local woman. He took real good care of it."

"Fine, what'll you do for me on mine?"

They walked back over and the salesman slid in behind the wheel, ran his hands almost tenderly over the steering wheel.

"Got the keys?"

Bobby handed him the car keys and the salesman turned on the ignition to check the mileage. Stared a moment, said, "Why it says there ain't but fifty-three grand on it. Can that be right?"

"Far as I know. My old daddy left it to me. He was a fool for collecting cars. He's dead, mama too."

The salesman studied the leather, said, "Perfect" and "Mint." Then climbed out and walked around to the rear, sniffed, said, "Somethin' smells don't it? Damn skunks come around at night."

He inserted the key and popped the lid and took three quick steps back.

"Jesus Christ!" Bobby saw it too—the body of a dead girl wrapped in blood smeared plastic, looking the pale color of a mannequin. *That fucken Johnny Pearl had murdered this woman.*

The salesman turned to Bobby for explanation, and that is when he saw the .45, cocked and aimed.

"I know you're not going to believe me," Bobby said. "I can't even explain this."

"Don't shoot me, Mister. I never saw a goddamn thing, I swear I ain't."

"Go on in the office," Bobby ordered and followed the guy inside just as Nina was coming out. She stopped and stared as Bobby marched the salesman inside, then followed.

"Hold the gun on him," Bobby said, looking around for something to tie the guy's hands. Then when he couldn't, he loosed the man's white belt and used that to truss his hands behind his back. He looked around some more, decided on a pair of coat hangers and used these to truss the guy's feet after putting him into the bathroom and closing the door. He took the gun from Nina who hadn't said another thing until they stepped back outside.

"What the fuck?" she said.

"There's a dead girl in the trunk," he said.

"What the fuck?"

"Yeah. We got to ditch the car, take one of his."

"But then they'll know you stole a car and the cops will be on the lookout."

What the fuck were they going to do, take the Windsor or steal one of the guy's cars?

"Okay then, drive it around back," he said, and she got in and drove it around back and he went inside the office and found a set of keys for one of the cars—a Buick BLK 4Dr instead of one of the trucks. Then he searched the filing cabinet for paperwork on the vehicle, found it and went outside again and around back to where Nina had parked the Windsor.

"Shit," he said and went back inside and found a screwdriver and came out again and switched plates with the Windsor and the Buick.

"Wipe our prints off the inside," he said, and they worked together to do just that. Then, when finished Bobby told Nina they were taking the Buick and leaving the Windsor.

"It will slow them down a bit if they're checking plates," he said. "Get in, let's go."

But then he got out again and went inside the office and into the small john, said to the salesman, "I'm sorry about all this, I really didn't know about the body. But here's the thing, I don't want to go down for a murder I didn't commit. And if the cops ask you, give them the name Johnny Pearl, he's the fuck owns that car and killed that girl."

He glanced down and saw the guy had wetted his trousers, punched the inner lock so nobody could just go in there, and then stepped out and pulled the door shut with the requisite wipe job. When he reached the front door, he turned the OPEN sign to CLOSED, then twisted the cheap lock and went out closing the door behind him.

Nina was waiting with the motor running and soon as he got in, she drove off, not in a hurry, but not slow either.

"I take it this is the best deal you could make," she said.

"You are a real piece of work," he said.

"Ain't I though, R2D2."

Texas seemed big and endless and a lot of landscape to get lost in, but a lot of cops, too.

Chapter Eighteen

"Is that a pistol in your pocket or are you just happy to see me?"
—Mae West

Max searched around Cherry's apartment disarrayed with clothes, shoes, etcetera, etcetera. He thinks he smells cigar smoke, says, "I smell cigar smoke."

"Oh, Max, I was smoking a blunt. You want one, honey?"

He stalked back into the bedroom—sheets on the bed are disarrayed, sniffed them, smelled a mixture of scents, perfume, aftershave, sex.

"Who was in here?"

"Nobody," she said.

"I don't want you seeing any other men, Cherry."

"Now baby, you know that ain't possible. Girl's got to make a living, you know."

He's so hot for her he can't stand still. He's been thinking about her, about them. So what if she's half his age and black, and a non-Jew. He doesn't care. He'd decided he wants to marry her. Even stopped off at Hegleman's Jewelry store and purchased a ring—not an expensive one, but a ring, nonetheless.

He sits down and tells her to sit next to him on the couch, when she does, he takes her hands in his, said, "Will you marry me?"

This caught her off-guard. He's rich, that's true. But he's also an old fat white man with hair on his back. Oh, and a small dick, the size of a gherkin, about the shape of one too, only it ain't green.

"Max, is you nuts or something?"

"Goddamn it, I'm serious as a fucken heart attack. I'm in love with you. I want to make an honest woman out of you."

"Honey, it's going to take a lot more than putting a cheap ass ring on my finger to make an honest woman out of me. This time she does laugh and it causes Max's face to turn tomato red.

"Look, you planning on dancing and fucking men the rest of your life? I seen girls go down that path, it leads nowhere. And what happens when you turn forty and your tits sag and your cooch is all loose and shit. Is that how you want to end up?"

"No, Max, and I ain't goin' to, neither. I got plans. I want to go back to college and get me a degree and make something of myself. I ain't gonna marry yo' old white ass. I don't know what you been smokin'.'"

It infuriated Max, the insults of somebody he told himself he was in love with. What the fuck was wrong with this whore, anyway? Said, "What the fuck is wrong with you? You're just a cheap whore and I could get a hundred of you anytime I wanted."

She said, "Well go on and get you some, then. Don't let the door hit you in your saggy old ass."

He grabbed her and drew back his fist. He was going to teach this bitch a lesson. Whatever made him think she was any more than what she was.

When he grabbed her, she slapped him open handed hard across the face. Big mistake. He jerked her to her feet and used his fist to hit her. The blow stunned her and she looked at him with a hurt cruel stare.

"You muthafucka!"

"Yeah, try this," he said and hit her again, harder, the blow causing her to fall, but for the couch, she would have slammed to the floor.

She wiped blood from her wounded mouth, looked at it on her finger-tips. Now she was fearful, began pleading with him not to hit her no more, but Max was beyond the point of listening, or reason. She had insulted his very desire for her, her words wounding. What a damn fool he'd been to think the two of them could be together.

As a young guy, he ran with a Jewish gang of toughs who mugged and strong armed people, among other crimes. Max was the hitter of the bunch. He got off on punching some guy in the face and knocking him out cold. It drew cheers and hoots from his comrades.

But now in his sixties, he hadn't punched anybody out in years and it felt good punching a face again. The odd thing was, rather than her pleas for mercy, for forgiveness, it only encouraged him more, and so he hit her again, and again and again until she was limp and unresponsive.

He grabbed her by the wrist and dragged her into the bedroom and lifted her onto the bed. She moaned and he went in and got a glass of water from the bathroom and filled it, then came back into the bedroom and tossed the water in her face. Her eyes fluttered open.

"Cherry," he said. "You could have handled this better, but you're one of those stupid broads who can't see the future, can you? Cut off your nose to spite your face."

She was hearing little of what he was saying, and comprehending even less.

He got on top of her, straddling her there on the bed and put his hands around her throat, said, "If I can't have you nobody can, baby. You might as well be fucken dead."

And did not loosen his grip until he was pretty sure she *was* dead. He got off, sweat dripping into his eyes, his throat dry and went into the small kitchen and opened the fridge door, found a bottle of vodka in the freezer. How come these cunts always kept their vodka in the freezer.

He got a glass from the cupboard and sat down at the table and poured himself a glass. It was good, cold like that, he had to admit. It tasted like fire and ice going down. He drank a second glass, and though he now felt bad for killing her, what's a guy supposed to do when he's disrespected like that—just let it go?

Thinking about it, he wondered if Cowboy had caught that prick Bobby Lee. He hoped that he had. Bobby Lee was another prick who'd disrespected him. Can't let that shit go.

He poured some more and downed it, then got up and went back in the bedroom and stared at Cherry's body for a moment, thinking, What the fuck am I supposed to do with you now. Thinking of how to get rid of the body.

"Well," he said. "I guess one more for old time's sake ain't going to hurt nothing, honey."

Then took off his clothes and got up on the bed with her. He talked to her the whole time, and for once she had no comments like: "Jeez Max, you could stand to lose some weight, you too damn heavy, I can't breathe." Or, "Fuck Max, a shower wouldn't hurt nothing now and then." Or, "Hurry up, I gotta pee."

It sort of gave him a little extra thrill, too, knowing he could do whatever he wanted to her and in whatever way he wanted to.

He'd never had a dead woman before, and you know something, he thought, it ain't too bad.

Chapter Nineteen

"I like my whiskey old and my women young."
—Errol Flynn

The salesman's name was Al Herbert and he'd pissed himself there in the bathroom trying to free himself. And even though he was alone and trussed up, he was embarrassed by it. He considered himself a good Christian man, faithful to his wife, but that one time, well, two, when he'd gone to the Used Car auctions and got a little drunk—well, more than a little. He'd been married to the same woman for almost thirty years and they had three children, grown now, and well, let's face it, married thirty years to the same woman could get a little stale, even she admitted it sometimes, acted relieved when he didn't want to fool with her. It really was a chore, you know, same old same old. He figured that was why she was always finding an excuse to get out of the house and play cards or shop with her girlfriends. Fine with him.

He hadn't meant to get into trouble that first time at the Econo Lodge there in Gulfport, Mississippi. No sir. Figured to go and have a few drinks and some laughs with the boys, swapping stories about the rubes who they'd had to deal with in the car business. And let's face it, there were some doozies, too.

They were all having a good time later that evening at a club nearby one of the guys said was a hell of a place. Said they had strippers that didn't leave nothing to the imagination.

Al Herbert was reluctant to go. After all, the only woman he'd seen naked in the last thirty years was his wife. He didn't know if it would be right to look at another woman that way. But they talked him into it, embarrassed him into it was more like it, calling him PW'd, saying nobody had to know, and "What happens in Gulfport stays in Gulfport."

So they'd all piled into a car, drove over there and went in after paying a five-dollar cover charge; Al thinking that was a bit steep, but then the drinks were at least five dollars each and the doorman who took their cover charge told them it was a two-drink minimum.

Al was feeling already like he was throwing money away he didn't really have or would have to explain to Martha when he got home.

They sat down front of the stage and there was already a girl dancing up on stage wearing just a G-string and Al was almost too afraid to look at her, but finally she got right down in front of him and the boys were sticking dollar bills into her—whatever that was barely covering her—and she looked him directly in the eyes when he glanced up and it was like getting hit with a cattle prod.

She was on hands and knees and even with the loud music she leaned in close and whispered, "Would you like a private dance with me?"

"Go on," they said, these other car dealers, slapping him on the back and saying, "Jesus, would you look at that ass, Herbert!"

He felt terribly uncomfortable and made an excuse to leave, said he wasn't feeling too good, and even though they begged him to stay, he went anyway. He was sweating by the time he got outside into the cool night air.

What would Martha think if she knew he'd gone to a strip club? She'd be mad as hell, might even throw him out. She was very religious, so much so she'd practically turned herself into a virgin again. Even early on in their marriage she'd warned him about talking dirty, even in the intimacy of the marriage bed. And she always insisted the lights be out when they did it, even though she would let him see her in her night dress which she also wore to bed.

He caught a cab back to the Econ Lodge and intended to call his wife as soon as he got back in the room. But there was a young woman standing out front of the place and when he got out of the cab she asked him if he had a light for her cigarette. She was very good looking. Long thick red hair and he said, yeah, and reached in his pocket for his lighter. Matter of fact, he could use a cigarette himself and got one out for himself and lighted hers, then his.

"Thank you," she said so politely. "My boyfriend was supposed to pick me up, but he didn't show and I've no money for a cab. I live clear across town. I don't suppose there's any way I could bum a lift off you. I'd really, really appreciate it."

Well, he didn't know. It was late, but she seemed so vulnerable out there alone with the traffic going up and down.

"Gee, Miss, I . . ."

"Oh, it's okay if you can't. I'll just walk and hope nobody grabs me up and murders me," giving a little nervous laugh.

"Well, I suppose maybe I could," he relented. "I'd hate to see something bad happen to you. I'd feel responsible."

"Oh, that's really nice of you," she said and touched his hand as they stood there. He still had the vision of that stripper in his mind. God, she couldn't have been much more than eighteen or nineteen and had a perfect body. Then as quickly berated himself for thinking that way.

He said his car was parked down around back and she said she'd walk with him, she talked very pleasantly, asking where he was from and he told her and so on and so forth and they reached his car—a big Lincoln Continental—and he held the door open so she could get in. When she did, he saw how short her skirt was because it rode up her leg.

You better stop it, Al. Stop thinking the way you're thinking. Those drinks are making you goofy.

He went around and got in the other side, dug around and started to put the key in the ignition, but she stopped his hand from getting there.

"Can I tell you something?"

"Sure."

"I think you're a very good looking man," she said.

He swallowed, said, "And you're a very nice looking young lady."

"Do you really think so?"

"I do. Really."

"Would you mind if we just sat here awhile. It's nice like this. I've been on my feet all day it seems like," and just like that she reached down and took her heels off and massaged her feet.

"This is a niece car," she said looking around. "The seats are really big."

He nodded, at a loss for words, but then said, "Okay, I suppose I should get you home, it is sort of late."

Then she leaned against him, said, "I know you're not the kind of guy who would take advantage of me. But maybe you should."

"Huh?"

"I mean, it's sort of dark and nice and quiet and nobody would know."

But by then she had one hand in his lap massaging his groin, and damn, she smelled so good and was so young and pretty, so that when she reached up and kissed him on the mouth, it just felt so natural that he greedily kissed her back. Somewhere in there he heard and felt his zipper unraveling, but he didn't try and stop her. It was already too late, he told himself. And besides, nobody would know, not even the other guys.

"Do you like me, honey?"

"Mmmhuh."

"Would you like me to take care of you?"

"Mmmhuh."

"I hate to bring it up, baby, but, if I take care of you, do you think you could give me cab fare home?"

He was by now disoriented, lost in a rush of hot desire, said, "I can drive you."

"No, that's probably not a good idea, my boyfriend is very jealous and he would hurt you if he saw us together."

He felt electrified with what she was doing to him, but then she stopped, waited for an answer but all the time touching him down there.

"Well?"

"Okay, how much?"

"Just fifty dollars," she said.

"Cabs must be awfully expensive around here," he said as she started nibbling at his ear.

"This late, yeah," she said.

"Okay, don't stop, not now."

"I won't sugar."

"Mmmmm . . ."

By the time Herbert had gotten back to his room it was too late to call Martha and he was just as relieved, for he didn't think he could lie to her well enough in the state he was in except, "Gee darling, you sure don't get much for your money these days, I just paid fifty bucks for a two minute blowjob." No, Martha wouldn't be too happy about that.

Now, as he struggled to get free from being tied up by the couple with a dead girl in their trunk, he heard somebody knocking and ringing the front door of the office, yelled: "Help! Help!" as loud as he could.

He heard glass breaking, then the knob of the bathroom turning but not opening because the son of a bitch had pressed the lock button from the inside.

"Help, call the police, I've been robbed!"

Suddenly there was a loud crash and the door flew open and he looked up to see a guy in a ten-gallon hat and thought, Jesus Christ, John Wayne has come to rescue me. Only when he looked closer he could see it wasn't John Wayne, who'd been dead for like ten years, but a guy who might could have passed for him.

"You look like you've had some trouble, friend, accident?" looking down at the wet spot on the front of Al's powder blue polyester trousers.

"You think? How about cutting me loose?"

"Will do. But I need to ask you about that classic old car around back, the aqua marine Chrysler. Who'd you trade with to get it?"

"Trade, fuck I didn't trade. There's a dead body in the trunk. Don't tell me that son of a bitch left it?"

"What did the guy look like you traded it for?"

"Are you fucken dense? He didn't trade it for nothing. You think I'd trade for a car's got a corpse in the trunk? Now cut me loose, Tex."

"One last question, sir, was he alone or was he with somebody."

"He was with a sweet little slut that looked like she could suck the chrome off a trailer hitch is what she looked like." And immediately he had a flashback.

"Okay, thanks, see you around."

"Hey wait, cut me loose you prick!"

But all Al Herbert got in response was the knocking of boot heels as they walked out and closed the front door again.

Al looked down at the front of his pants. This is God's way of making me pay for my sins. That girl in the car at the Econ Lodge in Gulfport, and after that, he'd told Margaret about some phony convention once a year so he could drive to Gulfport and find another sweet young hooker and offer her fifty dollars for a repeat performance in the front seat of his car. But you know something, those never did match that original experience.

There was just something about that first time that wouldn't leave him alone and he'd found himself often daydreaming about the hooker over and over again. He knew God could read minds and even though he prayed, it hadn't done a bit of good. He'd sinned against both God and Martha, a real bad combination.

And now he was paying for it. Besides, he felt a bowel movement coming on with urgency. Oh, Jesus. Oh, Jesus.

Chapter Twenty

"Dream as if you'll live forever, live as if you'll die today."
—James Dean

Midnight found them on the Texas back roads when a small roadside Inn popped into view out of the darkness. It looked lonely and sad, shoved back up against the pines and only one other car in the lot.

"I'm beat," Bobby said. "Let's get a room and rest for the night and head out early."

"Sure, sure, you just want to get in my pants again," she grumbled, half asleep.

"Well, that's a thought, but I think I'm way too tired for messing around."

"Is that what you old guys call it, 'messing around' instead of what it is?"

"What is it?" he said as he glided the stolen car into the parking lot.

"Well, I call it fucking," she said.

"Is that so?"

He parked in front of the office that looked like a tiny log cabin and got out and went in. Sounds from a television drifted from somewhere in the back. He lightly rang the bell there on the counter. Looked around as he was waiting. There was a large fish mounted on the wall, its mouth open, a red and white lure dangling from its lip. A black and white photograph of a man in a white shirt with his sleeves rolled up and wearing black trousers was holding the big fish up.

An old man came from the back looking bleary-eyed, mumbled, "I forget to turn that damn Vacancy sign off again?"

Bobby nodded, said, "Sorry to disturb you so late, but my wife and I have been traveling all day, all the way from Miami. Would it be too late to get a room?"

The man looked him over with faded blue eyes as if Bobby was something he was looking to buy at a flea market.

"Well, I reckon not, let me turn that damn light off first."

He had Bobby sign the register and asked if he wanted a room with one or two beds, said, "It ain't as if we're in the height of tourist season or nothing. Hell we've not been in the height of tourist season since FDR was in the White House."

"Room with two beds," Bobby said. "Sometimes my wife likes her own space when she's real tired."

The man nodded turned and took down a key, said, "I know that, young fellow. Women, they are some real strange creatures. Mine, before she up and died claimed she could communicate with the dead. I guess now, she won't have to do it long distance. Room Fourteen, way toward the back—only one I got has two beds."

Bobby Lee paid the man forty dollars, took the key and went out and drove them back to the room.

They got out, once again, Nina grabbing her garbage bag along with her purse before they went in.

The room smelled old but didn't stink. The night air was muggy so Bobby turned on the AC full blast.

"Two beds, huh?" she said setting her bag down on the far bed.

"Thought maybe you might want to sleep alone," he said.

"Yeah, good thinking."

He went into the john and relieved himself and oddly she felt reassured at the sound of a man peeing. You're a very strange girl, Nina, she told herself.

He came out, said, "I think I'll sit outside and have a cigarette, care to join me?"

"Yeah, I'll be out in minute."

He went outside, there was a pop machine down by the office and he walked down there and got two Cokes and carried them back and sat down in one of the handmade vine chairs out front. He lighted a cigarette and let the weariness drain from him as he smoked. The ice-cold soda tasted like the best champagne in the world, better.

Then the image of the dead girl came back into his thoughts and he silently cursed Johnny Pearl for a no good son of a bitch. Johnny was gay, but there was nothing sissified about him. A stone cold killer, but not the kind to face you head on. Johnny would sneak up on a person and run an ice pick through their kidneys. He wondered if that's what he did to the girl. The question was, why would he have killed her. Wondered if it was something Max had ordered him to do, maybe a girl who'd rebuffed him.

But no, that didn't sound like Max's style. Max could get all the women he wanted by giving them jobs and threatening to cut them loose if they didn't cooperate in his sexual needs. Lots of those girls were either dumb or needed the work and pay they took in dancing to support their families. Every once in awhile, a college girl or a hot looking married woman would come in just for the experience of dancing naked in front of strangers. And when Max invited them to feast on his teeny weeny, they walked rather than accept his invite.

Nina came out, her hair wet from a quick shower, sat down in the chair next to him and he handed her the bottle of soda.

"Thanks," she said. "You're a true gentleman. Got a smoke for a girl on the run?"

He gave her one and then held the flame of his lighter to it and she naturally cupped her hand around his, then removed it as she took her first drag.

And for a time they sat smoking and sipping from their pop bottles until she said, "This is nice."

"Ain't it, though."

"How's your cut doing?"

"I think maybe it's gotten infected."

"We can stop somewhere tomorrow and get some stuff from the drugstore, or, I can take you to an emergency room."

"Drugstore stuff will be fine. Just wash it out real good and pour peroxide over it. I don't think it's too bad."

"I'm kinda looking forward to seeing my dad again."

"Been a long time, huh?"

"Twenty-two years. I wonder what he looks like. He sounded old over the phone. I think he had a rough time in prison."

"But he didn't do it, right?"

"So he and his lawyers say. I want to believe, and part of the reason I want to see him again is to have him look me in the face and tell me the truth."

"You want another cigarette?" he said grinding the butt of his under heel and reaching for another one."

"I've a confession to make," she said.

"What could you possibly say that would surprise me," he said holding the flame of his lighter to the end of his cigarette.

"My name's not Kelly, it's Nina."

"I sort of guessed all was not as it seemed with you."

"I'm from Texas, originally. Left before I could get the drawl, y'all."

"Now I have a confession to make,"

"Shoot, Gunga Din."

"I'd like another time with you. But only if you sincerely are into it."

"Little ol' moi? I figured since you rented a room with two beds you weren't into me that much."

"Like most things you think of me, you were wrong," he said.

He finished his cigarette and swallowed the last of the soda, stood, said, "Well, I'm going in and shower and hit the rack. Enjoy the night."

He did as he said he would and showered and turned off the light at his bedside. He could barely keep his eyes open.

Sometime after, he felt her behind him, wrapping her arms around him enough to awaken him slightly, reached down below his belly.

"Sure," she murmured. "I'd like another time with you, too."

"Maybe wait till morning?"

"Whatever you like, Bobby."

He smiled to himself. She'd finally called him by his name, said, "You know what that old man in the office told me?"

"What?"

"That his wife claimed she could communicate with the dead, then he laughed and said now that she's passed on she wouldn't have to do it long distance." Bobby laughed.

"Well, I believe in some of that stuff," she said.

"You screwing with me again?"'

"Not yet," she said

And in a matter of moments he heard her soft purring snore and smiled again. Thought, she's going to end up making me fall in love with her, goddamn it. Then the oddest sensation came over him: he felt like singing a spiritual, only he didn't know any by heart. And pretty soon after that, sleep snatched him from wakefulness and flung him down a dark cave.

Chapter Twenty-One

"Never give the devil a ride, he will always want the reins."
—Cowboy Wisdom

Back at the club Max called Johnny who answered on the fifth ring, still hung over from a lot of poppers and hard ass sex with Levi, the bartender who he finally convinced to do his bidding with promises of things to come, saying, "Once I take over from Max, you can be my second in command." Convinced him it would be in his best interest, career wise to let Johnny take care of him, set him up in an apartment of his own, new car, clothes and money. The kid was no different than a lot of these young college aged girls who would let some older rich guy take care of them—what were they called, Sugar Daddies. Well, that's how Johnny put it to Levi, said, "You want to tend bar the rest of your life, or would you rather own your own place some day?"

That's all it took to get him in the sack—that and plenty of booze and nose powder to go along with the promises. Of course Johnny had no intention of doing any of it. He'd made such promises to other young guys in the past and then, when he grew tired of them, cut them loose. They were after all just whores.

"I need you to get over here to the club," Max said. "Not later today or tonight, but get your ass over here right now. I got something important I need you to do."

"Christ, Max, can't it wait for at least a few hours. I'm not feeling too well. Might be I'm coming down with the flu or something."

"I don't give a shit if you're coming down with black plague, get your ass over here now!"

Click.

Levi moaned and rolled over, but did not awaken.

"Stay there, lover boy, I be back." Using that Arnold Schwarzenegger accent, then did a quick shower and fresh clothes and on down to the parking garage where he had the rental—that upside down bathtub Taurus—and vowed once more to kill that fucker Bobby Lee. But how and when, he wasn't sure.

Max was for once, neither stuffing his face or stuffing his prick down some girl's throat. Instead he was working on what looked like a bottle of Chivas over ice cubes.

"Okay, what is it you're so worked up about?" Johnny said flopping down in a chair across the desk from Max. "A little early isn't it to be hitting the sauce?"

"What're you, my mother? I'll hit the sauce any time I want. I own the fucken place and everything in it, including you, and don't you fucken forget it."

Johnny felt duly chastised and hated the prick Max even more. If he could, he'd kill him and take over the club right now—turn it into a gay club with male dancers instead, maybe call it the Open Closet, or what about, The Meat Locker. Yeah, he liked that.

"I want you to take a drive over to Cherry's place and get rid of her," Max said, sweating and wiping his brow with tissues from a box he kept on his desk for other purposes.

"What do you mean, get rid of her? You want me to fire the broad?"

"No, she's fucken dead. I want you to get rid of the body."

"Well, Jesus Christ, Max, here I thought it was something simple!" Johnny mocked. "How the fuck'd she end up dead?"

"I killed her."

"What?"

"Yeah, she pissed me off, about like what you're starting to do."

"What'd she used too much teeth on your schlong?"

"Just shut up and go over there like I told you and get rid of her. Take her to the dump. Who cares."

"What's this worth to you, Max?"

"What do you mean. You work for me. I pay you to handle shit like this."

"Not like this. I get caught, I'm an accessory to murder. I couldn't do any time in jail."

"Oh for chrissakes," Max groaned. It had not been thus far a good twenty-four hours in the life of Max and now he had to negotiate with Queenie.

"What do you want?"

"You know, I've been thinking about that," Johnny said. "I want a piece of the action. I'm thinking a third straight up to start with. And there is one more thing. I want to bring in male strippers a couple of nights a week."

"What? You want to turn this into a pole smoking bar?"

"Let me tell you something," Johnny said. "I go to clubs all over the city and they draw big fucken crowds of guys who spend a lot of dough drinking in them. A lot of dough. Now you take for instance how slow we are during the week. What, maybe ten guys at the most come in here to look at the cooze, spend a few bucks on beer. Weekends, Friday and Saturday, yeah, we get a good crowd. Why not let me take care of during the week?"

"And when the girls I got walk, then what?"

"Shit, Max, girls are a dime a dozen. Let 'em walk. Who cares?"

"I don't think so," Max said.

"Then handle that dead broad yourself. I quit."

Johnny stood and turned to walk out, got as far as the door. Max's heart was tripping over itself, had tightness in his chest.

"Wait!" he yelped. Johnny turned. "Okay, okay. One condition. I'll give it a try for a month or two, and if I don't make more money as you claim, then that's it, back to the girls full time."

"And I get fifty percent?"

"You just said a third!"

"I get a third for the girls nights and fifty for the boys nights since it's my idea. We got a deal or do I take a hike."

Max shook his head; he was at the end of his rope. When shit went bad, it really went bad. Max wondering what he ever did to deserve this. Hadn't he given the Cuban janitor a hundred bucks just the other day—right out of the kindness of his heart. Where was this shit, karma, everybody talked about. It sure the fuck wasn't anywhere around him.

"Okay, fine."

"Have your cheesy lawyer draw it up and have it ready by the time I get back."

Max knew he was over a barrel. If he tried to screw Johnny now, it would be just like that prick to go to the police.

"See you around Max. I'll call you when it's done."

Max could but nod and pour himself another one, and lastly croaked, "Send in Louise, I need a little relief."

"Sure Max, you look like you do."

Then thankfully Johnny was out of sight and in a few minutes that new pixie haired girl with the small tits came in, said, "You wanted to see me, Boss?"

"Yeah, I did. Have a seat."

She'd heard from the other girls what the deal was when Max called you into his office. She thought he was a two-bit slob, and besides she was into girls, not men. Had been in a half dozen porn films doing all kinds of shit with all kinds of people, men and women. So it wasn't like she was innocent or nothing. She'd gotten canned when she didn't pass a VD test—"Herpes," the doctor said. Fuck.

So she got on dancing, best she could do under the circumstances.

"How about taking off your clothes and laying back on the couch," Max said. "There's something I want to give you, sweetheart."

She did as he ordered and when he was doing it, she thought, Yeah, and there's something I want to give you too, you fat fuck.

Chapter Twenty-Two

"Do not judge my story by the chapter you walked in on."
—Anonymous

Frank Dodge checked in with his pal and ex-partner Joe Ivanhoe, said, "You get anything more on that triple homicide the other day?"

"Yeah, those guys, two of them anyway were tied in with The Devil's Own, a biker gang known to run drugs, women and whatever else they can make a dollar at. They're some pretty serious people, Frank."

"Yeah, I know of them," Frank said fixing himself a cup of coffee back in the break room where he'd found Joe Ivanhoe trying to choose between an éclair and a jelly ball from a box nearly empty.

"I checked with the gang squad and they're investigating, too."

"You said two of them were affiliated with the Devil's Own, which one wasn't?"

The punk named Ray something . . . I'll have to get my file on my desk, you want me to check for you."

"No, that's okay," Frank said.

"Thought you'd be at some lake feeding the fish worms."

"Yeah, well, I'm heading there soon. You learn anything else about that shooting?"

Ivanhoe shook his head as he went for the éclair, picking it up with a napkin.

"Just that there might have been a girl with them according to a neighbor across the street who saw her going into that house about an hour or two before the shooting."

"So maybe a live witness to the slaughter?"

"Possibly. Let's go to the desk and I'll call down to the gangbangers crew and see if they got anywhere with that."

Gangbangers is what they called the unit that dealt with the gangs, bragging anyone was going to do any gangbanging it was going to be them, not the punks out on the streets with their Glocks and Nines and Street Sweepers. The little pricks were as well armed if not better than the police. Half their weapons they got from break-ins, getting them from good upstanding citizens who wanted guns to protect themselves, when really what they should have been doing was burglar proofing their homes.

Back at Ivanhoe's desk he set down his éclair and picked up the phone and rang downstairs and asked the cop who answered if they'd gotten a name yet on the girl seen going into the house. He listened a second and then scribbled a name on his notepad, said, "Thanks" and hung up.

"Nina Summers, a gal pal of this Ray kid, apparently. She's been known to run with him. Hell, maybe she did it," Joe theorizing because he was a cop, but not believing a dude's girl pal blew away three dudes, bang, bang, bang, like that.

"They're still trying to follow up on the lead, it's probably nothing. This looks like the work of a rival gang, most likely. You want half this éclair?"

"Shit," Frank said. "I was to even think about it, I'd pull back a stub."

Ivanhoe laughed that deep full-throated laugh he had.

"See you around partner."

Even as he was walking out, Ivanhoe called, "What's your interest in this Frank? Hell you retired man, go on and catch you some of them little fishes and forget about all this shit. I know I would."

Frank just waved, drove over to Wendy's.

Once inside, they sat at the kitchen table. He could tell by her anxiousness she was waiting for an answer.

"You know about the girlfriend Ray had, the last one, I mean?"

"Yeah, well, not too much. She seemed alright the couple of times he brought her around. Cute kid, sexy as hell. Be honest with you, I wasn't sure why they were together. I mean I can see why Ray would like her, for her looks, but she seemed a bit of a wise ass with the cracks and so forth."

"You know where she lived."

"With him. They kept a place in Hialeah, one bedroom, nothing much."

"So maybe she was with him the night of the shooting?"

Wendy shrugged. She was dressed in a Miami Dolphins short sleeve sports shirt, slim fitting jeans, still barefoot. There was music playing in the living room, some female blues singer, all very atmospherically mournful in a way. But then he didn't suppose she'd be up for anything but feeling mournful.

"Give me the address," he said. She wrote it down for him. He stood to leave.

"Are you forgetting something?" she said.

"Oh," he said, and turned to kiss her thinking that's what she meant, but she turned her head away when he tried.

"I mean you are going to take care of this right?" she said.

"That's what I'm doing," he said.

Now she let him kiss her.

On the way to the apartment, he had a funny feeling about it all, about finding whoever the shooter was and taking care of them, off the books, so to speak. That wasn't him, to just fucking kill somebody. And why if she loved him would she even ask that of him?

The traffic was heavy as usual. The snowbirds hadn't left for back up North yet, so you still had them, your old and dying, and everybody else on the roadways and all the damn construction didn't help any, either.

He finally got to the apartment building. It was one of those old places, squat, red brick, two-story, maybe forty apartments in all. The yard needed help, there were some kids toys, plastic bicycles and shit lying around. He could hear music coming from some of the open windows. He entered the front door and looked for the names on the mailboxes, there it was Ray Deleon. 222. He climbed the short set of steps, walked down a short carpeted hall and knocked on the door. Waited, knocked again. No answer. Went back to the mailboxes, found one that said "OFFICE APT 102" and found that and rang the doorbell.

A nice looking black woman answered. He flashed his now defunct police ID at her, told her he was looking into a homicide and needed to have a look in 222. She studied him a moment, shrugged and went back inside and came forth with a key and walked him up to the apartment.

"Okay, thanks," he said. "I've got it from here." She didn't look too certain but shrugged and left.

Inside was something of a mess. Found some old blunts in an ash tray and what might be some residue coke powder on a mirror on the kitchen table. Searched the bedroom dresser drawers, lots of thongs, found a small bundle of letters addressed to Nina Summers. Read the return address, Buscando Junction, TX. He opened the top one. It was from her father apparently begging her to come see him, said he had gotten out of jail and would like to reconnect. It was dated ten months ago. He folded it and put it into his pocket.

If she was alive and on the run, it made sense she might go there.

Okay then, I'll maybe just go out there and see if I can find this girl and what came down the other night. At least I'll have some news for Wendy and we can take it from there, see where it goes. What was it that one writer said, how you can never go home again. He wondered if that applied to ex-wives. He told himself probably not, but maybe so.

Chapter Twenty-Three

"A thousand dreams within me, softly burn."
—Arthur Rimbaud

That morning they made love until almost noon, then went and got breakfast. He was still curious about her. If he was going to like her, really like her, he needed to know more about what made her tick, asked her to go over the killings again. She didn't seem to mind as she dug into her sausage biscuit and gravy.

"Well, Buzzard and Ray I killed for payback—Dime Bag, I don't know. Maybe I did him just for the hell of it, because he was closer to Ray than I was, because I knew if Ray told him to off me he would have been happy to do it. They were all shit heels."

Bobby Lee felt torn between his desire for her and what he knows will not have a happy ending, no doubt. They can run, as the man said, but they can't hide forever. Not with a shitload of stolen drugs and cash, not from drugsters as Bobby thought of them. He had never personally taken drugs, didn't understand the whole psychology of the shit. Why a person wanted to get stoned just to nod off, was fucken nuts to him. He'd been thinking about them being pursued by drugsters and by Max's guys, probably Cowboy, if he knew Max, and whether he and Nina split up or stayed together, it didn't seem to make much difference in the long run. They'd either be caught together and killed, or caught separately and killed. Both would find graves that were cold and dark.

"What's wrong?" she said.

"Nothing."

"You're hardly eating."

He started eating.

"Got to keep your strength up Daddy-O, I'm a lot younger than you. I'd hate to have you drop over of a heart attack or something."

"Honey, I might look old, but I'm in better physical shape than most guys even ten years younger."

"That, I do not have a doubt about," she smiled coyly. "No doubt whatsoever."

He paid the tab and they got back into the car. But before he started it, said, "I think maybe it's a good idea to ditch the drugs."

"What do you mean, ditch them? Do you mean throw them out the window?"

"Yeah, better that than to be caught with them by the cops."

"We might be safer if we were caught by the cops."

"Maybe for a little while," he said. "But if they pick us up and run a trace on you and tie you into the murders, it's a long time to spend in one of those Florida prisons. And I sure as shit don't want to end up severing a stretch at one either."

"If I throw away the drugs, then all this has been for nothing."

"It's all been for nothing anyway."

"But with the money I can get selling this stuff, I can buy a new identity, hop a flight to Rio or somewhere, buy a beach house."

"You think?"

"Yeah, I do, why, do you doubt me?"

"Honey, I hardly know you well enough to doubt you. I just know what I know. Those drugs aren't worth the trouble."

"They are to me."

Right then he was thinking he'd have to find a bus station or someplace to drop her off. She just didn't understand the trouble she was in, or, she did but refused to accept it.

They drove on in silence—her because she was hurt and him because he was in full blown turmoil. Let's face it, he liked her a lot, and mostly he could imagine them having a life together, but not if they were dead or in prison.

It was as though she could read his mind, said, "Look, next city we hit, you want to drop me off, I'll go my own way and you go yours. I'm not riding with anyone I can't trust or who doesn't want me, and right now, you're both."

"Fine," he said. "If that's what you want."

"You know it isn't, but I'm tired of being told what to do by a man. I've done that all my life, never had one I could count on, and I guess you're just one more, so let's part company and call it a day."

He nodded but said nothing. His entire insides were churning with mixed feelings.

Another hour and half they came to a town that had a Greyhound station. She got out and he got out with her, not sure if he'd try and talk her into staying or cut her loose. It was best to cut her loose. No, shit, how many girls do you meet like her who would just coldly gun down three guys who'd hurt her. Fuck, he couldn't decide. Walked in the bus station with her, stood there while she bought a ticket to Manzanita, Texas—the closest she could get to this place her old man lived, Buscando Junction. The guy said it was only about thirty miles apart, "Sorry, Miss, Buscando Junction isn't even on our route."

"Fine, I'll take it," she said and paid the one-fifty-two for the passage, turned with her purse over one shoulder and her drug garbage bag over the other and walked to a bench and sat down.

He stood there.

Bus left at seven thirty, it wasn't even eleven in the morning yet.

He went over and sat down next to her, said, "I don't know why it has to be like this."

"You want what you want and I want what I want," she said coldly. "Is that too hard for you to understand?"

"What I want is you, but what I don't want is to see you go away in some system I'll never see you again. That would be worse for me than if I was to go."

She refused to look at him, said, "Time's a-wasting slugger. Seems to me you better get on down the road yourself."

He stood then, too mad and hurt to even speak. He'd never been in this situation before. Never had anyone he'd cared so much about so quickly. Walked outside and sat in the car with the door open, one foot on the ground, and smoked a cigarette and turned on the radio. All he could get was preachers and hillbilly singers. He chose the singers and it seemed like they played ten really, really sad fucken songs in a row, songs about heartbreak and lost love, and when the last one finished he turned the radio off and went back inside and stood in front of her until she looked up and she had tears in her eyes when she did and he said, "Come on, let's go."

She got up and followed him out and they drove for at least an hour without talking until she said, "Tell me you love me and I'll jump right out of this damn car doing sixty miles an hour, I swear."

"I love you."

"Goddamn it! Do you want me to fucken jump!"

"No."

"I love you too, you, you . . ." She couldn't find the word, said, "How'd things get so fucked up that we met like this?"

"You tell me and we'll both know."

She slid over against him, leaned her head on his shoulder. She was just as lost and confused as he was and they both knew it; they both knew what waited for them at the end of the line was going to be something writers and poets would write tragic love stories about, like Bonnie and Clyde, Romeo and Juliet.

It was just a heartbreaking fucking mess is what it was—like that guy singing about on the radio—"I'm so lonesome I could cry . . ."

Chapter Twenty-Four

"What's one less person on this earth anyway?"
—Ted Bundy

Johnny slipped the key in the lock to Cherry's apartment. He had a big sheet of plastic like painters use for drop cloths, a roll of yellow nylon rope, and beyond that he didn't know what the fuck was needed to dispose of a dead body. He still couldn't believe Max would have killed his main squeeze. It just proved to Johnny that Max was clearly insane. Wouldn't he think the cops would trace her death back to him?

The man's temper was outrageous.

He entered the nicely decorated apartment's entry with its Italian marble tile that flowed into a thick white carpet. He sniffed the air for the scent of death. Wasn't precisely sure when Johnny had killed her. Jesus, all he'd need was to gag on the smell of a dead stripper. But no, if any-thing the air was slightly cloying like dying flowers. He entered the living room with its white leather furniture and big screen TV and looked about. No dead woman. Had to be in the bedroom. Shit, he sure didn't want to go in there, open that door and find Cherry's corpse. But he'd struck a deal with Max and needed to carry it through. So he opened the door and it felt like the whole goddamn world fell in on him.

A loud crashing of metal and glass knocked him to his knees and Cherry was winding up to swing that big ass lamp at him again calling him ten kinds of cocksuckers. Screaming every curse word she had in her vocabulary, which was considerable, raining down epithets on him like he was the devil.

She struck him another glancing blow across the side of his cheek busting the glass base of the lamp and it sliced him like a straight razor even as he did his best to fight her off him.

"You dirty son of a bitch, come over her to finish me off. That muthafucka Max sent you to clean up his mess, didn't he! Well, you the only mess he gonna get cleaned you fruit bowl."

Johnny scrambled crab-like to the corner, but she came after him hitting him over and over swinging that son of a bitching busted lamp like it was a Louisville slugger and it was the bottom of the ninth, bases loaded and she was batting clean up with the team two runs down.

"I'll show you who it is gonna get taken care of. I'm goin' bury your ass right here and now."

He got under the bed which only pissed her more when she could no longer get at him, because try as she did, she couldn't move that big heavy bed off him.

"You best get your rat ass out from under there, Johnny Pearl, you deviant little bastard. Come'n, take your whoopin, bitch!"

His face was cut and bleeding in a couple of places and he pulled a piece of light bulb out of his cheek, thinking, What the fuck, Max, you said she was dead, said you'd strangled her. Well she sure as shit was *not* dead.

"And when I get through with your honky ass, Pearl, I'mma go over there and bust some caps in that muthafucker's Jew ass. I'll teach you two to be messin' with me; shit, you ain't never seen nothing like a black woman's fury, you muthafucka!"

It was almost comical, except Johnny didn't find that much to laugh about, but every time she called him a name, he wanted to blurt one back. He just couldn't come up with anything right then.

"Hey, hey! Wait a goddamn minute," he shouted from under the bed. "Max sent me over her to check on you—he was worried he'd maybe roughed you up too much. He wanted me to look in on you and take you shopping to make up for it. Said he just lost his temper."

She'd gotten up on the bed and was jumping up and down on it threatening to break the staves holding up the mattress and box springs. He was fearful if it gave way, he was really fucked.

"Yah, temper my ass," she shouted. "That muthafucka tried to murder me with them puny little soft ass hands he's got ain't good for nothin' but counting his money and pulling his meat."

Jump! Jump! Jump!

"Lucky for me I passed out and when I come to he was riding me and talkin' crazy shit, sayin' how much he liked fucken a corpse. Jesus Christ, the muthafucka is sick in the head. I just pretend I was dead is all, knowing he'd send you or one of his flunkies over her to get rid of me. Well now, bitch it is your turn to be dead."

Johnny scrambled out from under the bed just a second before it broke, but hadn't got quite all the way out from under. The weight of it trapped his legs causing him to yelp like a spanked dog.

Cherry leapt on his back and grabbed his hair and started slamming his forehead into the floor, but without a ton of damage because of the thick carpet. Still after about the fifth hard slam he was dazed.

Then she climbed off him quickly and got something out of one of her two matching nightstands. Johnny was fearful it might be a gun and tried desperately to work his legs free from under the broken bed frame and mattress set.

"Don't shoot me!" he squealed.

"I ain't gonna shoot you, you worthless bastard. You ain't worth a damn bullet. But I am going to do this to your ass."

He felt a jolt of electricity that left him glassy-eyed and foaming at the mouth. She'd used a taser on him, one of those personal purse models. Hit him two or three times with it.

"How you like that, bitch! Yeah, I didn't think so"

He found himself unable to move, even when she took the yellow nylon rope he'd brought over from the hardware store to truss her up. Only now it was he being trussed up.

And when she finished, she sat on the edge of the bed catching her breath.

"I ain't in the shape I used to be," she said, as if they were just having a friendly little chat. It a lot of work beatin' you ass."

It took him a few minutes to be able to speak, her looking down on him like some demon, if demons had coca brown skin and big 44 Ds and a malevolent smile.

"How you like being like you is now, sucka?"

"I honestly, I really only came to check on you," he sputtered, afraid she'd use that stun gun on him again. Shit hurt like ten thousand kinds of hell.

"Yeah, then why all this rope and that piece of plastic?"

"No, I was running an errand and . . ." He could hear himself how lame he was sounding.

"I'mma stomp your hairy little balls into something looks like the currant jelly my Memaw usta make you don't stop your lyin'."

"You're right," he confessed. "Max sent me over to get rid of your body. He thought for sure he'd killed you. You know how he is. Shit I don't do it, I'm out of a job and he's got someone else coming over here. And another thing, and I want you to really consider this, Cherry. He knew that once he told me he'd kill you and I didn't do what he told me, I'd be the next one ended up dead."

"Yeah, that little weasel is a son of a bitch, too bad for both of us."

She sat fooling with the taser trying to decide what to do with him. She sure didn't want to go to jail for murder, but on the other hand she didn't want to just let him up and leave because no telling if he'd return or not, maybe with a gun next time.

"Max tells me you is into boys, that right?"

For some reason with her asking, he felt embarrassed. He didn't know why. But he nodded his head hoping she wouldn't ridicule him.

"So has you ever had you no woman?"

He shook his head.

"Nevah?"

"No."

"So what would you do if somebody put a gun to your head and told you to screw some woman, would you do it?"

"I'm not sure if I could."

"What you mean you ain't sure?"

"I mean it doesn't work like that."

"What in the hell is you be talkin' 'bout?"

He shrugged, angry and embarrassed by her line of questioning.

"It just something I probably can't explain."

"Well what if I was to put this taser to you and told you to fuck me or I'd zap your ass with it."

"No," he said. "I couldn't do it."

She leaned over and unzipped his trousers, took it out, then got down and straddled him, then put the taser against the side of his head, said, "Pretend this a gun and you got about one minute to get it going or else I pull the trigger."

Now he was weeping with fear and anger pleading with her not to do it. She counted down to twenty-five and when Johnny couldn't get his anatomy to work, she gave him a good long shot to the temple until he started jerking beneath her.

She climbed off and watched as his eyes rolled back up in his head, said, "Goddamn. You was right. I could get more action out of a eggplant." Then she noticed his recovering eyeballs following her as she got dressed in tight fitting black jeans over black thong panties, over the calf leather boots, and finally a red bra before slipping on a silk blouse and completed the look with a blonde wig.

"I'll be back, bitch. I'm gonna go see me some Max."

Johnny took his first good breath when he heard the door slam shut, thinking, First thing you got to do if you get out of this alive is to kill Max, take over the business, deal with nothing but rent boys and never a woman again. And for the first time in a very long time, he prayed to the Catholic version of God, having himself been a lapsed believer, and asked Jesus to let Cherry kill that fucker Max for him and make the world right again.

Chapter Twenty-Five

*"We either make ourselves miserable or we make ourselves
Strong, the amount of work is the same."*
—Carlos Castaneda

Jerry Summers liked sitting out front of his trailer in the evening watching the sky turning to an orgasm of color and reading the Western novel—*Stolen Horses*—about this damn fool boy trying to steal an old outlaw's horse, only he didn't quite get away with it. Then the two joined forces and went down to Mexico to steal a large herd of horses and run them back across the border to sell to some wealthy fellow who owned a big spread and had a sexy wife.

Jerry got to reading Westerns when he was in prison up there at Huntsville. He liked them because they weren't complex or silly. He liked the characters in them because they were hard as hell but good hearted, mostly. The sort of man he saw himself as.

He had a stack of them in paperback inside his small accommodations and many he'd read more than once.

As the evening drew down around him, he could hear the mourning doves dusting themselves and cooing out in the scrub. A hot dry wind came up from the south and he could almost smell the river. Rivers had existed before man and existed still and would be there long after man had disappeared. They had both given and taken life, such was the spirit of rivers, he thought.

He smoked a hand rolled cigarette, another habit he'd picked up in prison. He didn't have to smoke them, he just enjoyed the meditative act of it. A cold sweating can of partially drunk beer set atop the heavy plastic cooler that mostly lived in the bottom of his beat up old fridge within the trailer. Jerry would take it with its contents of beer and luncheon meat and bread and cheeses outside and park himself in the shade, moving his chair as the sun shifted.

He would eat his breakfast and lunch and dinner that way and it suited him fine. The trailer was just a place to lay down and rest and the other things a human required doing. But he didn't like it in there much—too much like a jail cell.

Way out on a two-lane that ran west to Terlingua and north to Marathon before swinging southeast to Del Rio—if you wanted big city and all it beheld.

The wind kicked up temporary dust devils that spun themselves out in unraveling spools of sand. Gus, his dog, got up and went off and lifted his leg against some creosote bushes, sniffed around, then stood with his nose scenting the air, then casually came back and settled near Jerry's old green metal chair. Jerry took out a hotdog from the cooler, said, "You think you done anything to deserve this?"

Gus stood then watching with pleading eyes but made no move to grab it, stood patiently till Jerry said, "I reckon probably so, have at it partner."

Gus woofed it down and looked for more but Jerry said, "Wait, you'll ruin your supper." Gus settled down again. Damn dog was smarter than most people Jerry thought, but then that didn't take a whole hell of a lot.

He'd hoped to hear from Nina again. Wondered where she was and when she'd get there. She sounded sort of awful on the telephone and he hoped she wasn't in some sort of trouble. God, he wanted so much of the best for that girl. He hoped he could make up for a little of the lost time, repair whatever pain he'd given her by not being around for her.

But when he really thought about it all, he told himself he'd kill that son of a bitch again for what he'd done to his beautiful sweet wife.

So even when it got full on dark, Jerry would set watching the distant highway, the headlights of the passing cars and trucks until night really grew deep and the traffic dwindled down to only an occasional wayfaring stranger. But thus far not a single one had turned off and come over the rutted desert road up to his place.

He could see his only neighbor's light on—the hot white glow of the Coleman lantern of Mingo White Deer who claimed Chiracahua blood and himself an ex-con, with the jailhouse tats to prove it. Mingo had been part of a motorcycle club sent up on manslaughter charges from a gang fight in reservation casino that left three rival gang members dead on the floor by the slot machines.

Mingo White Deer was a tall skinny dude, wore his hair in braids and didn't say much—always the most dangerous sort of men—the quiet ones. But he was a good neighbor to Jerry and sometimes they sat and drank beer together and spoke of their jail experiences, Mingo saying, "You ever notice how everybody is a member of one tribe or another these days—just like in the long ago days."

Mingo often did peyote for two reasons, he said. One was to give him spiritual enlightenment, and the other was because the cops couldn't do anything about it, as peyote had been ruled part of the native religion. He got Jerry to try it once, but Jerry didn't care for the experience—said he saw the gates of hell. Mingo said it was because Jerry's spirit guide was bad, but that could be fixed easily enough.

Mingo would often disappear for days in search of the peyote. He was always in company of a good looking woman, usually white when he was home. Jerry couldn't quite figure out where he met these women and asked him once about it and Mingo said, "Oh, anywhere. They just seem to show up where I'm at and they like the idea of associating with an Apache." Would laugh and shake his head. Sometimes the women would stay at his place for upwards of a week and then they'd just be gone and in a little while more another would be over there. Mingo's place was just a cobbled together tin shack.

Mingo's peyote rituals were always carried out in the early evening before a huge bonfire. And once the drug was consumed, Mingo would beat a small drum and chant loudly for hours as whichever woman Mingo was seeing at the time would dance around the fire, usually fully naked. Then after a bit Mingo and she would switch places and she'd beat the drums while he danced naked. This would go on until the bonfire would burn down to just glowing embers and then Jerry would hear her screams of passion as she and Mingo went at it like a pair of drug induced badgers.

Jerry considered Mingo nuts, but at least gave him credit for getting some good-looking women. Maybe the women just did it to get high on the mushrooms, but then again, as Jerry could plainly see, Mingo was hung like a Shetland pony.

It was Mingo who most often gave Jerry a lift into town whenever he needed to go there, but many times Jerry would have to either walk back—a distance of five miles—or hitch a ride from someone else. Mingo was almost as unreliable as he was mysterious.

While sitting in his green metal lawn chair, cowboy book in one hand, cigarette smoldering in the other, he imagined the desert around him was full of the ghosts of the old ones like John Wesley Hardin, Billy the Kid, Doc Holliday, Cherokee Bill, Jesse and Frank James and all the rest—still roaming the land, looking for trouble and looking for their own particular brand of pleasure.

He thought too about the men who hunted them down, Hickok, Garrett, Bill Tilghman, Bat Masterson.

Bullets, blood, death, some lived, some didn't.

The question became, he believed, were you a bad man if you killed out of a sense of honor or retribution, or a good man if you killed because you were paid to do it?

He sure wished Mingo had a woman over there this evening dancing naked. The beauty of a naked woman dancing in and out of the flickering firelight was a thing of wonder, of art in motion, of poetry spoken, and seemed to bless the very ground upon which she moved with added beauty.

"Well, Gus, I'm gonna retire for the evening. Don't know about you, but that last beer topped me off." he said to the dog.

He stood and stepped into the doorway of the trailer, said, "You coming, or sleeping outside tonight. You better not. Them damn coyotes will gang up on you and tear you to shreds. Ain't no kinda way to go. Come on."

The dog rose slowly to its feet and followed him in, then he closed the screen door, set the hook. Then he found his bed and flopped down.

Tomorrow was another day, and tomorrow and tomorrow until the last one came—as it did for everyone, and after that, who knew.

Shortly he heard the call of coyotes out in the hills, not too very distant and said to the now rested dog on the floor at the end of the bed, "See. I told you."

It was sometime in the blackest hour the phone rang and he stumbled out of bed and went to the front where it sat, and it rang three times before he was able to find it in the dark and pick it up.

"Nina?"

"Yes, we're in Texas, we'll be there soon."

"We?"

"See you soon."

Click.

He set the receiver down and returned to bed and lay there a long time staring into the darkness. He wished he could see the stars and read his own fortune and that of his only flesh and blood.

And as he began to drowse, he was awakened again by the thudding of hooves, the whinny of horses and he sat up and listened as they ran passed, but by the time he got to the door they were gone, as if winged creatures from some mystical past.

Only rarely did wild horses come this way and rarer too to see them in daylight this close to humanity. The dog was at his feet staring out into the night as well.

"Too late, too late," he said. "We missed them."

His daughter's voice still in his head as he returned once more to the bed and the dog lay down as well.

And thus it was.

Chapter Twenty-Six

*"If someone has a gun and trying to kill you, it would
be reasonable to shoot back with your own gun."*
—Dalai Lama

He heard the door latch click and grabbed the .45 under the pillow. Dark as hell in the room, went to roust her, but the bed was empty.

"Don't shoot," she said, "it's just me."

He flicked on the nightstand lamp as she entered the room, closed the door behind her and locked it.

"Where'd you go?" he said.

"I went down to the payphone by the office and called my dad. I thought he should know we're still coming."

She slipped out of her jeans and shirt, wearing no panties, got into bed with him and wrapped her body around his. Something had definitely changed between them, beginning back there at the bus station when he told himself to move on and leave this trouble behind. But man, he just couldn't fucking do it. She was into him in ways no woman ever had been and if you asked him to explain it by putting a gun to his head, he couldn't come close to an answer why.

Her body felt warm and soft, her breath sweet from some sort of chewing gum that she chewed softly as she took his face into her hands, drew her mouth close to his and kissed him playfully, said, "I'm glad you changed your mind."

"I'm glad too."

"What made you do it?"

"I don't know, I just knew I couldn't drive off and leave you."

"Worried about me, were you, slick?" she said playfully.

"Bobby Lee," he said, "that's my name."

She nibbled his ear and worked her body against him, lean and muscular as if it and she knew every erotic spot on him. She gripped his waist and pulled him to her, ran her hands over his buttocks and continued to kiss him running and flicking her tongue across his mouth.

"I like your hard body," she said, thinking of Ray's puny drug emaciated self. He hadn't always been thus, but too much rock and smoke and later sticking a needle in his veins had left him puny and she never told him what a turn off it had been whenever he wanted to have sex. She'd obliged him only because she was in love with him, or thought she was. She believed it was what women did, they overlooked the frailties and disappointments, for the sake of love, be it real or be it false. But with Bobby, it was different, really different.

Bobby might not be handsome or nearly as pretty as Ray had once been, but he was all hard muscle and strong hands. His jaw was like granite, and let's face it, he would never make *People's Sexiest Man of the Year.* But he was gentle and kind and easy to care for. She wasn't sure it was full blown love for her, not yet, but it was edging in that direction, if only, and this was a big fucken if, they weren't tracked down and killed.

"Come on," she whispered and drew him atop her as she spread her legs to accept him and thought about all those animal shows she watched on Nat Geo, how the males fight for the right to mate with the females and how the females accepted the alpha male. Bobby sure as hell was an alpha male and she wanted to accept him.

He rose above her and she took him inside and then time itself didn't mean anything, their situation didn't mean anything. Men coming to kill them didn't mean anything. Nothing meant anything but the now of who they were and what they were doing with each other.

"Yes, baby," she whispered and arched her back and racked her nails across his ridged and knotted back muscles. "Yes, just like that."

Just the touch of her spun him nearly out of control. He could hardly believe what had happened between them—the happenstance first meeting and then on from there to here and now. It was almost as if it was destined to be, for how else could it be explained?

Afterwards they slept hard and woke at a little after nine-thirty.

"I can't believe we slept so late," he said.

***

She stretched, yawned, looked at him and smiled, and reached out and touched his face again as gently as if it was made of the dust of butter-flies.

"I can," she said. "That was some action Gunga Din."

"Christ, are you ever going to stop calling me names?"

She laughed, said, "Never. You're my pet and I can call you what I want. Now kiss me and lets get dressed and go eat. I'm dying for some French Toast."

They dressed and found a café. It was Western themed; reminding them they were in the great state of Texas. The place was called Bronco Willy's and there was Western swing music coming over the speakers. The waitress had a jolly smile and a nice accent. They ordered the French Toast, bacon, coffee and orange juice and hardly said two words while they ate.

"Wow, that was pretty good," Nina said after they polished it off, "don't you think?"

"Yeah, and if I keep eating this way, I'm going to put on fifty pounds by the time we get to wherever we're going."

"What weight class did you fight in?" she asked.

"You know about that stuff?"

"I told you, Ray used to make me watch those pay-for-views big fights. I liked watching the middleweights best."

"Why was that?"

"I don't know exactly, but they were all really built well, they moved around good and were quick handed. Not like those big lumbering heavyweights who always hugged each other and danced around like a drunken gay couple at a wedding."

He laughed.

"Well, I was either a super middleweight or a cruiserweight, depending. I just naturally grew into it and I liked it, but some of those other classes have some real good fighters, too. I personally think the Mexican fighters are the best, and by far the toughest of them all."

"The guy you were supposed to lose to," she said.

"Up and comer who everybody was predicting to become a champion in another year, year and a half. Had a hell of a promoter too—turned out to be mine. The kid had won twenty-two straight fights, nineteen of them by knockout, and most of those before the fifth round," Bobby said shaking his head.

"Was he fast, did he hit hard?"

"Fast as a lightning bolt, and yeah, if he tagged you, it hurt. He almost got me out in the second round. Dropped me like third period algebra class and I damn near couldn't get up. But then I heard Max and his crew yelling at me to stay down. Max you see was my manager, the guy who wanted me to throw the fight because he'd secretly had fifty-one percent of the golden boy. Max knew on account of my age I was basically finished, so why not."

"Sounds like a crummy game," she said working on her second cup of coffee.

"Yeah, well what isn't anymore," he said. "Jesus, I have to tell you something."

He'd leaned in close, conspiratorially.

"You see that guy came in and sitting at the counter."

She looked around.

"Which one?"

"The one wearing the baseball cap, jeans, white sneakers."

"Yeah, I see him. What about him?"

"Nothing," he said. "I just wanted to whisper how much I dig you."

"Dig me? Jeez Pop, I dig you too."

"Goddamn but you've got a great smile."

"Shut up or you're going to have to take me back to bed and we'll never get down to the border."

She kissed him and he kissed her back, then got up, paid the check, went out into the sunshine and got into the sedan, and out onto the highway, the radio nothing but shit kicking music and mad preachers and some guy advertising Cialis, for "Whenever the mood strikes."

She laughed, said, "Should we stop at a drugstore and get you some, Grandpa?" Then quickly added: "Nah, you don't need any."

"Maybe I use it and you just don't know it."

"Maybe I don't care, how's that strike you, Butch?"

He shook his head and found the classic country and Merle and Willie were singing "Pancho and Lefty."

"That's better than listening to dick supplements, isn't it?" he said with a grin.

"Yeah, maybe. Can we get a pecan roll next station we gas up? I keep seeing them advertised."

"How the hell do you eat so much and don't weigh a hundred pounds?"

"I work out a lot, slugger."

"I can sure as hell attest to that."

They loved the teasing and Bobby thought he sure was smiling a lot these days.

He wondered as they drove in the moderate heavy traffic, as Merle sang about how Lefty didn't sing the blues like he used to, and was leaving a cheap hotel, just how many men she'd had. Was it just this Ray guy or were there others. She was still young yet, but in a somewhat hardened way. Some live lives of ease and others get it all done and over with in a short fast and very hard time.

She leaned her back against the door and put her bare feet in his lap and wiggled her toes. He laid his free hand on those small feet and it suddenly made no difference at all how many other men she might have been with. She was with *him* now.

Chapter Twenty-Seven

"Part of the loot went for gambling and part on women
The rest I spent foolishly"
—George Raft

Max was eating a bowl of chicken noodle soup when Cowboy phoned in.

"What's the word, have you taken care of that business yet?" Max said. He was still somewhat stricken with the murder he believed he had committed. Especially it being Cherry, whom he falsely thought he'd loved and foolishly proposed marriage to. That was why he'd gone over there, to pop the question, make her his exclusive. He knew she tricked for other men, had once hired a private eye to check on her. The report wasn't positive for Max's mind and one of the reason's he wanted to take her off the market. He didn't want her doing that anymore. He didn't want her dancing and showing herself to these creeps who came in his place either on the belief they could score one of the girls, get them to fall in love, run off and live in a double-wide while the sucker was off driving truck five days a week. Yeah sure, that's exactly what these hot young broads were looking for.

The soup he'd had the kid, Levi, run and get him from the deli because Max wasn't hungry for a big fucken sandwich, his stomach wasn't. The soup was good, nice thick noodles the way he liked. Chicken soup was good for the soul, wasn't it?

"Not yet," Cowboy said, sounded like he was chewing something. "But I got feelers out all the way from here to the coast. But here's the thing, he ditched Johnny's classic at some used car lot. Thing is, there was a dead girl's body in it according to the guy who owned the place. What do you know about that, Max?"

Max, caught off guard about the mention of Johnny having a dead body in the trunk of his car, coughed and sputtered soup all over the front of him, grabbed a paper napkin and did his best to mop it up.

"What the fuck you saying?'" Max yelled.

"I'm just telling you what was told me. I checked, and yes there was indeed a not so good looking body of a girl in there, dead maybe two, three days. Why the fuck do you think Johnny would kill a woman and stuff her into the trunk?"

"Johnny wasn't even into girls. I bet it was that fucker, Bobby did it."

"What reason would he have, Max?"

"Fuck, you're asking me? How the hell do I know?"

"Well, I'll get back out there, but maybe you ought to ask Johnny about this when you see him. Just saying. See you around, Max."

Click.

Goddamn, first me, I kill a broad and now I learn Johnny's killed a broad, too. Must be the moon or something.

He finished his soup and thought maybe he'd take a snooze on the sofa there in his office, the one he'd gotten a lot of strange on. Thinking of it, he'd like to give that new girl came in yesterday and was hanging around waiting for Johnny to come in for his stamp of approval. Johnny might be as queer as a three-dollar bill, but he had an eye for the type of girls could milk the most money out of the customers, whether or not they could dance.

Let's see, what was her name. Ah shit, it didn't matter. He got up and went to the door, walked out into the club and saw her sitting at the bar with a drink she was stirring with one of those little green plastic straws as she chatted with Levi.

Max called her over, said, "Pardon me, honey, but come on in the office and we'll move ahead with your application. I don't know when my floor manager will get back and I'm sure you're in a hurry to get back to your kids."

She stood. She was some fine looking piece of tail, tall and willowy with a whole bunch of hair the color of a lion's mane that reminded him of his favorite girl of all time, Farah Fawcett, who he'd been in love with since he was a teen. Used to jerk off to her poster regularly till his mother told him to stop it or wash his own sheets.

Max held the door for her, then followed her into his office. He asked her to take a seat on the sofa, picked up a blank sheet of paper from his desk and looked over it as if it was an application.

"So you got experience at dancing?" he said.

"Some," she said. "My husband got laid off at the factory—which happens a couple of times a year, then they call him back. But when that happens I do what I do best for making money."

"Dancing?" he said. Wanted to see if there were other things she did for money, she looked the type, but then you never knew. She had a good sized silver crucifix around her neck.

"Yeah, dancing," she said.

"That's all?"

She nodded.

"Take off your clothes."

She stared at him, blinking.

"I didn't bring what I normally dance in," she said.

"Don't know where you been dancing round here, honey, but in this place, you don't need clothes."

Saw her swallow hard, get those deer in the headlight eyes.

"Well, I mean it's up to you," Max said. "I get all kinds of girls coming in for work and some of them can cut it and others can't. I mean I really don't know what you broads think when you come into a strip club, but that's what it means. You strip. So if you can't for me, then you can't for them out there."

She swallowed again, then slowly started unbuttoning her blouse, Max thinking, Yeah, let's see those babies.

She got out of her blouse and was working on the button on the side of her skirt when this raving black madwoman came in screaming and cussing and calling Max vile names. The stripper grabbed her blouse and ran out.

Max couldn't believe it, she had to be a fucken ghost. His heart was hammering in his chest. What the fuck! How'd this bitch not be dead? And why hadn't Johnny buried her ass in the ground already.

"Max, you dirty white muthafucka, tryin' to kill me after all the shit I put up with you old white ass! Well, we'll by god, see who eats it!"

She pulled a meat cleaver from her handbag.

"I'm gonna slaughter you like one of Auntie Rose's chickens, like she do for the cook pot."

He raised his hands in fear.

"Don't, don't! It was all a mistake. I can't tell you how bad I felt afterward. I've done nothing but cry over you, Cherry. Put that damn thing down and let's go to the Justice of the Peace right now and get married."

"Max, you such a goddamn dumb ass. You think I'd marry you just so you could kill me in my sleep? What kinda shit you been smokin'?'"

She came toward him and swiped at him with that cleaver. He blocked most of it with an arm, but still it got some meat and he yelped and made a dash for the door, but she blocked him and beat him over the head with the flat of the blade and each time she hit him, he went, "Oh, oh, oh, oh."

"I'm gonna cut you dick off, though that won't take much doin', then I'm gonna feed it to the first damn dog I sees."

Max, streamers of blood from where she'd smacked his skull with that cleaver, ran down his face. He retreated to his office, grabbed the chair and huddled there like a frightened child as he begged and sobbed.

"You stupid muthafucka."

Bang.

She stiffened then fell face down to the floor, hard.

Max with his fists to his mouth looked at her in amazement. She was so still and dead he thought a miracle had happened. Then he turned to look at where the sound of the lightning bolt had come from and there stood young Levi with a silver pistol in his hand bleeding blue smoke.

"I figured you needed help when I saw her come in and heard the screaming," he said.

"Oh, Jesus Christ, kid, you don't know the half of it. The broad was going to kill me with that cleaver. You saved my ass."

"I know," Levi said. "Seems to me that should be worth something."

"You bet, how about five-hundred, a grand maybe, what'll you say?"

Levi aimed the gun at Max and took a piece of paper from his hip pocket, said, "I think it's probably worth more than that, sir. I think if I hadn't come in when I did, you'd be chopped liver, literally. And if that was to have happened, nothing would have meant anything to you. So, since I saved your life, seems to me half of everything would be about fair. All you have to do is sign this contract."

"Are you crazy?"

"Hardly," Levi said. "I mean you hired that gay blade to manage this place and he's just one big fuck up, and you hire these women to make you money and keep you happy. And you hired me to make drinks and stand on my feet all night for a few bucks and some tips. No sir, I am not crazy. So sign this please or I will put a bullet in your brain and plant the gun on Missy here and well, I suppose I can still get Johnny to give me half seeing as how I took you out for him, if that's the way you want to play it. Your choice."

Max could see this fucken junior was serious. He'd already come close once to dying at the hands of the crazy broad. He didn't think he wanted to risk being killed again. This fucken kid was a lot smarter than he looked.

"Alright, goddamn it, I'll sign it."

"Oh, and in case you're thinking you'll renege later, well, take this." The kid reached inside that bartender's vest and took out a second gun and handed it to Max, said, "Don't worry, it's not loaded. Now go over there and point it down at her while I take a picture with my cell phone."

Max of course did what he was told and when the kid finished taking a couple of shots, he told Max to confess on the phone's voice recorder that he'd murdered Cherry.

"That's perfect, Max. I'll keep this in a nice safe place where only one other person will know about it and have a friend of mine send it to the police if anything were to happen to me. Now sign and let's get on with this."

Max signed and his whole body sagged into the chair as if his main parts had been removed.

"Okay, Max, I've the van parked out back. Help me carry her out and put her in it and I'll take care of your little problem here. You might want to clean up the blood in your office. Just saying, partner."

Max helped him get Cherry into the van, his only consolation was she was damn well dead this time and wouldn't be showing up again with meat cleavers and shit. Of all the women in the world he could have lost his mind over, it would have to be a psycho with nice tits. Well, goodbye and so long, lover.

Chapter Twenty-Eight

"The whole world is about three drinks behind."
—Humphrey Bogart

Wendy answered the door to her ex-husband and most recently retired city detective, Frank Dodge. She was still fraught with sadness with more than a pinch of anger and hatred at the guys who killed her brother. It seemed to Frank that it had drained all the beauty out of her. First time he really noticed it.

"Did you learn anything more, Frank?"

Frank waited to see if she would invite him in, if maybe she had someone over, like the last dude walking around in his boxers when Frank showed up.

"Come on in?"

Well, finally, there it was, entrance into the castle of Queen Wendy where she diddled whoever she pleased, and thus far the final settlement on property, et al, had not fully been completed. Frank was a loving generous guy living in a cheap two room apartment so that he wouldn't upset her applecart, on the hopes they could get back together. Didn't seem so far she was in any generous mood.

They walked into the kitchen, Wendy wearing a shorty robe that came just to mid-thigh.

"You want coffee, Frank?"

"Sure, when don't I."

She poured them each coffee mixing into his sugar and hers just cream—like comes with marital familiarity—and sat down at the table.

He sipped at his while she ran the name Nina through her brain.

"I've got a line on Ray's girlfriend, this Nina Summers. I think maybe if I can locate her, I can either eliminate her as a suspect, or at the least find out what she might know about Ray's killing."

"So if you find her, you're going to arrest her?"

"Well, depends," he said.

***

Wendy lighted herself a cigarette and smoked it, one elbow resting on the table with her hand that held the cigarette in the air, and for a second Frank became mesmerized with the swirl of the smoke as it rose and drifted.

"I need to know something," he said.

Those amber eyes turned toward him, coolly as a cat's.

"Sure, go ahead," she said.

"What if this thing wasn't about Ray, would you really be interested in getting back together. I ask because before you didn't seem like that was even a remote possibility.

She dropped her gaze to the red Formica table top. He hated that fucken thing, thought it was garish, a sentimental thing left over from her first husband. He had planned some day to ask her if Jack, husband number one, had ever fucked her on it. In the early stages of their dating, and with a few drinks in her, she'd tell stories about Jack and his insatiable appetite and where all they'd done it. Frank thought maybe it was a test to see if he'd stick, because she'd also said more than once how she wasn't sure she'd ever trust a man enough to marry one again. But then she did. He didn't really believe she kept the table for that reason, but still he hated it.

"Honestly," she said, "I'm not sure. This thing about my brother has me all torn up. I just want to be happy again, feel safe from the bastard world, you know? What can I tell you, Frank?"

"That's okay," he said. "I told you I'd do what I could to find the people who killed your brother, and after that, things will work out between us or they won't."

Her eyes grew wet, she said, "Thank you, honey."

He got up from the table, said, "I'll let you know Wendy.'

She didn't get up and walk him to the door, just sat there smoking and thinking about poor dead Ray, that, or the clown she'd had over the other day. Hell, maybe he was upstairs right now listening. Well, fuck him if he was, and fuck her too.

When he put a call into Joe Ivanhoe, the detective said, Yes, they'd tracked down Nina Summers old man's address to a P.O. Box in Texas."

"Where in Texas?"

"Some little place twenty or so miles north of the Mexican border down there, place called Buscando Junction. You ever heard of it?" The information confirmed what Frank had found on the envelope to the letter he had in his pocket.

"Buscando, that's Mexican for "looking for, or to search for, something like that, isn't it?"

"Hell if I know. I'm African American."

"Go on."

"Dude's name is, Summers, Jerry K. Said he killed his wife and blamed it on another man, someone Summers claimed she had a relationship with or some such. Trouble was they could never find this other guy, even though they found out he was an actual person. But gone in the wind. So Summers took the fall, guilty or not."

"Okay, thanks Ivanhoe."

"You was a cop and now you playing a cop, Frank? Question is, why?"

"Ah shit, just something to do between shuffleboard tournaments, I guess. See you around, and stay safe."

"Safe as ribbed Trojans, my man."

Frank got out his Atlas from the back seat of the car, opened it and looked up Buscando Junction. Well, shit, there wasn't even any listing."

He drove to a bar he liked and went in just to relieve himself of the day's heat. When Miami sun gets to hammering down on you like Thor's hammer, something cold is required.

The Tres Jack's Bar was just the right place. Hardly ever crowded, and thus hardly ever loud. He took a place at a back booth and loosened his tie, then wondered why he even wore one now that he wasn't on the job. Just a damn old habit, so took it off, folded it and put it in his jacket pocket.

Ronnie came over with one already uncapped and set it down on a napkin.

"Haven't seen you around in a while," she said.

She was a good-looking red-head with a personality to match her looks, and whenever, he was in there and she waited on him, he would tease her by saying, "Someday I'm going to marry you, Ronnie" to which she would reply, "I'm waiting, Frank."

"How's the copper business, Frank?"

"Retired, my young and innocent friend. Day before yesterday was my twenty. Hung 'em up."

"Well, congratulations and the first one's on me."

He smiled as she leaned down and kissed him on the cheek. Her scent was just right. She was just one of those women who knew what to wear and how to be in any given situation.

He handed her a five, said, "Keep the change."

"No," she said. "I refuse your filthy lucre."

"You been watching that show again, that thing about mythical kingdoms where they're either fighting with swords or fornicating?"

She laughed. "I love that show."

"Yeah, me too, but don't tell anyone. The boys all think I'm macho."

"The boys," she said. "What do they know."

"You ever get back together with your ex, Frank?"

He shook his head, took another swallow of that good cold beer, said, "No, not really. I thought there for a second there was a chance, but I don't know."

"You know I'm still available," she said with a large smile.

"If only," he said.

She started to say something else, but Logan called from the bar and she quickly said, "Let's take this up again soon, Frank."

He nodded, thought what're you, nuts? The idea of being hooked up with a woman maybe fifteen years younger was intriguing. It would be nice on one hand, but on the other, he wondered if men his age who married women Ronnie's age—he didn't know exactly but guessed her to be mid-thirties to his fifty-seven, or was it eight?—didn't that age difference just make the men feel older at some point?

He took out his phone and dialed the operator and asked for the police in Buscando Junction Texas. In a moment she said, "I'm sorry sir, there isn't a number listed." Looking down at his notes he said, "Well, how about Manzanita, Texas?"

"No, there is no number listed for there either. Is there another number you'd like me to try, the Holt County Sheriff's department?" No, he said and hung up and put the phone back. He detested them only because he had trouble using them, but otherwise they were swell.

He finished his beer, casting glances toward Ronnie who was busy with an all of a sudden lunch bunch of guys from a nearby construction crew ordering beer and burgers. Well, another time, maybe.

He headed for the door and she broke away from a table she was taking orders from, said, "Frank. I'm serious about continuing our discussion. Will you call me later?"

"Yeah," he said and walked out knowing he didn't have her phone number, thinking, just too much damn temptation. I told Wendy I'd look into Ray's death, and so that's what I'm going to do. But he didn't feel magnanimous or heroic or any of that horseshit.

He just simply felt bereft.

Chapter Twenty-Nine

"The path to paradise begins in hell"
—Dante Alighieri

Nina took out the scrap of paper with an address she'd written on it, looked up through the dusty windshield, the sun's glare making it hard to see much and the desert landscape looking all the same—tans and whites and hills and canyons scarring it all.

"Christ," she said. "Everything looks the same. I'm wondering if we should have taken that last road. We may be lost."

"Or found," Bobby Lee said.

She thought he looked ruggedly good with a three-day-old growth of reddish beard.

"I like you like that," she said.

"Like what?"

"Like the way your beard looks on you. You could be a movie star."

"In a horror film maybe."

She smiled and touched the side of his face.

"I think we better stop at a gas station or whatever so we can find out if we're even near this place."

"Sounds like a swift idea."

"Real swift, daddy-O," she teased him with her feet in his groin.

"You had best stop doing that," he said.

"Or what?"

"Or, I'm going to find a place to pull over."

"Oh, baby cakes, this front seat is way too cramped for you to do to me what you're thinking."

"But you forget that the outside is just one big empty world."

"You wouldn't."

"I damn well would."

She sat up, leaned over and kissed him, and since it was one big empty world, he wasn't worried about hitting anything. They hadn't even seen another car for two hours.

But he did hit something—something significantly big to jolt them as he slammed on the brake pedal and came to a sliding crunching stop.

"What the hell!"

It had banged Nina's head a glancing blow off the dash.

"Ow!"

They both got out and saw the right front fender was bent into the wheel. Looked around and there off to the side was an emaciated mule deer struggling to get to its feet, but its foreleg dangled uselessly, the sounds of its pain and struggle were strange and wrenching. There was also a deep gash just behind the leg.

"Get the gun, Bobby," she implored.

He reached in under the seat and took out the .45 and came back out and stepped in close, but Nina stopped him, reached for the gun.

"I caused this to happen," she said. "It should be me that takes care of it."

"No," he said, stepped forward and fired a round into the animal. "Damn shame."

They both stood staring, then Bobby dragged it off into the ditch, then slowly got back in the car and drove on, more slowly because of the way the fender was rubbing against the tire, drove on in silence.

"I just hated killing that poor animal," she said.

He wondered when she said it if she as much hated killing three men, didn't say anything.

A few miles up the dusty road, they came to a blacktop crossing north and south. He looked both ways, saw with a sense of relief some sort of business quarter mile or so down the road to the south and turned that direction.

It proved to be a sort of catchall, gas station, repair shop, café and motel with the M nearly rubbed away from wind and sand scour.

He pulled in, parked and they got out together, the heat rising from the earth's floor about what you'd get when you opened the oven door to check the pot roast.

There weren't any cars parked at the two pumps but they heard the whir of a power tool and stepped into the open garage door bay where a man in greasy overalls was changing a tire on an old truck up on a lift.

They waited until he fastened the last lug, then he turned and said, "Hep you?"

"Got a fender that needs bending out, hit a mule deer not far back."

The guy set down his power tool and wiped his hands on a rag from his back pocket and came forth into the light. His gaze rested on Nina as if he'd never seen a female in his life.

"Where's it?"

Bobby pointed to the sedan and together the trio went forth as if in homage to all things mechanical that needed fixing.

The mechanic bent to examine the fender, stood, said, "Sure enough did. Wonder you did tear that tire up."

"Can you fix it?" Bobby said.

"Sure, fix anything needs it," the mechanic said, Bobby thinking it a double entendre by the way he was eyeing Nina.

"Okay," Bobby said. "Any idea when?"

"Won't be but tomorrow, earliest I can get at it. Got three others ahead of you."

"Well, we'll see about getting a room at that motel," Bobby said. "Maybe if when you get it fixed you could let us know over there?"

The man looked in the direction Bobby indicated as if for the first time in his existence he'd noticed the place.

"Sure. You all go on."

They walked across the cracked paved parking lot to the motel's office and were greeted by a fey young man who spoke with a lisp and they asked to rent a room, Bobby explaining about the truck and he looked at Bobby about the same way as the mechanic had at Nina.

"Yes, yes, just for one or two nights?"

"Hopefully just the one our car's getting fixed over at the garage."

He had Bobby register. Bobby said, "I don't remember the plate number but it's over at the garage.'

"Not a problem, you're my only guests anyway. Usually happens only when somebody breaks down and has to leave their cars, or a couple of kids running away to Mexico to get married and can't wait for the honeymoon to start."

"The food any good at the café?"

"Can't actually vouch for it, but then what's a poor body to do when in need of nourishment, if you know what I mean. Was me, I'd go with the chili, though."

"Thanks."

They went over to the café that was a combination eatery, souvenir shop and also where you could pay for gasoline, and grabbed a window booth.

"This is how we first met," said Nina.

"Don't go getting all sloppy on me," Bobby joked.

They ordered Cokes and chili, and the chili was pretty damn good and the cold sodas refreshing.

"It's only middle of the day," Nina said. "What in the world do you think there is to do to kill time?"

"I've an idea," Bobby said standing with Nina following his lead. He paid the bill and once more crossed the parking lot to their room. Small, walls painted bright white with a single cheap print of some Indians riding hell bent for leather somewhere undefined.

Bobby cranked up the AC all the way and then together they squeezed into the shower bathtub and turned on the spray standing face to face.

Bobby tore the wrapper off on the small bar of soap then used it on her neck to feet, taking his time and she stood like a patient creature absorbing the tenderness of his hands. Then she took the soap from him and did the same thing, lingering around his sex and he hugged her to him when suddenly a dark feeling passed through him like a shadow.

"You think we could in here?" she said.

"Probably, but we'd break something if we did."

She laughed and kissed him standing up on tiptoes. He turned off the faucet and they climbed out, he dried her first and then she him.

The room had cooled from the efforts of the clanking AC and they pulled the coverlet back on one of the beds and Nina got him to lay down on his back and then straddled him circling her palms over his chest while bending and kissing him passionately as he held her hips in his hands.

"Do you like me, Bobby?"

"Yes, I like you, Nina."

"I mean really, really like me?"

"I really, really do."

She sat up and reached behind her until she had hold of him. He was already hard and she made mewing sounds as she rubbed him.

"Damn it," he said softly, "You better do something soon or you're going to miss all the action."

She raised herself and then came slowly back down onto him, said, "Not till I tell you to, baby. Stay with me now. Stay with me."

And he did.

Chapter Thirty

"If you're going to do something wrong do it big
because the punishment is the same either way."
—Jayne Mansfield

Late nights searching wasn't no kind of job for a lesser man, Cowboy thought as he sat in the Midnight Lounge somewhere in Bumfuck, Texas working on his third Manhattan. He fucking loved the stuff, maybe a little too much. But hey, a man had to have his likes, or what was the point?

It was a nice, fairly quiet place, the décor from the '60s, he guessed, but more than he expected when the hotel clerk told him about it, a cadaverous middle-aged man with what looked like penciled on eyebrows.

"Just a mile up the highway on your right, can't miss it."

Well, he did miss it and had to take a U-turn and when he did that, a cop pulled him over, some slick on a big white Harley, all the bells and whistles, of which there were many.

The cop asked for the usual papers, shined the light on him then in the car and wrote him a ticket for a hundred dollars. He asked if he couldn't just pay the cop instead of having to show up in court.

"You wouldn't be trying to bribe me, now would you, sir?"

"No, just in a hurry to get home is all."

"Home being California? The Golden state, land of fruits and nuts?" The cop was starting to piss him off big time, the little fucken twerp.

"Yes sir, Officer."

"Well, you just take that ticket on into courthouse there in Del Rio and get it paid or we'll put out a warrant to suspend your license, if it's not paid in thirty days."

"Okay."

"You have a good evening now." He wanted to say, You too, asshole.

***

Cowboy kept his cool, though. He hated cops. Just fucken hated them. But he had a job to do—to find the boxer. So he drove back to the lounge and ordered his first drink along with a t-bone and house salad.

After he ate, he sat and listened to the woman up on the little stage with piano accompaniment sing torch songs. It reminded him of his boyhood, the music his mother liked to play on radio.

She was good, velvety voice, but it was hard to tell what she really looked like under the small spotlight from where he sat along the bar. And by the time she finished her last number before taking a break and coming over to the bar, he said, "Could I buy you a drink?"

She wasn't great looking, but she wasn't bad.

"Sure, why not, cowboy."

"You know my name," he said.

She looked at the hat, said, "Just a wild guess."

She sat down next to him and said, "Got a smoke for lady?"

"Sure," he said and fished her one from his pack and lighted it and then one for himself.

"I've not seen you in here before," she said, "but then I only work here every couple of months."

"You have other employment?"

"No, I just sing whenever I feel like it. You know, that whole professional music career thing is way in the rearview mirror. This is just something that makes me happy."

"Well, I like what you do, Miss . . ."

"Eva," she said, "Eva Montrose. And it's Missus."

"Oh. I imagine your husband enjoys your singing."

"Wouldn't know, he never says."

Up close like this he guessed, early forties, still not too bad though. He liked them a little older anyways. The young ones were fine, good tight bodies, but the older ones, well, they were like philosophers of sex, didn't have to tell them what to do, what you liked, they just knew.

"Why doesn't he?"

She eyed him through the haze of cigarette smoke, her smile sardonic.

"You ever been married, Cowboy?"

"No, least not yet."

"If you had been, you'd know why not. You've heard it said, familiarity breeds contempt?"

"I get your point, still, if you don't mind my saying, you are an attractive woman. Be hard for me to not take notice."

She leaned in, whispered, "I bet you tell all of them that."

"No, some I do, most I don't."

She smelled good, animalistic, from the perfume and light sweat and maybe a little musk, or that could be his imagination.

"Stick around then," she said. "I've got another set, thirty minutes or so, and we'll see how cheap your talk is."

"Cheers," he said raising his tumbler to hers and they touched glasses before she downed hers and slid off her stool to go back on stage.

Later she said, "Just follow me in your car."

He did not question because by the time she told him to follow her home, he was already for whatever the night would bring. She seemed classier than most you met in watering holes, and he was never the kind to go out just to try and meet girls, nor would he ever consider one of those dating sites. In his line of work always better to keep a low profile, don't get involved, and so Cowboy's main source of lady friends were the higher escorts, the two, three hundred dollar a session types. But to tell the truth, that started getting old after awhile. They were all nice, just not real engaging. But once in awhile he met a woman like this Eva who he was following home in her older Mercedes tank. He didn't know where she was leading him nor did he much care.

She pulled into a subdivision of cookie cutter faux adobe two stories with the desert landscaping and just about every other one it seemed with a For Sale sign out front.

The garage door opened, she pulled in and then walked back out and said, "Might be best if you pulled in over there at 2007—its vacant. Some of my neighbors are what you call busybodies.

"Sure," he said and did as requested, walked back across and entered the garage where she waited for him.

The inside was fairly nice, good carpet, granite counter tops, cherry wood cabinetry, open floor plan.

"What do you want to drink?" she said standing in the kitchen.

"Whatever you're having."

She gave him a big smile, said, "I like your style, Cowboy."

He figured sooner or later she'd ask his real name, like most of them did, but she served him the drink and never did, said instead, "Why don't we take these upstairs."

He followed her up, her round heart-shaped ass straight in front of him and he had a feeling she knew it, too. Coy. He liked that too.

They went down a short plushy hall and she entered a room on their right, he followed her in. She snapped on a light switch that turned on two small bedside table lamps, each covered with a red scarf so that light around the bed was a diaphanous rose glow.

"Why don't you get undressed, Cowboy, I'll be right out."

She disappeared into the bathroom and closed the door.

Well, maybe she wasn't up for any more conversation, which was fine with him. What the hell, hadn't they pretty much said all the important stuff already?

He got undressed, carefully laying his trousers and suit jacket atop a tufted footstool with his 9mm Taurus under the coat jacket, then set his hat atop those before climbing into bed in just his underwear. It wasn't that he was shy, he just wanted her to take them off for him.

Sitting up with his back against the headboard, he sipped whiskey—good stuff, too—and looked around at the room. Lots of straw hats and scarves, and frilly ornamentation. He noted nothing masculine to indicate a husband. Maybe they didn't live together.

She came out just then wearing a black teddy and he liked that, and got into bed next to him. Her breath was sweet from the whiskey.

"Let me have a look at you, Cowboy."

"Doesn't cost anything to look," he said.

"How original."

"Yeah, well, I'm just an old boy trying to get by."

"Shit, I just bet you are. I noticed your western suit, those fancy boots, and that hat probably ran you five-hundred easily."

"A grand, actually."

"Jesus Christ but I want to fuck you so bad my teeth hurt."

"Well, fuck away, little darling and I'll see what I can do to help you."

And like that they were at it—the most intimacy a man and woman can share, and even more so when they are strangers.

It was as they say, 'Fast and furious' and over almost as soon as it begun. A really hot fire doesn't burn long.

And then they were sitting up again smoking and drinking their whiskies.

"Just passing through, I assume?" she said. "No plans to stick around so maybe we could have a repeat some time?"

"Wish I could," he said. "But duty calls."

"Mind if I ask what you do for a living?"

He started to tell her a lie, then said, "Why do you ask?"

"I noticed that you had bulging under you jacket looked a lot like a gun maybe."

"Observant," he said.

"Well?"

"I'm actually a bounty hunter," he said. "Looking for this dude. The pay's good, that's all I'll say."

"Bounty hunter? No kidding?"

"True as I am tall."

She gave a little derisive laugh.

"What?" he said.

"Count on me to pick the guys who carry guns for a living, my husband's a cop."

That put him on the alert.

"That might have been something you mentioned before bringing me over here," he said.

"I didn't bring you, you followed, remember. And, you didn't seem to be interested in what my husband did back at the lounge when I told you I had one."

Well, there it was—the change that occurs once they get what they want. He tried to keep it light for a minute, then thought fuck, I need to get out of here. Last thing he needed was to tangle with a fucken cop.

"Okay," he said. "It's been swell, but I better get going. Got to get an early start tomorrow, you know, early bird gets the worm and all that."

"Oh, relax," she said. "I didn't mean nothing by it. Let's have another drink and talk. I really would love to talk."

He got out of bed, found his shorts on the carpet and was tugging them on when he heard the distinct thud of a car door that sounded like it was just outside the door.

"Ooops," she said. "Ernie must have finished his shift early. What time is it?"

"How the hell would I know?" as he pulled on his trousers and sat on the edge of the bed to pull on the boot socks he'd stuffed down the shaft of the Tony Lama elk skin boots.

He heard the door downstairs open and close, turned to her. She hadn't moved, but sat still with her back against the headboard holding her drink as casually as if everyone was going to be good friends.

"You better get up and do something," he said.

"What would you have me do?"

"I don't know, but if he comes in here and starts shit . . ."

"Oh, don't be so dramatic Cowboy, my husband knows I fuck other men."

"And this he is good with?"

She shrugged.

He could hear the guy coming up the stairs calling her name, only he was saying "LuAnne, you taking a bath honey?"

Cowboy looked at her, said, "I thought you said Eve was your name?"

"So I lied. We all lie sometime. Besides, your name isn't really Cowboy. It's just something you go by."

One boot on and the other not, Cowboy went for his gun, but in diving for it, it fell on the floor just as the guy came in—the same fucken motorcycle cop who had stopped him earlier: little prick with a moustache.

Three words shouted: "What the fuck?" followed by an exchange of gunfire. The one that caught hubby dearest flung him back into the hallway, gurgling and kicking his feet. The one that caught Cowboy felt like the hot end of a poker in his abdomen. And for a full minute it seemed, he couldn't breathe. He just sat there bleeding on the plush carpet trying to hold most of it in.

She leaned over the edge of the bed and looked at him.

"Gee, doll, I'm truly sorry about that. But really, you ought to know not to fuck around with other men's wives. Down here in Texas it's a real sin. Would you like me to call an ambulance? For you, I mean, I think poor Ernie there probably won't make it. You got him good with that heater. And I want to thank you for getting rid of my problem and turning me into the grieving widow who will collect the insurance money, and this lovely house, also insured by the way, you know, in case something were to happen to my husband with the dangerous work he does."

"You cunt" he breathed with every effort he could summon.

He struggled to his feet and she looked up at him from the bed, said, "Yeah that works for me."

Raising the gun, he fired a round into her forehead. "It sure the hell works for me too."

He made it downstairs and out the front door, his entire front sopped with blood and the pain so terrible he wanted to bite his tongue off.

He made it to his car and reached for the door handle, but had no strength to open it and let go. His hand and arm slid slowly down the car door leaving four red streaks from his finger tips.

"You stupid son of a bitch," was his final thought.

And when in minutes sirens were cutting through the night coming closer, he lay in the driveway on his back—belly up, ain't it always how a dead creature ends up? The cops who found the body figured it was a burglary gone bad, that this guy they found in the driveway with no real identification on him and six-hundred in cash had followed Officer Ernest Blando's wife home and raped her and then Officer Blando came upon them and there was a final shootout. The coroner's report confirmed it, she had the suspect's semen in her as proved by DNA.

Tragic, tragic, tragic, all agreed. Case closed.

Chapter Thirty-One

"Sometimes I am God, if I say a man dies, he dies that same day."
—Pablo Escobar

The Black Dude and the White Dude sat inside the ebony black Escalade smoking joints and watching the place from a distance with high power binoculars.

"See anything yet?" the White Dude said.

"Just some skinny old guy in striped shorts and a green wife beater and a raggedy ass dog sitting out there. Guy's still reading a book and drinking beer from his cooler. Nothing changed."

"Nobody else showed up overnight?"

"If they did, they ghosts."

"This is some fucken country, huh. Just fucken rocks and sand and cactus."

"Snakes too. I see one fucken snake, he's gonna be a dead muthafucka."

"You know the man didn't pay us to come out here to shoot snakes, least not them kind crawl on the ground."

"Why you think that bitch did it? I thought her and Ray was tight, all the time kissing on each other? Why a woman do her man like that, shoot him in the goddamn face, fuck up his looks and shit?"

"Ray never had no kind of looks to begin with, like looking at a rat's face."

"He must've pissed that bitch off bad, 'cause she wiped out the whole fucken crew. I can't even feature that shit, can you?"

"No, it don't seem likely. Had to be something else. Maybe she got herself a toy boy on the side and they went in on it together."

"Then why was it they say Buzzard was found with his dick out lying there on the sofa?"

"Buzzard was a beast like to jerk himself off, I guess. Who would ever screw that ugly bastard?"

The sun blazed without hint of relief. They had the windows rolled down, but all it was, was a hot ass wind blowing in on them. They had their own cooler full of iced down Lone Star, about all they could buy from the market they'd stopped at, and by noon had cut it down to a third of what was in there, but nothing seemed to bring relief.

"Man, I thought Miami was a bitch, but this shit is unreal, this heat. Shit, lets drive on back down the highway and hit that place, that air conditioned Mex Restaurant, get some chili dogs. Man ain't had me a chili dog since I don't know when. Let's get the fuck out from under this sun for awhile. He ain't going nowhere and we be back in an hour's time."

"Good thing the man paying you by the job and not by the hour."

"He's paying me to put people in the grave is what he's paying me to do."

"What you think, you just gonna shoot that bitch dead away, no chance to hear what she have to say?"

"No, I'll give her a chance, long as she gives up the dope or tells me where the fuck it is, then I'll shoot her."

"Maybe we should fuck her before we shoot her."

"You a cold mother."

"Us or them, baby, us are them."

"Right on."

The white dude started the engine and pulled away from the top of the ridge and cruised over the crumbly caliche, the loose earth grinding under the big tires, and headed back to that spot in the road with a shot up sign of white letters over green—Buscando Junction, and pulled in at the café within spitting distance of the auto repair and filling station, parked and went inside.

Jerry Summers had seen them, saw the glint of sun running off that strip of chrome, big black beast that spoke of cops, FBI, Secret Service, something. Whatever they were, there was a particular reason they were watching his place. Well, let them watch, he hadn't done anything.

Still it irritated him to be watched after all those years in the penitentiary. He'd paid his dues, dues he didn't even owe. If they'd found Robbie Winterfield and charged him with that murder, yeah—guilty as fucken charged, and he would do it ten times over again. But they charged him with the wrong crime at the wrong time and no matter how you sliced it, it was Justice gone awry.

"What goes around comes around," he said fishing out another cold one from the cooler. The dog raised its eyebrows at his voice, but knew by the tone the man wasn't asking him to go for a walk or nothing ambitious and so simply stayed belly to the shaded ground.

Jerry wondered if those men up there in the big black car had anything to do with his daughter. Seemed kind of odd she'd called out of the blue just a few days ago wanting to come see him—or "home" as she'd put it. He did not discount the idea. But they were gone off that ridge now so nothing to worry about, no need to go in and get that old Colt he bought off that broken down rodeo rider who'd made fantastic claims about it having once been owned by the outlaw Bill Doolin. Shit, if true, then the old boy would have been asking a lot more than two-hundred dollars for it. It needed a new firing pin and one of the wood grips was cracked so bad it needed replacing, but it shot true and it felt good in his hand, and did not every single fucken soul in American need a gun these days? He was a felon and wasn't supposed to own a firearm, but actually he owned two; the Colt and a lever action rifle, a Marlin 30.06.

No, he wasn't too concerned about those guys. Fuck 'em. Let them come down and play their games, he'd play with them. Twenty-two years in the pen had hardened him in ways most of the population could not conceive or believe. When you're locked in with a couple of thousand other guys, many of which would kill you for a deck of smokes, well, you learned how to survive or you perished, if not physically, then in every other way.

That thing, they used to say: "I'd rather die on my feet than live on my knees" was what it was all about. You were either a man or some man's bitch, and Jerry Summers was nobody's bitch.

***

No, he hadn't killed his wife, just the guy who had killed his wife, and let's face it, killing was killing no matter what was behind it.

So yeah, if those boys in the big black shiny ride wanted to tangle, Jerry was more than willing.

"What about you, you little bastard?" he said to the dog. This time it sat up and cocked its head at him, first this way and then that. Barked once as if to ask, "What'd you say?"

Jerry tossed it a hot dog from the cooler and watched with pleasure as it finished it off then looked to him for more.

"Man, what you think I am, doggy welfare? You best go learn to make a living and support me."

He thought about the woman, Nancy, what his pal had referred to as a Comfort Woman, and she was indeed that. Jerry had thought about inviting her out to a cookout. He had a small charcoal grill and could save up and get some sort of steak, wrap some potatoes in tin foil to put on with it. But thus far, he felt too far impoverished to invite her out, and doubted she would come anyway. What woman would trust a guy who'd been in prison for the accused crime of killing his wife, besides, she was in a way like himself, needing to survive, not go to cookouts.

Don't be a sucker, he told himself. Just go see her when you can afford to and she has an afternoon to see you and be content with that much.

He had been forced to learn a certain self-discipline in not wanting too much of anything good, because for those long years in lockup—there was hardly anything good to want—a sort of Zen thing a guy in prison told him.

He sat there for a long time—until the sun sank beyond the distant scribble of mountains and flung up its final prayer against the sky that seemed to bleed from the artist's brush. Sat there until he could barely keep his eyes open from all the beer—the cans lined up like some miniature Stonehenge that only he knew the meaning behind.

Then he rose, went in and fried a slab of ham that filled the entire skillet, heated some pork and beans, took this back out and sat in the cooler night air after having lighted his Coleman lantern and ate, sharing the meat with the dog and finished the very last can of beer.

"What's say we go to town tomorrow for more beer?" he asked the dog. It scratched a hind leg behind its ear. "Okay then, it's a date."

And soon the coyotes sang to one another far out and then he noticed a pair of headlights riding the ridge, saw them stop and go out.

Yeah, that was trouble right there.

Chapter Thirty-Two

"There's a difference between crooks and criminals
Crooks steal. Criminals blow some guy's brains out."
—Ronald Biggs, English Criminal

Bobby went over to the garage that next morning to check on the progress on the car. The mechanic was still wiping his greasy hands on his greasy hip pocket rag and standing now under another truck using a torch to cut away a monstrous exhaust system that had rusted bolts and clamps.

Bobby stood patiently just inside the service bay. His own car parked outside where he'd left it, only now with a skin of dust covering it.

He wondered what sort of person would live way out in the middle of nowhere and fix cars all day, become so begrimed he maybe could never get the grease out of the creases of his skin. What sort of man would that take, he wondered.

Between working on the undercarriage, the mechanic had to go out and pump gas and check oil on cars that pulled into the two pumps and he didn't even seem to take notice of Bobby those two or three times until the last time when Bobby said, "Any estimate on when you might get to my ride?"

The guy stopped and fished a cigarette out of his coverall's pocket and lighted it and blew a stream of smoke into the air, one boot rested against the garage's wall.

"I'll get to her as soon as I can," he said and eyed Bobby carefully. "Say, ain't you a fighter, light heavyweight?"

"Yeah, I used to be," Bobby said.

"I thought I seen you on the TV. "The mechanic was running the names of boxers he knew of, snapped his fingers, "Bobby . . . Bobby The Rebel Lee, that's it, ain't it?"

Bobby nodded.

"Goddamn, whatever happened to you?"

Bobby did his best to keep from smiling and saying nothing ever happened to me, I'm standing right here, but instead he said, "A whole lot of bad and not much good."

"No, man, you was good. I seen you knock out Pinky Alverez down in El Paso. Me and my uncle went, what was it, three, four years ago. And Alverez was no punk either."

"Lucky shot," I guess."

"Man, for a white fighter, you were pretty damn good."

"Yeah," Bobby said glancing over at his car with the smashed in front fender. "You have any idea when you can get to it, I've got a fight in Albuquerque this Friday, is the only reason I'm hoping for a rush on this."

"Yeah, who you fighting?"

Bobby had to quick come up with a name, said, "Big stud calls himself Butterball, something, is all I know. I don't book them, I just fight them."

The mechanic laughed, said, "Butterball? Now him I never heard of. Must be some new hayseed. What're you in training for a title match?"

"Possible. You like a pair of tickets?"

"Shit yeah."

"Well, if I can get down there in time, I'll see my manager overnights you a pair, ringside."

"Deal, brother."

Bobby Lee found Nina sitting out by an empty swimming pool on a lounge chair, shades on and wearing just her panties and bra.

"Jesus, woman, have you no decency," he said coming up and leaning over and giving her a kiss.

"I could take these off," she said, "you want indecent."

He smiled and sat down beside her and handed her one of two Cokes he'd gotten out of the machine out front and they both took long swallows. It was not yet ten in the morning, but already the sun was brutal.

"You thought anymore about what I said?" he asked.

"About getting rid of the dope?"

He nodded, said, "The longer we hold onto it the more likely we are to be caught with it."

"You're right," she said. "But just give me a little more time to think this through—how I can turn it into a future—for us."

He looked at her, but with wearing her shades he couldn't see her eyes, but she sounded sincere.

"You're thinking there's an Us then?"

She nodded, said, "Pretty much, wouldn't you say, after our little dust up at the bus station."

"Yeah, I would say."

"Then if we're in this together, all the way to the end, don't you think it's fair we make decisions together?"

He nodded, however he'd been around enough of the underworld side of boxing to know there was just some shit you did not mess with, and a couple of bundles of dope stolen from men who would probably kill, if not torture first, to get it back, were not men you wanted to mess with. Too, he had in the back of his mind what guys like that might do to her, maybe in front of him, before they blew their brains out. The thought became a knot in his stomach.

"Can we agree that once we get to your father's place we can make that decision then. For me, it's like riding around sitting on top of a bomb about to go off any time."

"I promise," she said. He hoped that was sincerity he heard in her voice. But to tell the truth, maybe it was just what he wanted it to sound like.

He watched her tip the soda to her mouth, her head tilted back, the motion of her throat drinking. She even did that sexy and so he let the subject rest for now. The mechanic said into the phone, "That woman you're looking for is still here. She's with a boxer. No not a fucken dog, I mean a professional fighter. Bobby the Rebel Lee. You ever heard of him? No? Maybe if you did more than pull your pud and look at fuck books, you might know something Ellison. Yeah, well, he's pushing me to get his car ready, you may want to drive the hundred and ten miles and get here. Yeah, I know. Just make sure I get my cut of the wanted money or I'll tell my sister to throw your ass out of the house. I'll tell her you got the clap off some truck stop lizard. No? You don't think I would? You just go on and bet me I would. Alright then. Okay, get your ass in gear dick weed. What? Yeah, I know you're a goddamn deputy sheriff. So the fuck what? See ya."

He hung up the phone in his cramped little office with a gray metal desk covered in various invoices and a few parts, grabbed himself a Payday candy bar from a box that had dust on it and went back out under that big ass truck and its troublesome exhaust and right off he hit it a lick and some rust flacks got in his eye.

"You cocksucker!" he cursed.

Chapter Thirty-Three

"The great nations have always acted like criminals
And the small nations like prostitutes."
—Stanley Kubrick

Max was sweating so bad he kept drinking seltzer water. Between Johnny Pearl and now this fucking Levi, he'd have shit left of his business. Well, fuck that, he thought sitting in his office. He had worked too hard, screwed too many people, cheated and schemed all his life to get where he was. He'd really counted on that big payday for the fight that bastard Bobby Lee was supposed to throw—laid off two-hundred and fifty K using Cherry to bet the money for him with a bookie that didn't know either of them. Who'd figure some dumb bimbo would know what she was doing? But he should have figured Bobby would screw him. The bum had too much self-pride to take it on the chin, even though he was at the end of his game, that his glory days were well in the past.

Now Cherry was dead and both his fucken body-guard and this tipsy-toes bartender were squeezing him, holding him over a barrel. Well, there was only one solution. And why hadn't that goddamn Cowboy called back, been going on two days and not a peep.

Max was too upset even for a blowjob or piece of tail, and that was too bad since that new girl, Marilyn had started temporarily to see if she'd work out. Real looker, and young too. Said she was eighteen and a senior in high school and wanted to make some quick money to bail her boyfriend out of jail, that one of her friends had suggested she do a little prostituting, but, she told Max when she came in looking to dance a few nights, that she was a good Christian girl and was saving herself for marriage. Max thinking, yeah, sugar, I'll just bet you are. She was sweet looking with long straight brown hair that hung to her waist. She didn't have a lot on top, which was a big thing with guys who came in the place, tit crazy, no matter if they were plastic or not. Max figured most of their wives didn't have that much either, that's why they loved the girls with big boobs they could stick their creased dollar bills between.

Max had Marilyn do a little strip tease, but not all the way, he didn't want to scare her off like that last little slut. Let her think he was a nice old guy. Max was tempted to bang her right there when he saw her stripped down to her panties and padded bra. Her panties had little hearts all over them. Talk about innocence, Jesus.

He couldn't be sure but thought maybe she was scheduled to dance tonight. He hadn't yet decided whether to close the joint down for the evening anyway.

Then out of the blue Johnny Pearl came straggling in looking like he'd fell down a couple of flights of stairs.

"What the fuck?" Max yelled. "You were suppose to take care of that broad, and instead she turns into one of the living dead and comes back to try and kill me with a fucken meat cleaver."

"Yeah, well, she sure as fuck was *not* dead, as you can plainly see. I went over there to wrap her in a sheet and she jumped on me and god-damn the woman was like one of them badgers you see on them nature shows on TV. Caught me off guard. I'm thinking she's a fucken zombie or some shit. My heart damn near stopped. I need a drink."

Max could but shake his head in disbelief, said, "I thought you was a tough guy—you can't take care of a half dead woman and you wanted to take care of Bobby Lee? Gimme a break."

Soon as he downed his whiskey Johnny said, "What's that big blood stain on the floor—you finally kill that broad?"

"No, your boyfriend did."

"Levi?"

"You got more than one boyfriend in the place? Yeah, he walked in and popped her in the back of the head."

"Levi?" Johnny said disbelieving.

"What are you, hard of hearing?" Max so frustrated he was pacing.

"I been thinking," Max said.

Johnny poured himself another glass of whiskey.

"Way I see it, I'll give you one more chance to make up for fucken up the deal with Cherry, or, I could cut you out and put Levi in. It don't matter to me long as somebody does what I tell them."

"We got a contract Max."

"Contract? You don't think my lawyer can't testify I signed that under duress, that you threatened to kill me if I didn't sign, or some shit?"

"You dirty prick."

"Guilty," Max said. "But we can make it square and I'll cut you back in, all legal, we'll go to my lawyers this time. If, you want to settle things with that kid for me. He's trying to blackmail me over Cherry's death, saying he'll go to the cops and say he saw me shoot her unless I give him half the club. That, or he was going to fucken kill me and blame it on her. Fact is, I was surprised he didn't. I guess he didn't want to take the chance and be charged with my murder. But here's what I know, once a blackmailer, always a blackmailer. I can't have that."

"So it's okay for you to screw me, but not him to screw you?"

"How long we go back, Johnny? Besides you're my fucken nephew. We're family. Come on, think smart. I know you like that punk, but the world is full of punks like him. 'Sides, one more thing, I'm thinking about retiring, letting you run the whole thing, the management of the fighters too. Everything. Go down to the islands and get me a boat, catch them sailfish and shit. I need to know you can get the work done."

That did the trick. Max could see it in Johnny's face, the idea of him taking over the business, probably turn it into a gay club like he wanted, get rid of all the girls. Who knew, maybe he could make more money and have less headaches.

"I'll handle it," Johnny said eagerly. "You know I will, Max, and this time I'll be ready. No fuckups. Where is he, anyway?"

"Out somewhere burying my true love, kid. Hopefully deep enough the coyotes won't dig her up. He should be back in a few hours. But listen, do it away from the club, okay? And in the meantime, can you clean up that blood on the floor there, it breaks my fucken heart to have to look at it. Poor Cherry, me and her had something for a time. But love, kid, love is just another word for everything to lose. Remember who told you that. I gotta go to her place and clean out anything of mine I mighta left there. I think for sure I left a bottle of Aqua Velva and a pair of silk boxers over there."

Johnny drank more glasses of whiskey thinking about taking over things. That fat fuck was finally going to quit and turn things over to him. It was about damn time. There was no room in this world for old fat perverts like Max. Yeah, things are finally falling into place.

He looked around the office as if seeing it for the first time. He didn't any longer have to worry about taking Max out of the picture, he was taking himself out. Good things come to him who wait. Somebody said that once, he thought.

Fuck yeah.

Chapter Thirty-Four

"A cop came to my door and asked where I was between five and six.
He got irritated when I said Kindergarten."
—Stephen Wright

She answered the phone, it was Frank on the other end. She heard a lot of background noise, said, "Where you calling from?"

"The airport," he said. "Waiting for my flight to El Paso."

"El Paso? Why are you going to El Paso?"

"I might have a line of those who are responsible for Ray. I don't want to say too much, you understand, in case later certain things were to come up that required you to testify."

"What are you talking about, testify?"

"How long were you married to a cop, Wendy?"

"Oh, okay, I see what you're saying. You want, I could go with you."

"No. You stay where you are and if anything comes of this, I'll call you, let you know."

Then there was a long pause, one waiting for the other to say something, but nobody did. She could hear a woman's voice asking if he wanted another, Frank saying, "No thank you."

Then, "Wendy?"

"Yes."

"I just want you to know something."

"What is it, Frank?" She thought he was about to tell her how much he loved her.

"Whatever comes of this, I'm not doing it out of love or wanting to get back together with you. I've thought about it a lot after our conversation and I've decided that if it's broke, I'm not going to try and fix it. You shouldn't either. If what we had was any good, it would have never come to our separating. We're two different people. So, I just wanted to let you know."

"Then why are you even going, if you feel that way, Frank?" the anger overriding her words was obvious and confirmed what he already felt.

"Because, in spite of everything, I loved you once and maybe I still do a little, and knowing you, if I didn't go, you'd try and hire somebody to do something to revenge your worthless brother and I wouldn't want to see you jammed up over somebody like him. No promises, I'll do what I can, but then you won't hear from me again after that. Goodbye."

He felt a degree of satisfaction when he hung up, then told the bar girl in the airport lounge on second thought he'd have one more Bloody Mary and when she served it, he gave her a five-dollar tip, said, "You just don't know how much I hate flying."

She gave him a cute smile and even patted his hand, said, "It's safer than driving."

Yeah, well, he wasn't so sure. Least you wreck a car you had a chance of walking away.

He went and waited to board this flight to El Paso. He'd never been there before—hadn't even been to Texas. He'd purchased a small chapbook in one of the airport shops called *Fun Facts of El Paso* perused it waiting for his boarding to be called.

He read that the Margarita was supposedly invented there, that General John Pershing had once used a high school football stadium there to stage his troops in pursuit of Pancho Villa. But the one thing that caught Frank's eye was the town's former moniker, The Six Shooter Capital. Now, that he liked.

He'd packed his own gun in his luggage. It wasn't a six shooter, it was a fifteen shooter. Those old cowboys would have shot up more towns if they'd had that little Beretta PX4 Storm, he smiled.

In a way, he hoped he'd not catch a sniff of this girl Nina Summers.

The call came for him to board his flight and he stood, but left the Fun Facts book on the chair. It wasn't worth the two dollars he'd spent for it, figured somebody else could get something from it and boarded the 727, which for Frank, seemed the size of a sardine can and felt like one too, with the two seats down one side and one on the other side.

Luckily, he got seated next to a stewardess on her way home, vacation trip, and she was not only good looking but very conversational. And, she smelled nice. Triple bonus.

They talked the whole flight out, got into El Paso late afternoon, and the two of them had exchanged phone numbers.

Her name was Donna Mesa, single, thirty-two, lived alone with just her cat. Did he like cats? she'd asked. He loved cats, he lied. But shit, she was so good looking and personable, she could have kept armadillos for all he cared. Said even though her home was El Paso, she was stationed out of Miami.

"Maybe if you're in El Paso for a few days, we can grab dinner," she said, "and I can show you my cat."

He wasn't sure the full meaning of that comment was, but he readily agreed. When they de-boarded, she'd given him a sweet and promising goodbye and he thought briefly about saying, fuck you, Ray, you're on your own. He would go get a hotel room and call this Donna up later and see if she wanted to go out for drinks tonight, dinner tomorrow night; that the business he was supposed to have there had been cancelled, so he had extra time on his hands.

But the cop part of him wouldn't allow it. Even though he wasn't a cop anymore, in a way he still felt this obligation to see this thing through. He'd try and hurry and wrap it up fast and if his sources hadn't yet come up with an address of a door he could knock on, then—what was it Arnold said in those Terminator movies, "Hasta la vista, baby."

El Paso was of course hot, like Miami was hot, but a different kind of hot. Miami was a wet hot and El Paso was dry and hot. But then when the temp is hovering around one-hundred, it was all fucken hot, no matter how you thought about it.

He thought about his dream cabin where he was going to fish all day, thought maybe Alaska or Montana might be a good place to have it. Nah, that Berretta wouldn't stop any grizzly bears.

He didn't know why, but by the time he caught a cab into downtown, he was feeling pretty good. He thought he could still smell her perfume.

Play this right Frank, and who knows. Maybe it's meant to be, you know, like everything else, wondered if that stewardess liked to fish, feed the heads to her cat.

Chapter Thirty-Five

"You never run out of things that can go wrong."
—Murphy's Law

"What's taking so long with the car, Bobby?"

"Hell if I know. I'm not sure that mechanic is too swift. I told him to rush the job. Said it would maybe be not too much longer. I mean all he's got to do is straighten it out far enough away from the tire to get us on down the road and hopefully to your dad's place."

"Maybe we should just see about getting another vehicle?"

"Not sure where we'd get one without stealing it."

"Well, we stole the last one," Nina said sitting on the side of the bed so that the morning light coming into the room fell on her like God's own grace. Bobby thought she was beautiful in that near perfect moment.

Ever since that morning, and after a lingering breakfast at the small café, they'd pretty much been cooped up in the small motel room. Of course they took up some time once Bobby had returned from the garage making love. But the room was now confining.

Nina got up and went to the window to glance out toward the garage in hopes she'd see their car gone inside, started to say that she thought she'd go to the empty swimming pool and get some more sun when she suddenly said, "Bobby, there's a cop car just pulled in out there at the garage."

He hurried over and looked as well. Sure enough. Sheriff's patrol car.

"Now what's the story?" he said.

"The guy couldn't possibly be here for us," she said. "How would he even know we were here?"

The answer came soon enough when the saw the mechanic talking to the officer and pointing toward the motel.

"Yeah," Bobby said. "He called them."

"But how in hell would that grease monkey even know about us?"

Bobby didn't say it, but he knew that Max had a long reach into the world at large and that somehow that reach extended to a desert garage in south Texas.

"What do we do?" Nina said.

"Gather your things," Bobby said as he gathered up his own.

"He'll see us if we make a run for it, and besides where the hell would we run to?"

"We're not running," Bobby said. "He's coming to us. Just play it cool. Take your things into the bathroom and wait for me to call you out."

He saw her grab her gun.

"And don't shoot the guy. Killing a cop is a sure way to punch our ticket."

"I'm not letting him take me in," Nina said.

"There could be worse things."

"You do what you want, but if he comes into the bathroom, only one of us is walking out."

He had to admire her grit, but it scared the shit out of him too.

She grabbed her stuff and ducked into the bathroom and closed the door. Bobby waited patiently for the knock to come. He didn't have to wait long.

"Big Bend Sheriff's Department," the cop said.

Bobby opened the door.

The cop stood there under his Stetson, his gold plated badge gleaming under that broiler of a Texas sun. He was trying to look into the room around Bobby.

"I need to come in," he said.

"What's the problem officer?"

"No problem. There's been the report of a robbery nearby and that fellow outside said you matched the description. Please step back into the room and keep your hands where I can see them."

***

Bobby saw the cop's hand resting on the big handle of his revolver—not the more modern semi-autos most cops carried. Between it and the hat and the pointed toed cowboy boots this guy could have been Wyatt Earp's brother.

Bobby stepped back far enough to let the cop into the room, his hands slightly raised.

"I'm told you're with a woman?" the cop said.

"No, you must have heard wrong. I'm alone, officer."

That's when the cop went to pull his gun and Bobby brought an overhand right down against the side of his face, squarely on the temple and he never so much as made a sound, just went face down into the shitty carpet that had probably been stained with everything from baby piss to semen over the years. He lay still.

"Come on out, Nina."

She opened the door, gun in hand, said, "You got him."

"Yeah. Let's drag him into the bathroom." She helped though it was kind of counterproductive the three of them squeezing into the small space. Bobby took the cop's cuffs and clamped one around his wrist and the other to the sink's plumbing, then pocketed the key.

"We probably need to gag him," Bobby said, "to keep him from screaming his head off."

Nina took off her panties, balled them and stuffed them into the officer's mouth.

216

"Well, I'm sure he won't complain about that," Bobby said.

"Pervert," she said.

"Let's go," Bobby said, and they started to hurry out, but Nina stopped him.

"Wait, what about his gun?"

"No, we're not going to take it."

"Why not?"

"Just make them look for us harder. Cops hate having their guns stolen."

"Oh, and like getting knocked out they don't mind so much?"

"Jesus woman, do you have to question everything?"

"Well, I'm taking it and tossing it out the window soon as we get a couple miles down the road, better that than having that prick shoot us with it."

Bobby was tired of fighting her on her headstrong ways. And, after all, how much more trouble could they really get in?

They quickly crossed the parking lot toward the garage where the mechanic saw them and ducked back inside and grabbed a wrench as a defensive weapon. It was Nina who took charge, "Said, you stupid asshole. Call the cops on us. You really think that is going to stop a goddamn bullet?" Nina waving her big ass gun at the guy. He dropped the wrench and started begging for his life.

"How'd you know to call the cops?" Bobby said.

"I . . . I . . ."

"Forget about it. Where's the keys to your ride?"

The mechanic reached in his coverall pocket, said, "The 300."

A dark blue Chrysler parked alongside the building. Bobby gave the keys to Nina, told her to throw their stuff in the trunk then bring it out front of the motel while he took the mechanic over to their room, led him inside and chained the other cuff to the mechanic's wrist—the cop's on one side and the mechanic's on the other side around the porcelain base of john.

Then he went back into the bedroom and took a pillowcase and stuffed it into the mechanic's mouth, said, "Sorry, your friend here got the only pair of panties my girl has."

Bobby went out and started to get into the 300, but hesitated and had her go back around to the garage where he took a screwdriver and switched plates with their Buick, while Nina got out, grabbed a county map from inside the office, a couple of Cokes from the cooler and some Zagnut bars.

She'd always had a thing for Zagnuts.

Chapter Thirty-Six

"It's only murder if they find the body,
otherwise it's just a missing person."
—Unknown

Johnny was glassy-eyed from drinking so much when Levi came strolling in big as you please.

"Johnny," he said. "Heard you had a little trouble with Max's squeeze?" making a joke of it, like Ha, Ha.

"The prick told me he'd killed her, sent me over there to take care of it. Only she wasn't even close to dead. Bitch jumped me, raving mad. Hit me from behind or I'd have torn her ass up." Johnny playing it off, playing as though he was unaware of what Levi had done in killing Cherry right there in the office. As if he didn't know shit of Levi's involvement. Catch him off guard then end him and once he was gone, Max would soon follow.

Levi acting quite the innocent too.

"Where you been?" Johnny asked.

"Max had me run an errand for him. Told me to go over and clean up any evidence of his being at Cherry's place."

"Oh yeah? What he do with her?"

"She came over here all irate and Max shot her right between the eyes, said, 'I guess this time you really are dead you stupid twat.'"

"So what he do with the body?"

"I helped him load her onto the van. Said he was going to take her out and drop her in the desert."

"That Max, he's a piece of work, ain't he?"

Levi went over and helped himself to a glass of whiskey, said, "He's full of surprises."

"Never ceases to amaze," Johnny said. Told himself he shouldn't have drunk so much, now he was having trouble keeping focused on how to take out Levi. Had a thought.

"Say, the other night, at my place," he said. "We had a pretty good time, huh?"

"Yeah, I guess so," Levi said, but thinking it was the worst damn thing he'd ever done—being with another guy—and had only done it because Johnny had gotten him drunk and coerced him with talk of the two of them taking over the business together from Max.

"So I was thinking," Johnny said. "Perhaps a good night for a repeat, you know relieve some of the stress we've all been under. Besides, I want to talk more about how we're going to fuck ol' Max right out of this club and everything else he has. Divvy it up, fifty-fifty, right down the middle."

Levi still acting the innocent, said, "Yeah, we should do that, you know before ol' Max gets wise to us, huh?"

"How about you drive, I'm too drunk."

"Sure."

Johnny handed Levi the keys to his rental. Pretty soon he was going to buy something new—a Porsche maybe. Soon as he took care of Levi and Max and changed the venue, he was thinking of calling it JOHNNY'S BIG JOINT, something like that, you know, like that guy said, "Do what you love, the money will follow."

Miami at night was aglow with lights, like all the rich in all the world had suddenly lost all their diamonds and they were scattered all over the city.

The night air was warm and humid as it always was, not so much as a breeze coming in off the ocean.

They took 41 east to 9 and then South on 9 to West on 272—headlights coming at them a double vision blur for Johnny, red taillights like a string of rubies ahead of them.

Johnny pretended to doze, but had one eye open and on Levi to see if he tried anything. Johnny thinking if they hadn't been moving, he would have just shot Levi and kicked his body out of the car.

They reached Johnny's pad in about twenty, twenty-five minutes and got out and went inside. It was a nice place, if old, with glass on three sides so that you could still see the glowing lights of the city off in the distance.

"Want a drink?" Levi said.

"Sure. Fix yourself one too. I'm going in and taking a shower. I like to be squeaky clean for my man," Johnny said.

It turned Levi's stomach to hear him say it. told himself he wasn't a queer and it had been just that one-time thing—you know, to get ahead. He didn't always want to be a damn mixologist—what they called it these days.

Johnny disappeared into the bathroom. And though still a bit unsteady, he had it planned out, how he would kill Levi and get away with it. Say the guy had come and broken into his house and demanded money, he had a gun and threatened to shoot Johnny. Shoot him under the 'Stand your ground' law. But before he pulled the trigger, he'd get Johnny to tell him where he'd taken the body so he could hold that over Max. Two birds with one big ass stone.

He got out the snub-nose .38 from his dresser drawer and waited for Levi to come slip in, figuring no doubt to shoot Johnny in the shower, disappear and let the cops chalk it up to a home invasion gone wrong. Yeah, show me a smart bartender and I'll show you a miracle wrought by Mother Teresa herself, he smiled.

In the other room Levi listened for the shower water to start. He had the same gun he'd killed Cherry with. Bang! One to the back of the head. Figured he'd give Johnny the same treatment and still have a few rounds left over for ol' Max if need be. Who would suspect a dumbass bartender for such cleverness. Everybody knew bartenders were only good for two things—mixing drinks and picking up middle-aged married women.

Johnny turned on the shower full blast leaving the bathroom door open for Levi to better hear by. He didn't fully relish the fact of killing Levi, he quite liked the boy, thought, but for the current circumstances, they might have even had something of a future together.

Oh, he knew Levi wasn't completely gay—but he could have learned to like it given time, just like some broads learn to love some men that's got money. Yeah, it would be a bit of a shame, but after all, business was business and love was just a concept fronted by straight people who wanted to get married and have babies.

It didn't really exist, did it, Love?

Levi heard the shower going, thought, Now or never, thought: It's always easier if you don't like the person.

He removed the gun, made sure there was one in the chamber and went up and slowly twisted the doorknob leading to the master.

On the other side, Johnny calmly watched the knob turn.

Come on, kid, let me show you how to mix a bloody Levi.

The door open. One stepped in, the other stepped out of the steam coming from the shower.

Two sharp reports.

And then silence.

Chapter Thirty-Seven

"Waiting is painful. Forgetting is painful.
But not knowing which to do is the worse kind of suffering."
—Paul Coelho

"Dude, how long you think we're going to have to sit up here watching for them two?"

"Dude, like if I knew I'd fucking say, okay?"

"I mean like it's been what, two, three fucken days already. I ain't seen shit, but that old man and that scroungy dog. Maybe she ain't gonna show?"

"Yeah, you want to tell the man back home you can't sit your ass still for a few days, or would you rather me tell him?"

"Fuck, man. I'm just saying, we could be out here who knows how long? Why don't we just go down there and get that old fool to tell us if she's coming or not?"

"And if he don't know, then what? You done already tipped him off."

"So we kill his ass and wait inside?"

"You think it's hot out here, sit inside one of them fucken trailers. I know, man, I grew up in one of them in Lemon City. So fucken hot you wanted to cut your throat. No fucken thanks, I'll sit my ass right here where I am. Least they's a breeze ever once in awhile."

"Sheeit, man. You fucken crazy. I bet that old man got himself some AC, something to keep cooled off with."

"Gimme them binoculars."

Black dude glasses the aluminum Airstream below, hands the binoculars to the second dude, said, "You see any fucken AC sticking outta that thing?"

"Hand me a beer outta that cooler, one of them beef sticks."

***

Jerry Summers saw they were back. They might not have been there during the night, might have gone into Manzanita—if they were smart they would have.

What is it you pricks are really after? Surely not this place. And you sure as hell aren't law enforcement or you'd have come down here and asked me questions.

Tell me, boys, what did my lovely little Nina get herself into this time to warrant a couple of guys on a stakeout?

He stood, went inside and got his rifle and came out again and said, "Let's go see if we can get a rabbit or two for supper" and the dog stood quickly, tail wagging eager to go do something, anything. Jerry thinking, Let them see it—the gun, as he carried it one handed. He didn't really believe they'd find so much as a rabbit in the heat of the day. Maybe just do some target practice. Let them hear the shots up there. See what they thought of it.

And, it was just as much a walk in solitude as anything. There was a rare beauty and grace to the desert one had to pay attention to in order to notice.

"Hey lookit?" the Black Dude said.

"What?" the White Dude said sipping on a beer in the shade of the big SUV.

"He's got a gun and leaving the trailer."

"Where's he going?"

"How the fuck I'm suppose to know?"

"He coming up this way?"

"Nah, he's heading out into the desert, looks like, him and that mongrel. He's carrying a rifle with him."

"Well, long as he'd not coming up here, fuck it."

"Let's say, if she don't show up by dark, we go back into that shithole of a town and see about getting laid. Even we got to cross the border, get some of that Mex puss."

"Why don't we just concentrate on what our mission is here."

"Yeah, but we got to eat, right? All I'm saying, long as we got to eat, we could take what, thirty minutes to get our dicks wet?"

"Your mama told me you couldn't last thirty minutes."

"Fuck you."

"Okay, the girl doesn't show up before dark we'll drive into town. I need a shower so bad I am starting to rot. Now keep an eye out while I take a little siesta. I don't want that old bastard circling around and getting in behind us."

***

Jerry could almost feel their eyes on him, even at that distance, but he got soon lost in the chaparral as he headed up to an old abandoned camp of an uninhabitable place of three adobe walls, no roof and wondered the history of the place. He liked to think maybe it was an outlaw hangout back in the old days, a place where men came to count their stolen bank loot, drink and bring their women.

There was no evidence of anything, of course, but it left plenty of room to fire the imagination. Thing was, when knocking around those old abandoned places you had to be careful of snakes, so he kept the rifle handy and called the dog to stay close to him.

"Don't you go getting bit now," he warned. "You'd be dead before I could get you anywhere they could help you."

The dog looked back at him quizzically then trotted on.

He spent about an hour out in the brush before the heat got to be too much and headed back. When he got close to his place, he glanced up there on the ridge and they were still there.

Well, you boys enjoy the Texas weather, he thought. I'm going to grab me a beer and take a nap.

But first he made sure the dog had water in its bowl and shook in some fresh dog food from what was left of a fifty pound bag.

Thought: I hope she doesn't come. I'd just as soon not, if it means trouble for her.

He lay in the narrow bunk at the back of the trailer after firing up the generator so he could run one small fan, and nursed his beer.

He knew the dog would warn him if or when anyone came. He'd learned to be fatalistic. If something was going to take him out, then it would, otherwise, why worry about it.

He lay there in the dry airless heat and thought not of danger lurking up on the ridge, but of Nancy, the comfort woman. Thought she was the sort of woman, that if he had anything to offer her long term, he sure as hell might.

She wasn't anything like his late wife, but for the fact she had a kindness in her put there by heartache and misfortune that would turn most women bitter.

The dog lay there on the cracked linoleum floor beside his cot and he lightly rested a hand over the side and petted its skull, thinking nothing brings out a man's kindness like women and dogs.

Then he dozed.

Chapter Thirty-Eight

*"If you don't believe there is a price for this sweet
paradise, remind me to show you the scars."*
—Bob Dylan

When Max pulled around back of the club into his private parking spot, he didn't see any lights on inside. Dark as a whore's soul, he liked to say. Hard for a man to earn a living running dancing girls and hookers if they weren't dancing or hooking. And boxers—*forgetaboutit.*

He wondered which one—Johnny or Levi had taken care of business with the other. Levi was younger and maybe even a bit more cold-blooded, but Johnny was an old hand at the killing game. Well, whoever wins, I'll personally take care of him, Max thought as he exited his car and softly closed the door. Can't have any tales told out of school.

He approached the back door, but just in case, took out the small Taurus P22 with the pearl grips he carried for personal protection. What was it Johnny called it, "A lady stinger" —anybody would know it would be Johnny. What lots of people didn't know was that the twenty-two was the gun of choice among professional killers. Two in the back of the head, one in the heart. Did the trick no matter the caliber. Well, maybe if Johnny had been the survivor of Max's little plot, Johnny would learn just what a "woman's gun" it really was.

As a kid, Max grew up watching and loving gangster movies with Jimmy Cagney, Edward G. Robinson and his personal favorite, George Raft. Raft was a good looking suave guy and Max emulated him, even though he only grew to five-foot eight in elevated heels.

So now he had his gat in his hand, his roscoe, his heater, his rod, and he was going to put one of those yobs on ice real quick, and it didn't matter which one.

He got out his keys, but had to lay the pistol down to find the right one holding it up to the night sky until he found it, slipped it in the lock and slowly turned the handle and stepped inside, but then stepped back out again to retrieve the gun he almost forgot, calling himself a dummy before easing the door closed. He stood listening. Nothing. Not so much as a sound from within.

Good.

He eased down the familiar back hall, passed the storage room and walk-in cooler where he kept cases of beer, passed that until he reached his office. Put his ear to the door and listened. Still nothing.

Opened it and stuck his hand in and flipped the light switch.

Nobody home. He exhaled a sigh of relief, said aloud, "You boys are lucky you weren't here, 'cause ol' Max was going to put you into the big sleep."

Set the gun atop his desk and mixed himself a drink, this time gin mixed with grapefruit soda over ice and sat down at his desk.

He saw then that that fucken Johnny hadn't cleaned up the bloodstain—it was still there on the floor big as two dinner plates.

"Cocksuckers," he muttered. "Why don't people do what I ask of them?"

He paced, he sat, got up and paced some more waiting word as to what happened between Johnny and Levi. If he was a betting man, he'd bet on Johnny. He poured himself another drink, still feeling out of sorts.

You know what I need, he thought, that new girl Marilyn. Sat down at his desk and rifled through his scattered paper and notes looking for her number. He was sure he'd written it down somewhere. But he couldn't find it.

"Goddamn it!" he said in frustration. There were other girls he could have called—Harmony, except she had those buck teeth that scratched his tool; Lucy, but she had an off eye and he couldn't stand to look at her—talk about losing your hard-on. Jennette? Maybe, but man Marilyn was stuck in his brain and the more he searched for her name and couldn't find it, the more he wanted to find it.

He went through every piece of paper, twice. Still no Marilyn.

"Max, you stupid ass, when you going to learn to file properly?" he berated himself.

The wastebasket. Check the fucken wastebasket.

He went through the wastebasket and there it was, crumpled up. He smoothed it out on his desk and dialed her number. A guy answered.

"Yah?" Deep voice.

"Hello, is Marilyn there?"

"Who's askin'?"

"Oh, I'm sorry, this is Max, I own the club. She was in the other day looking for some work as a dancer. I actually do need another dancer if she's still interested."

He heard the guy call her to the phone, and then she came on.

"Yes?"

Told her who he was and did she still want to dance.

"May I ask what it pays, Max? You see I got my boyfriend bailed out, so I'm not in as much of a need for a job right now. He's back working construction, and . . ."

"It pays twenty an hour, plus full benefits after thirty days, plus, most of the girls can make two, three hundred dollars a night in tips."

It was a lie of course, but whatever it took to get her over. Imagine, she gets the fucken boyfriend out of jail and suddenly she don't need the work so bad. This fucken generation was a lost cause.

"Wow, that is a lot of money. Just a minute."

He heard a muffled conversation she was having with the guy, then, "Yes, that sounds really good. But just for a few weeks, Max, until Freddy and I can get to California. I want to get into the movies, or television."

"Great. Can you come over now? One of my best girls called in sick and I'm really in need of a dancer right now."

Again with the conversation.

"Okay."

"Good, I'll meet you at the front door."

Max hung up and had another drink and patted the sweat on his forehead with a paper towel from the bathroom.

Yeah, a little bit of Marilyn could chill him right the fuck out. He always liked trying the new girls. Not all of them went along with it and he'd find a reason to let them go after a few nights, because, you know what, the world was full of women who'd take off their clothes for money. He'd read the really big thing nowadays was young women who wanted to become porn stars. Didn't their folks raise 'em right?

He wondered how Johnny was making out, if he'd killed the kid, or, maybe the other way around. Tell the truth, he sort of liked Johnny, being his nephew, even though he was gay, which, considering his many other sins, was the least of his problems in Max's way of thinking. He wasn't sure how he'd break the news to Audrey if Johnny bought it instead of Levi. Worse if it was Max who had to kill the kid, he'd really have to lie his ass off then. But Audrey and him weren't ever close in the first place, so no big deal.

Max heard somebody knocking on the front door and went up there, through the empty lounge and opened it.

Marilyn peering in, saying, "How come everything's so dark, Max?"

"Oh, well, we don't open till nine-thirty during the week and it's only eight-thirty. 'Sides, I'd kind of like to see your routine up there on stage.

Got a good section of taped music you can choose. Here I'll show you where the girls change at."

"Gee, you sure about this?"

"Yeah, yeah, not to worry, they'll be lined up at the door any minute now, pounding to get in."

Max led her to the back where the girl's dressing room was. Showed her a rack of outfits and costumes that looked more like Halloween for strippers.

"Go on and change, doll and I'll find you some music."

She nodded, he closed the door and went around to his office and pulled the wood plug to a peephole that looked directly into the dressing room. Watched every girl who ever came in the first time, thought, My new main squeeze—somebody to replace Cherry, Oh yeah, when he saw her naked.

He waited for her to come out of the dressing room, said, "Oh, before we get started, honey. I need you to sign a couple of papers, you know the usual—to keep the IRS off my back and so forth. Led her into his office and shut the door and then pretended to find the fake paperwork and laid them face down on his desk and handed her a pen, saying, "Just sign anywhere."

She leaned over and looked at them, said, "Max, this is a bill for laundered shirts."

"Really?"

She started to turn around but Max had her from behind, groping her top and bottom as she tried to wiggle free, saying "Max, stop it! What are you doing?"

"Honey, I know you're innocent, but you ain't that innocent. This is part of the job. Taking care of ol' Max."

"No, no! Let me go, damn you!"

"Yeah, like that's not going to happen. Just go along to get along. You'll still have plenty left over for that boyfriend of yours. He doesn't even have to know. Hell, I'll even give you a couple of hundred for the privilege, whadda ya, say, baby?"

She spun suddenly and slapped him open handed. It shocked him more than hurt. He slapped her back, harder and she screamed, whether in pain or fright, what difference.

They danced around the room in a struggle. She was a lot stronger than she looked. They kept slapping each other and she kept screaming and Max kept telling her how much he liked it.

The corner of her mouth was bleeding and her teeth were wet with blood too, and both sides of Max's face looked like he'd gotten sunburned over the cuts Cherry had laid on him with that goddamn cleaver.

He finally got her over to the well-used sofa and bent backwards onto it.

"You might as well stop all this damn foolishness," he warned.

"You goddamn right, amigo!"

Max snapped his head around at the deep voice. Who the fuck was this? Said, "Who the fuck are you?"

"I'm her boyfriend asshole, let her up."

The guy was holding a knife, light racing off its blade.

Max got up and so did Angel. She was crying and cursing him like a dirty grandpa.

"Go on, get in the truck, baby," the boyfriend said.

She scampered past and ran out of the room.

"Okay, I think we've some sort of misunderstanding here, friend," Max said holding up his hands like he was a stage passenger in the old West being robbed at gunpoint.

"No misunderstanding, asswipe. You tried to rape my girl, and where I come from, that shit don't fly."

"Rape? Ha. She told me she'd do whatever I wanted to get a job here. Then when I tried to collect, she reneged. That's what happened."

"Fuck you!"

The guy came forward, the knife held out front of him.

"I'm going to cut your balls off, you old bastard."

Max ran around his desk, was tugging at the drawer he'd put his gun in when the guy came across the top and swung the knife, Max felt something sharp, clean and painful touch his cheek, then the instant wet warmth of blood slide down onto his chin.

He jumped out of the way and ran toward the door, but the guy cut him off.

"Keep running dad and I'll keep cutting till there ain't nothing left but that cheap suit."

Max figured he was about to be killed over a piece of ass he never even got, oh what tragic irony.

But then the door flew open and Johnny Pearl stood with a gun in his hand, the other hung limp at his side, blood dripping off his fingertips.

He saw Max bleeding from the face, the boyfriend holding a knife and just fucken shot him, no questions asked. Boyfriend and knife banged to the floor.

"Jesus Christ!" Max said with relief. "I was hoping you'd show up. That son of a bitch was trying to cut me into a brisket."

Johnny stepped over the body, said, "You need to sign everything over to me right now, Max or I'm going to finish the job this guy started."

Max could see the madness in Johnny's distended eyes, the blood continuing to drip like red rain from his fingertip.

"Sure, I got the contract already there in my desk drawer. I'll sign it. Fuck this anyway. I've had enough. It's all yours kid."

Johnny stood waiting. Max could see he was hurting, pale and sweating.

Max sat down at his desk, pulled open the drawer and took out a contract, one he used to sign his fighters with and laid it on the desk. The .22 lay there like poison fruit.

"What happened, did you finish Levi?" he asked. "You look like you could use a drink, kid, let me pour you one."

Max got up and poured Johnny a glass of whiskey, set it on the desk and Johnny slumped wearily down across from him and took the drink and downed it.

"Yeah, I got him. It wasn't easy, but I got him. No more worries about Levi, Max. Your troubles are over on that account. Give me that contract."

"Let me sign it first," Max said pretended not to have a pen, said, "Wait, I got a pen right here and reached in the open drawer and came up with the .22—the one Johnny called a lady stinger and pulled the trigger just as Johnny pulled the trigger of his own gun.

Both men were hit and went down sideways out of their chairs and lay there looking into each other's faces not three feet apart.

"Did you really think I was that stupid?" Johnny gasped.

"Yah, I did," Max gasped back.

"Well, you were fucken wrong, weren't you?"

"I guess we both were," Max said, bleeding from the mouth now.

Max expired first, Johnny just seconds later.

The boyfriend came around, stood clutching his broken shoulder, staggered out through the front and out the door, got in the car and drove away in a hurry.

"What happened?" Marilyn cried when her boyfriend climbed in behind the wheel bleeding.

"Everybody got fucked up," the boyfriend said.

"Well, I'm glad I didn't go to work there," she said.

"Me too," the boyfriend said. "I think I should go to the hospital."

"Sure baby."

"I love you, baby."

"I love you too, honey."

Chapter Thirty-Nine

"I never meant to hurt anyone, I meant to kill them."
—Unknown

While the White Dude and the Black Dude were in a cheap motel room with a couple of even cheaper hookers, neither of which were a day under forty, Bobby Lee and Nina Summers eased up to something that looked like a spaceship, their headlights glancing off the aluminum skin of the trailer.

Inside the dog barked sharply and Jerry Summers reached for the pistol he kept under his pillow and swung his bare legs out of bed.

"Who the fuck is that?" he whispered to the dog, thinking it was those pricks he'd spotted up on the ridge finally come to do whatever they were there for. He slid back the gauzy curtain there in the kitchen, saw just a pair of headlights said, "Son of a bitch."

Then somebody stepped out of the passenger side and Jerry cocked back the hammer prepared to do what he had to. Twenty-two years in lockup and it had come to this, he thought. When can a man ever be left the fuck alone?

But then the person stepped in front of the headlights and he saw it was a woman and he knew right then it was Nina even though he had no idea what she looked like anymore. Last he'd seen her, she was just a girl.

He went to the door and called out, "Honey, is that you?"

"Yes, daddy."

Then Jerry flipped on the light overhead that filled the combination kitchen living room and said, "Jesus Christ, get up here."

She came to him with a rush, all her past reservations suddenly gone. There stood her daddy in a pair of boxer shorts and undershirt, but it mattered not. Jerry stepped out of the trailer to greet her, the soles of his feet onto the gravelly earth, but it felt to him like salvation at last.

They hugged and held each other for what seemed like eternity. What a blessed night, he thought, knowing they both had a million questions, but that could wait. He had his daughter, he had a family still, a congress too long belated. She was here.

After a long, long time she pulled apart, said, "Dad, I want you to meet a friend of mine."

Suddenly Jerry began to wonder, for the last he'd heard she'd taken off with some guy was in a band or something.

"Bobby," she called and he stepped out of the car. The night air was surprisingly cool after the day's heat. He came forward, hand extended, said, "Sir."

The two men stood looking at each other, measuring, reluctant, for that is how men are at first.

"If you're her friend," Jerry said, "then you're my friend," and offered his hand and they shook, Jerry noting the strength in Bobby's grip.

"Let me get something on," Jerry said. "Come on inside." He was a jangle of nervousness over finally seeing her again.

They entered the trailer and sat on the sofa at the far end—an old broken down brown thing they sank into. And when Jerry re-emerged with his trousers on, he sat straddle legged on a wood chair—his only one for eating inside whenever it rained out.

Then he quickly got up again and said, "I bet you could use some coffee, something to drink. I got a strawberry pop in the fridge—one of those big bottles. I might have a couple of beers . . ."

"A glass of water would be fine," Nina said.

Jerry got down plastic glasses with yellow flowers painted on the side he'd picked up at some yard sale, and poured two glasses of water from the kitchen sink, saying, "Got good water. Well struck an aquifer and you couldn't ask for any better" and handed them each a glass, then straddled the chair again and waited for them to speak. He couldn't believe how pretty she was, and how much she resembled her mother. He nearly wept looking at her.

"Dad, I know we have a lot of catching up to do and we will. But right now we've had a little trouble and I want to tell you that right up front. There are probably some very bad people after us."

"Funny," he said. "But I think I already knew that?"

"How?"

"There's been a strange black SUV parked up on the ridge east of here for the last few days. I thought maybe they were police, but then I figured if that were the case, they would have come down here and talked to me. Unless, well, unless this was something really serious and they were waiting for you to show up then swoop down."

Bobby and Nina exchanged looks, Bobby said, "If it's me, I'll take off so you don't have to deal with them."

"Yeah, but if it's me, you're taking off won't mean a thing," Nina said.

"I'm confused here, guys," Jerry said.

So they explained it, one at a time, first Nina and then Bobby.

"I didn't mean to kill them," she said. "but if I hadn't, I wouldn't be here today. My boyfriend—my ex-boyfriend—left me with a guy who raped me over a damn drug deal . . ."

"Oh, honey, I'm so sorry you had to go through that."

"It's okay," Nina said. "I'm not a bit sorry. People shouldn't treat other people like dogs, worse than dogs."

"What about you, son?" Jerry asked.

"My sin was not losing a fight I was supposed to. And the people who owned my contract would like to see me pay for it in a very bad way."

"What the hell is this world coming too?"

Jerry stood then and went to a cupboard over the sink and got down a pint of tequila and said, "I could use me a taste, you all?"

"None for me," Nina said.

"Son?"

"Sure, why not," Bobby agreed. "But I don't know how much longer I can keep my eyes open. It's been a long ride in a lot of ways."

"My bed's back there, you can crash any time."

"I can sleep in the car," Bobby said.

"To hell with that. You two sleep in my bed."

Bobby tossed back the tequila and it was semi sweet and fiery.

"Thank you," he said. "Nina, I'm going to turn in. Let you and your father talk." Then to Jerry Summers: "One more thing, that car outside is stolen."

"You two decide to get into trouble, you do it up right," is all Jerry said.

For a time, Bobby Lee could hear them out there talking. The bed was springy and lumpy, but it felt like a bed in a first class room. He lay there thinking about what the guy had said about people up on the ridge. Black SUV. Could be anybody. One of Max's people—the Cowboy most likely if it was—or those who were after Nina for the killings and the drugs she'd taken.

There was no comfort to be found in any of it. But finally, he had to let go of the long day with all that had transpired, and all before, and to say nothing of his feelings for Nina.

What the fuck were they going to do?

Sometime during the night, she got into the narrow bed with him, pressed herself up against him with an arm around him. She kissed his shoulder and then they both slept.

They awakened to the smell of bacon frying and each got up and used the lavatory before going to the other end where the kitchen sort of was, Jerry standing at the stove with two fry pans on the burners and a coffee pot brewing. It was all kitsch and mismatched, but it was doable and Jerry didn't mind a bit. Compared to prison, it was the Hilton.

They sat down to eat and Bobby and Nina both said it was the best breakfast they'd ever had.

"I learned to cook in prison," Jerry said. "Found I had a knack for it. Cooking can be very creative, like art. I like to cook everything in butter—like the French," he joked.

When they had finished and were working on a second cup of coffee, Jerry said, "I've got an idea."

Bobby and Nina listened.

"You two have enough money to buy a good used car?"

"Sure," Nina said. "More than enough."

"So, I was thinking here's what we'll do. You take me into Manzanita—there's a used car lot there. I know the guy runs it. Old con himself. We sometimes sit around in the bar over there and swap war stories. Fact is, he ended up introducing me to a nice gal who I sometimes see. I can get him to fix up the paperwork however I want it. On top of that, I know another guy over in Buscando Junction was a forger back in the day. I think with enough money, we could get him to fix you two some passports. Only thing is it might cost upwards of ten grand—five apiece."

It was Nina who proposed swapping the dope for the papers. "It's probably worth fifty, sixty grand and that's not even the street value, if he could use it."

Jerry whistled, said, "Damn. All I can do is ask. But all this might take a few days to pull off. And those boys atop the ridge might not wait that long now that they know you're here. Too bad we couldn't have hidden that car."

Bobby went to the door and looked out and up toward the ridge, said, "I don't see anybody up there?" Jerry had a look too.

"You're right. Let's get going."

They left in a hurry and drove first to Manzanita to the car lot.

Two miles across town the dudes were still recovering from a night of drinking and coke snortin and two forty something whores who had more mojo than either had expected.

But for a desire, a vigil was lost and but for a vigil three people escaped from the trailer in the desert who might not have otherwise.

***

The car deal was done with no problem—after all twenty grand of dope for a ten grand car was the best deal Leo Krist ever did in five years of buying and selling cars. Was lucky if he made fifty bucks a unit. He could buy a new necktie now, maybe one of those Texas jackets with the fringe on the sleeves.

Jelly Miscvige had started out life as an artist, had high hopes of becoming famous, but soon found out there were a million artists in Paris alone. So he started doing art forgeries of the great masters until the FBI busted him and all the money and women and good times were quickly enough finished—traded in for a prison uniform and working in the laundry.

These days he made and sold a few landscapes, but who the fuck bought desert landscapes in the desert when they could look out their car window and see the real thing? Still he sold enough to scrape by. It didn't take much to live in the back of an abandoned gas station.

When Jerry Summers came in carrying a sack of groceries and a case of beer and sat and talked to the artist with his paintings sitting around collecting dust, it didn't take a lot of convincing to make a couple of fake passports.

"Thing is," Jerry said. "These are for my daughter and her boyfriend. They got into a little trouble—something we both understand, eh, Jelly?"

"Costs money to do a job like that," Jelly explained. "I got a guy in Juarez who can do it, but he's not cheap."

"What about you, Jelly, couldn't you do it?"

"Nah. Shit, one thing I learned is I'm too old to go back to the can and besides, I learned to live this simple life."

"You think you could find out if your friend would do it?"

"I can give him a call."

"Before you do," Jerry said. "Instead of cash they've got about forty or fifty thousand in coke they need to dump. Ask your friend if he'd take that instead of cash."

"I don't know if I want to get involved with drug dealers," Jelly said.

Jerry explained the situation, that they weren't drug dealers, that his daughter had stole the dope from the guy who raped her and tried to kill her—though that part he embellished.

"The sins of the father, eh?" Jelly said.

"Yeah. I could really use your help, Jelly."

"Okay, I'll call and talk to him."

"Can I wait while you to call?"

"Sure."

Fact was Jerry was surprised Jelly even had a phone, but he did, and he called this friend and spoke to him and then said, "Yeah, he'll trade dope for passports. He needs two passport photos though. Send them overnight express."

"Done. And Jelly, for your help, here."

Jerry laid an envelope on the table. It had a thousand dollars in it.

"There's no need for this," Jelly said.

"I know. But us old cons need to stick together, Jelly. Who do I have the photos sent to?"

Jelly wrote down the address.

"Once he has them done, he'll meet us here, exchange the passports for the drugs. —day or two after he gets the photos."

"Thanks," Jerry said and went out and got into the car that was waiting with Nina and Bobby Lee in it.

"It's a deal," Jerry said. "All the dope for the passports. Need to get your photos taken and send them to this guy in Juarez who'll do it. Probably take a few more days."

"That's an eternity," Nina said.

"Don't know any other way."

They nodded, drove back into Manzanita to the Walgreens and got the photos made, then to the post office where Jerry over-nighted them to Juarez.

"Let's hangout until dark before we go back to my place—just in case those birds have returned and sitting up there watching."

They bought a cooler, some cold beer, luncheon meat, bread, cheese, potato chips and sweet snacks, drove out to a place that had shade and grass, sat around and talked and later ate lunch, then napped. Woke, drank a few beers, talked some more, mostly Nina and her dad catching up.

"I just need to know the truth about my mother," she said at one point. So he told her.

"I guess that makes us both murderers," she said after listening to his story about killing the man and dropping him down a mine shaft.

"By law, there is murder and then there is justifiable homicide," Jerry said.

Bobby Lee kept silent not wanting to intrude, wondering if those guys Jerry had spotted were after him or Nina, not that it made any damn difference in his mind. He'd do what he needed to do to protect her and himself.

Evening fell sooner than they thought, they stopped on the way back at a burger joint, had burgers and fries, then drove back to Jerry's place, but shut off the headlights a quarter mile out and pulled in and parked the car, went inside without turning on the lights.

They tried to spot whether or not there was a vehicle atop the ridge, could not tell.

"We better stand watch in case they are up there and saw us come in," Jerry said getting his rifle from the closet. "I'll take first watch. Nina and Bobby went to the back, got undressed and lay down on the bed.

"What do you think?" he said.

"I think if we can get across the border, we may just have a chance of getting out of this."

"My thinking, too."

"I'd like to live by the sea," she said. "I saw a TV show about the Sea of Cortez. I'd love to live there."

"Then shall it be," Bobby said.

"You know something?"

"What?"

"I love you."

"I love you too."

"Make love to me, Bobby. Sweet and slow. I want you to be tender with me."

They kissed, and the tenderness began.

***

"Guess who's here," the Black Dude said.

"Yeah?" the White Dude said taking the night vision glasses from his partner.

"Time for a little gun music," the Black Dude said.

"Let's play a concerto on their asses," the White Dude said.

"A what?"

It was sometime in the middle of the night when gunfire woke them. Bobby jumped out of bed grabbing the gun he'd kept on the nightstand and rushing outside.

Jerry was lying wounded on the ground.

"Sons a bitches!" he cried.

"Where are they?"

"I don't know."

A round whizzed past his head and tore into the metal sides of the trailer and shattered the coffeepot inside.

"They must have night scopes," Jerry groaned.

Bobby dragged him inside the trailer just as another round slammed just above the door.

Nina with her own gun crouched there.

"Get on the floor!" Bobby shouted.

She got down.

"He's been hit, see if you can find a towel or something to stop the bleeding.

She scrambled to the bathroom just as a window was blown out into a thousand sharp little pieces.

She got the towel and crawled on her hands and knees back to the men and Bobby pressed the towel to Jerry's wounded side.

"I guess they sure as shit ain't FBI or law enforcement," Jerry groaned.

Two more shots tore through the trailer.

"They're hoping to get lucky," Bobby said.

"Yeah, well, they damn sure just might," Nina said as she held the towel compress to Jerry's side. But he wasn't bleeding a lot and she thought it might not be as bad as first thought.

"I don't suppose they built a back door to this place?" Bobby said.

"If they did I haven't found it," Jerry groaned.

"What do we do, Bobby?" Nina asked.

"Just wait is about all we can do. Maybe if they think they got us they'll come down.

But they didn't come down and the firing kept up for another forty minutes, every round like death seeking them out blasting holes in the aluminum skin. They managed to crawl behind the sofa and three or four rounds tore into it causing batting to fly and some of the rounds went harmlessly over their heads.

"Maybe somebody will hear the gunfire and call the law," Nina suggested.

"Shit, gunfire out here is as common as firecrackers on the Fourth of July," Jerry said. 'Sides, the law wouldn't come out here after dark."

"Well, let's hope they don't get lucky," Bobby said.

After the forty or so minutes, the shooting stopped and the silence was almost deafening. They waited. And waited.

"What do you think?" Jerry asked Bobby.

"I think they're probably coming to see oh what slaughter they have wrought."

Jerry grunted.

"You read that in a book somewhere?"

"Probably."

"I don't think I can just sit here and wait to be murdered," Nina said. It felt like maybe Jerry's blood flow had stopped, but the towel was soaked so it was hard to tell.

"Let's just wait," Bobby said. "But if anyone opens that door, let them have it."

"You took the words out of my mouth," Nina said. "I've got some experience at that shit, remember." Thinking of when Ray and his buddy opened the door back at that shithole house.

"I wish you weren't here, honey?" Jerry said to his daughter.

"Me too, daddy."

They climbed out from behind the couch and took seats on its shredded upholstery, facing the door, guns in hand.

They listened.

Nothing.

They held their breaths.

"I think if they ain't dead, they sure the shit ought to be," the White Dude said.

"We put enough lead into that muthafucka even that mongrel is running around in doggy heaven," the Black Dude said.

"Well," the White Dude said after about ten minutes of listening to nothing but the nightfall around them. "Guess we ought to go down and do a body count."

"Yeah," the Black Dude said. "Like we usta over in Iraq, them towel heads.

The Dudes were approaching cautiously, night vision goggles and AR-15s—ex-military with but one real skill: killing the enemy, and right now those inside the trailer were the enemy.

They gestured to each other with hand signals as they advanced. Twenty feet, fifteen feet, ten feet. One reached for the trailer's door handle, was about to turn it when suddenly out of the darkness that damn ratty dog came charging, barking and clamping sharp teeth down on the White Dude's crotch causing him to yelp and tumble backwards and fire off a round into the dirt, slapping and cussing at the little bastard dog.

Jerry saying, "Oh shit, they're going to kill my dog."

More gunfire, more cursing, the dog howling.

"Fuck this," Jerry said and struggled to his feet.

"Dad, don't go out there!" Nina called, but Jerry had already reached the door, kicked it open, that Colt in hand, bleeding, cussing, firing that heater like Cagney in *White Heat.*

"Bobby!" Nina screamed.

"I'm on it, but you keep your cute little ass right where it's at and— well shit, you know what to do if they come through the door."

Bobby charged out firing the .45 at the shadowy figures, hoping to God one of them didn't cut him in half with their automatics.

Far as he could make out, Jerry was on the ground tussling with one of the guys while the other was shouting, saying, "Hold the fucker so I can kill him!" Jerry's dog in on it too biting the shit out of the guy,

Bobby quick fired at the dude still standing and saw him do a backward two-step. He obviously had been so focused on his partner wrestling the dog, intent on getting in a death shot, that he missed Bobby's presence entirely. Bobby unloaded on him some more and watched him do a crazy tango then hit the deck, his death grip pulling the trigger so that there was one long burrrr then nothing.

The guy Jerry was wrestling with was on top of him now, straddling him, even as the dog was getting tossed aside, and the White Dude now had a knife raised ready to plunge it into Jerry.

Bobby turned to end his career as a drug enforcer for some nameless fucks, but an explosion came from behind him and dude number two flopped dead.

Bobby turned in time to see Nina braced in the doorway.

Jesus, she was as hard as any of them, he thought. No hesitation, no fear, no fucken problem.

The dog came limping up sniffing the dead guys, probably to see if he still needed to protect his master from them. He didn't.

Bobby helped Jerry off the deck and got him in the house.

Lights were lit and Nina examined Jerry's side wound.

"We'll drive you into Manzanita to the clinic there," she said.

"Fuck that. Just give me some of that tequila. We can't afford to have any questions asked. There's a first aid kit somewhere in the closet back there."

Nina went to get it, Jerry said, "We got to get rid those guys before the law comes around."

"Yeah," Bobby said. "I can dig a grave."

"No," Jerry said. "There's another way."

Nina got her father patched up while Bobby took a flashlight and went looking for the dudes' car, found it a hundred yards down the road, off to the side, the keys on the dash. Got in, drove it back.

"Can you load them in their big black SUV?" Jerry asked. "I don't think I have the strength to."

Bobby got them loaded in the back. Nina drove, Jerry riding shotgun, directing her up those back roads.

"Good thing they did us the service of picking out a nice four-wheel drive," he said. "Out here in the desert the roads are few and you make your own."

"Where we going?"

"I'll show you."

She looked back to see Bobby following.

After an hour Jerry said, "Pull in here" and got out using the flashlight to look around, then he saw what he was looking for.

"Drop them down there," he told Bobby.

Bobby dropped them down there.

"Don't worry," Jerry told them, I remember now where I put the guy who killed your mother, they'll have company. Now let's get back to my place, I need a damn drink bad and I may have some oxy stored around there somewhere."

Chapter Forty

"Freedom is the oxygen of the soul"
—Moshe Dayan

Three days later, they drove into Buscando Junction, to Jelly's place, Jelly saying, "He'll be here any time." And, "What the fuck happened to you, Jerry?"

"Snake bit me?"

"Shit man, you ought to go over to the clinic in Manzanita and have that looked at."

"I ain't dead yet, I'm not going to be from this."

They sat around and drank Yellow Roses in front of a fan. They didn't have to wait long when a car pulled up outside, a fancy ass thing with steer horns on the hood, like what you'd see in the movies.

"You got that dope?"

"In the bag," Nina said.

Jelly picked it up, didn't bother to look and walked it out to the car. They watched through one of the windows as Jelly put it through the window, got a brown manila envelope in exchange and then the car took off raising a rooster tail of dust.

Jelly walked in and handed them the envelope, and true to his word, there were two passports with their photos and the names, Charlie Dickens and Fanny Cleaver.

"Do I look like a Fanny to you," Nina said with mock complaint.

"As much as I look like a Charlie," Bobby said.

"Okay," Jelly said. "Would you kindly get the fuck out of my house."

He and Jerry shook hands.

"Thanks, Jelly."

Outside Nina said, "So I guess we better split for the border, dad. But once we get settled we'll let you know. Maybe you can come down and hangout. I'd like that."

"Yeah, me too."

"We'll run you back to your place, then head out."

"How about just running me into Manzanita. There's a woman I'd like to visit. Help me recuperate."

"Sure. What about your dog?"

"Hell, that dog can take better care of himself than I can of me. That dog will be alright."

Two days after Nina and Ray leaving for Mexico, another vehicle pulled up and a man got out.

Jerry came to the door with his gun hidden in his hand behind his back.

"Help you with something?"

"Not sure," the man said. "This is some country and place you got here, looks like your trailer was used for target practice," Frank Dodge said eyeing all the bullet holes.

"Reason the rent's so cheap?" Jerry lied. "Suits my needs well enough."

"Are you Mister Jerry Summers?"

"Who wants to know?"

"Oh, pardon me. My name is Frank Dodge. I'm a former Miami detective, but now I'm just a plain old citizen like everybody else. I don't suppose you'd have a beer, something cold. Jesus, the heat."

"What is it you want, Mister Dodge, besides a cold beer?"

"Just to talk if that's alright."

Jerry got two beers from his fridge. The damn thing was sounding funny lately, like it was about to go kaput. But he had the satisfaction of knowing if it did, he could get a new one now with some of the money Nina insisted on leaving him.

"Let's sit out here in the shade," Jerry said handing the guy one of the beers.

They sat and Summers studied the guy—this Frank Dodge who used to be a Miami cop.

"Well, here's the thing," Frank began.

Then he told him his interest in finding Nina, about the shootout, but he didn't think she was responsible. Said, "My wife, my ex-wife that is, it was her brother who was one of the guys. And I promised her I'd look into it."

"I'm listening," Jerry said.

So they talked some more, about ex-wives and so forth and Frank told him he'd looked into Jerry's past, saw he'd been tried for killing a guy he claimed had attacked and murdered his wife and so forth.

"I understand, believe me I do," Frank said. "Shit, I would have done the same thing."

"She's gone, Nina is. I don't think you'll ever find her," Jerry said.

"Ah hell, that's okay. I didn't think I'd find her in the first place. I just promised my wife I'd do what I could and now I've done it as far as I'm concerned."

Jerry nodded.

Frank looked around, said, "You know I met this airline stewardess lives in El Paso that's not too far from here."

"Couple hours."

Frank nodded.

"What's it like living out here in the middle of nowhere?" Frank asked.

Jerry laughed, said, "Shit, never found nowhere better. And hell you can't beat the cost if you can find something abandoned, or you can buy a used Airstream from a woman over in Manzanita who'll put one on whatever piece of ground you can buy—few grand probably."

"It's pretty out here," Frank said finishing his beer and setting the bottle down. "That dog bite?" The dog had been damn quiet since the fight and getting kicked in the ribs and head.

"Only people he don't care for," Jerry said.

"Be good to have me another dog. Wendy, my ex, she didn't care for them. Didn't like how they shed and shit all over."

"Yeah, some wives are like that, I imagine," Jerry said.

"Well, I better get on. I'm supposed to hook up with that stewardess tonight, go out to dinner and dancing, she said. Hell, why not? I've not been dancing in a coon's age."

Both men stood then and shook hands, Frank saying, "Maybe I'll see you around or I get out this way or something. Next time I'll bring the beer."

"Sounds good," Jerry said.

He watched Frank get in his rental car covered in dust and drive off toward El Paso.

"Yeah," Jerry said. "See you around."

***

Three months later Jerry got a postcard with a picture of an azure sea and thatched roof huts and girls playing volleyball in bikinis. It was postmarked: *Isla Espiritu Santo* Mexico.

"Come on down, the water's fine here by the Sea of Cortez" is all it read on the back, but signed,

Charlie & Fanny.

On Sale Now!

Quint McCannon Adventures

For more information
visit: www.SpeakingVolumes.us

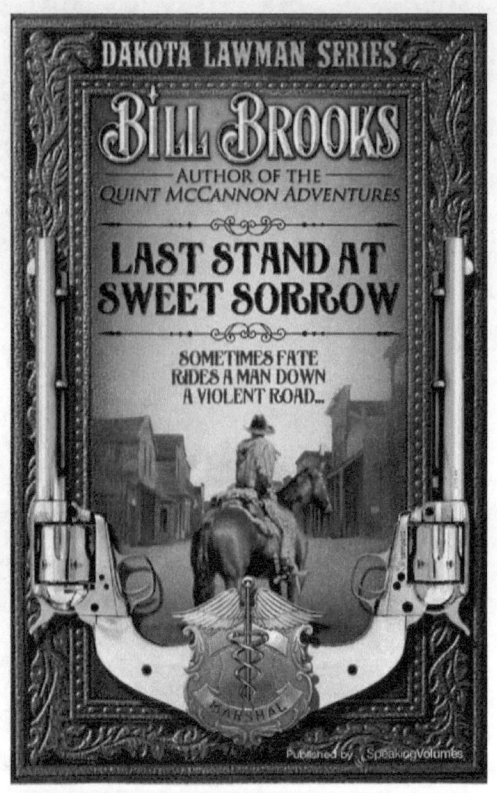

On Sale Now!

THE GUNSMITH *series*
Books 430 - 452

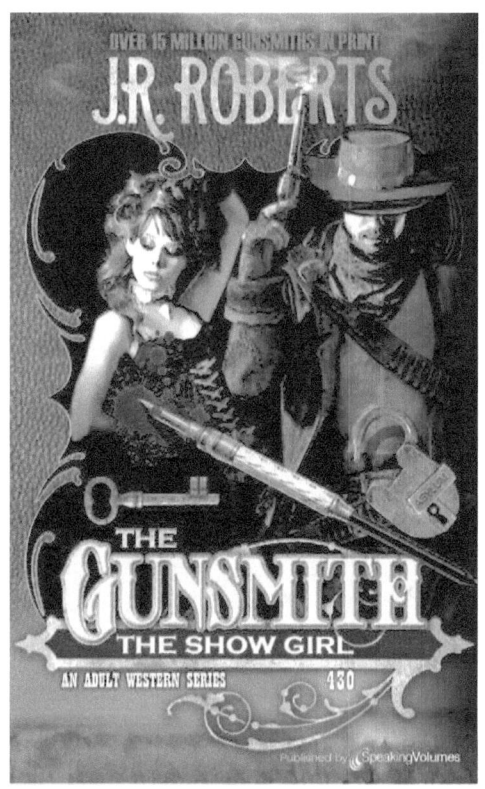

For more information
visit:

On Sale Now!

Lady Gunsmith *series*
Books 1-7

For more information
visit: www.SpeakingVolumes.us

Sign up for free and bargain books

Join the Speaking Volumes mailing list

Text

ILOVEBOOKS

to 22828 **to get started.**

Message and data rates may apply.